IN
DUE
TIME

J. KEITH

JONES

AMERICA'S FUTURE CAN ONLY
BE SAVED ... IN THE PAST!

Published by White Feather Press. (www.whitefeatherpress.com)

ISBN 978-1-4537883-6-3

Printed in the United States of America

Cover design created by Ron Bell of AdVision Design Group (www.advisiondesigngroup.com)

White Feather Press

Reaffirming Faith in God, Family, and Country!

Dedication

Dedicated to the three best women I have ever known: my mother, Betty; my wife, Melissa; and my daughter, Erin. Thanks for believing in me.

Acknowledgements

I would like to thank a few people for their roles in my growth as a writer and the development of this book. Skip Coryell: thanks for believing in this book enough to give it a life outside my computer. Lynn Salsi, Dr. Richard McCaslin and Wilton Earle: I could not think of three better mentors. All the members of the Bill Bray Writing Group, especially Al Perry whose leadership in the Winston Salem writing community is immeasurable; and of course, the late Bill Bray himself. Bill's knowledge and patience shaped my writing more than he could ever have known.

CHAPTER

1

FIRES had raged about Washington during the final battle of the revolution. I had taken time to stroll around the capital mall on the way to the White House. The monuments were heavily pock marked by bullets where they had shielded the rebels from the global forces. I rested for a time on the steps of the Lincoln Memorial, or at least what was left of it. Upon crossing the river from Arlington, the rebels had used it as a stronghold from which to stage a flanking movement around the tidal basin. Global artillery had reduced it to rubble. Still it had provided them the refuge they needed to direct their attacks.

I laughed at the irony. Lincoln had fought to destroy one set of rebels in order to enforce the will of greater central power upon them. Now he had protected a different band of rebels from the ultimate central power; a global government. Yes, old Abe had served them well this time as they struggled in the initial attack which drew a large portion of the reinforcements the International Union could muster down on their heads.

They fought valiantly and took heavy losses, the globalists were confident they could destroy them here if they threw all their weight against them. That's when the attack began from the north. The rebels were stronger than the IU had believed. The Arlington attack had been less than half of the forces. While the global army battled an attempted flanking movement around the site of the old Jefferson Memorial, the real flank attack began from the north.

In Due Time

The fires were all out and the globalists were gone, for now. They would try to return later, but General Birch knew this. He was wasting no time preparing to defend the country now that it was liberated. I wondered through all this if anyone had given any thought to restoring a statue of Thomas Jefferson to its former perch in the Memorial. The IU had pulled it down many years before, declaring that his values were inconsistent with the greater good of the "people." The only people whose greater good they were interested in were those in the government. The American republic had been slowly dying nearly from the day of its birth. Now it would have a second chance.

𝆑 𝆑 𝆑

The most amazing thing was not where I sat now, but that this room even existed at all. The globalists had attempted to lay the torch to the White House when it became obvious that they were cut off. The North American Governor had ordered several fires set as he gathered his personal guards to affect his escape under the cover of the flames. They misjudged how close the opposing forces were and they were overrun before many of the flames were set. There had been minimal damage to the building, so today I occupied a fine leather chair before an oak desk in the center of the oval office.

General Alexander Birch entered through a side door and I rose. He took my hand and quickly waved me back into the chair. He perched on the edge of the chair beside me rather than putting the desk between us. His hair was closely cropped and his face clean shaven. He looked like a different man cleaned and attired in a business suit. The army uniform of recent years was now put away.

"I suppose you are wondering why I asked you here." General Birch said after studying me for a long moment.

"Certainly General," I cleared my throat, "I mean Mr. President." I smiled and nodded. It had been a long road here, from a small band of malcontents gathered in the mountains of North Carolina. Birch had built them into a highly effective force that annoyed the global forces to no end. With each government atrocity and each successful strike, his numbers grew. His real genius came in attracting similar rebel bands and organizing them into a larger force. Other rebel leaders elsewhere were buoyed by this and followed his example.

"Actually, Mr. Spence," he smirked, "I rather prefer General to President."

"Yes sir," I grinned.

"I have a question for you," he leaned forward and squinted slightly. "Who is Joshua Lance?"

I chuckled quietly. That name had not crossed my ears in many a long year, yet seldom did a day go by that I did not think about him. I smiled sadly and looked back up at him, "What prompts you to ask about Joshua Lance, General?"

Birch rose and strode around behind his desk. He pulled a small gold colored key from the center drawer and held it up between us. "When I was a baby, my mother was given an envelope by a man. It contained instructions directing her to a law firm in Danville, Virginia."

"Faucett and Faucett?" I grunted.

"Yes," he arched an eyebrow, "Faucett and Faucett." His eyes bore into me for a moment. "When she went there, they told her that there was something on deposit there for me, but I couldn't have it yet." I grinned like someone who knew the punch line to an old joke. "You would expect that it would be held until I was eighteen or twenty-one, but…"

"But it was much longer than that wasn't it General?"

Birch stared back and slowly nodded. "Yes, it was, Mr. Spence, in fact it was only a month ago that I was allowed to access this. You know what it contained?"

"Hmm," I mused, "a key?"

"Yes, it was this key." He set it down and stared at it for a few seconds, "Do you know what the really strange thing about that key is?"

"I would only be guessing sir."

"It goes to a safety deposit box at a bank in Montana."

"Okay," I wanted to point out that Montana has banks too, but remembered who I was speaking to.

"I know," he waved a hand and smiled, "Montana has banks too.

The strange thing is that this bank wasn't built until five years ago."
He reached out and thumped the key with his index finger, "This key
has been sitting in that office for thirty-seven years for a bank that is
only five years old." He waved away the notion and reached for an
envelope on his desk, "Anyway, it contained an envelope with a note
in it. Do you know what it said?"

I shook my head.

"It said," he opened the envelope and pulled a letter from it, "this,
'By the time you read this, you will be an important man. But a deep
scandal will soon destroy everything you worked for. If you want to
prevent this, find the great writer, Howard Spence, and ask him to tell
you about Joshua Lance'" He then laid the letter back on the desk
beside the key and turned back to me.

"Mr. Spence," he propped his elbows on his knees and stared into
my eyes. "Who is Joshua Lance?"

"General Birch," I said, "it will take quite a while for me to tell
you about Joshua Lance."

"For this sir," his gaze bore into me, "I have all the time you
need."

The old man had told me that he would find a way and I guess he
did. I took my glasses off and rubbed my temples. These old eyes
tired more easily now. I sighed deeply.

"Well sir," I said, "Joshua Lance, in a different, um…" I struggled
for the right words, "time dimension… reality, perhaps…" I smiled
and put my glasses back on, "well, he would have been your step-
father." I watched him sit back in his chair as his eyes opened wider.

"In this reality," I continued, "he is a man you will never know,
because he sacrificed everything for you." I laughed ruefully, "And
he was the best friend I never had."

CHAPTER

2

IN the spring of 2001 I was working for a daily newspaper in Asheville, North Carolina. As a young reporter mostly writing about garden parties and local parades, I was eager to chase down any lead that seemed more promising than the latest community craft fair. So when I began getting tips concerning a rather unusual man up near Mount Mitchell I was willing to listen. He suddenly showed up one day with millions of dollars. He proceeded to buy a small mountain top and isolate himself in the tiny cabin at its peak. His anti-social attitude intrigued his neighbors. He seldom left his own land. People would see him buying groceries or picking up his mail from the post office at Micaville. He would speak, but would never entertain any real conversation.

Folks in the community burned to know where all his money came from. Someone had heard that he had won a lottery. Others thought he was a bank robber or connected to the mafia. The speculation was wild and I was wild about the speculation. I had a gift for drawing people out and hoped it wouldn't fail me now.

The leaves sprouted from the limbs above me just enough to give the trees an easy green glow as the sun peeked through. An earthy fragrance from the mountainside floated on the breezes streaming through my windows as the highway passed beneath my tires. The boring fluff pieces were complete and on my editor's desk, so I decided it was time to do some digging into this peculiar old man. Maybe I would strike a goldmine of human interest or at least find some interesting dirt along the way. Or maybe it was just a wasted trip. The truth lay at the other end of the driveway I turned into.

I rolled to a stop in front of a wooden gate a short ways up the drive and walked up to it. A stream gurgled over dark rocks and disappeared into a culvert running beneath my feet to reappear on the other side of the driveway and spill into a groove in a boulder. From this rock the water dropped about a foot onto some smooth stones creating a miniature waterfall. The sweet scent of the fertile humus wafted up from where it lay nestled about the trees; a flock of Canada geese flapped by overhead, honking as they went. Even if this James Mack guy proved to be a non-story, I decided that it was still worth the trip just to experience this.

I pulled through and closed the gate behind me. The narrow road wound around to the backside of the mountaintop. I held my breath as I looked down upon the treetops going by to my left. Finally there was a simple cabin nestled among the trees on a shelf of flat land just below the ridgeline. The vista spread out before the cabin to command my attention and I stood with my back to the log building. I closed the car door gently and stared. There was a valley between two larger mountains. A distant tiny town peeked out from the sprawling foliage. How could there ever be a trouble in the world with a view like this?

"Beautiful isn't it?" I snapped around; an older man, not as old as I had expected, but still a good bit older than I was, stood on the front porch.

"Mr. Mack?" I asked. He nodded slightly. "My name is How…"

"I know who you are Howard," he cut me off. I'm sure my surprise was obvious and it seemed to amuse him greatly. "I've been expecting you."

My stomach did a slight flip-flop as he waved me toward the porch and turned toward the house. I hesitated wondering if I should go up. I wasn't sure what I had expected, but this wasn't it. He stopped at the door and turned back raising his eyebrows.

"Are you coming?"

I mumbled a reply and nodded. I followed along as he disappeared into the house. The cabin was light and airy. Plenty of windows vented the air and brought in the sunlight as it filtered through the trees. Books jammed the shelves that lined the walls. A shotgun stood guard in the corner next to the now cold fireplace. Ashes lay as witness to recent nights when flames kissed the stones and chased away the night time chill.

The clinking of ice against glass came through the door Mack had disappeared through followed by the swooshing of pouring liquid. The old man emerged from the door carrying two glasses of iced tea and held one out for me. Being a native of the South, of course, iced tea was my favorite drink. I like it sweet with plenty of ice and no lemon. Lemon adds a certain tang and is an affront to properly sweetened tea. I took the glass from his hand noting the absence of lemon and took a sip. The man could certainly make tea.

He smiled and walked out the back door. I followed him out and around to the side where a set of chairs rested in the shade. We sat in silence for a few moments. He stared off across the valley and I studied him carefully. My nerves began to ease as I sipped the tea. This man was about as threatening as a domesticated teddy bear. He crossed one leg on the other, resting the side of his foot on the other knee, and smiled.

"It's good to see you buddy," he nodded. I leaned in and looked harder at the face, it wasn't familiar.

"Have we met?" I asked. The old man grunted out a soft laugh.

"That's a complex question," he grinned.

"Yeah, okay," I rolled my eyes. "I was wondering if I could ask you some questions."

"Sure," his gaze bore into me. "First let me tell you one thing."

"Um, alright."

"My name is not really James Mack," he smiled as if a great truth of the universe had been revealed. I sat back and pulled out my note pad. This might prove easier than expected.

"Why? I mean, why use the fake name?" What would it be; fugitive, witness protection, international spy, foreign legion deserter? The truth was beyond my ability to imagine.

"You'll see," he said.

"When?"

He sat back silent for a moment, "In due time."

"What is your real name then?"

"Joshua Lance," he said. I scribbled this down, guessing at the spelling.

"Well then," I looked up, "Joshua Lance, where are you from?" The old man smiled and stood up. He strode over to a pile of firewood sitting beside a tree about ten feet away.

"Do you like splitting wood Howard?" He set a stick of wood on end atop a stump and picked up an ax and sited down the point toward the log like a sniper sizing up a target.

"What does that have to do with anything?" I asked.

"Well," he lifted the ax and slammed the edge into the end of the log splitting it into two blocks. "You take a piece of wood that is too large to burn efficiently in the fireplace." He stooped and picked up one of the halves he had just split and set it back on the stump and swung the ax again turning the one half into two quarters. "Then you break it down into smaller parts that are more digestible." He leaned against the ax handle and looked back at me. "Do you get what I'm saying?"

"No," I ran my hands through my hair and sat forward.

"It's like this story… just too large to digest in one telling."

"What? So that's it!" This was no story.

"For today," he held up one quarter of the log he had just split. "This is what we discussed today. We've got to go through that whole woodpile." He gestured over his shoulder, "I don't think you're quite ready for all that today."

"Alright," I waved a hand and got up to head toward my car.

"Oh, by the way Howard," his face took on a more serious look as I turned back. "How are your parents?"

"Fine," I sputtered, "why?"

"See 'em much?"

"Some."

"Raleigh, right?"

I nodded dumbly. How did he know all this?

"I know you're busy," he set the ax down on the woodpile and straightened up, "but do yourself a favor. See them all you can. Call your mom, that doesn't cost you much time. And while you're at it talk to your dad, I know he doesn't like to talk on the phone, but make him anyway."

I narrowed my eyes and shrugged in a questioning manner.

He shrugged back, "You never know how long they'll be around."

"They're like," I feebly managed, "ten years younger than you."

"You just never know."

"Thank you for your time," I said after pausing a moment and turned to leave. I wondered what kind of game this man was playing.

"I'll see you when you come back."

I whirled back around scowling, "After the way you've wasted my time, Mr. Lance, you don't have to worry about my returning."

"You'll come back Howard."

"What makes you think so?"

"You'll have to," he said quietly.

After leaving the mountain, I wasted no more time returning to Asheville. I did call my parents from my cell phone, however; I talked to my father for twenty minutes.

CHAPTER
3

A COUPLE of months later I did manage to squeeze in a visit to my parents' house. To my shame, I probably wouldn't have otherwise, but that old man's words gnawed at my gut like a bad meal. On that day Raleigh was its usual self. The people quietly went about their business unawares while the politicians proceeded to rob them blind downtown in the state capital.

Dad was already up and lounging out in the screened in porch when I joined him. Two pigeons were fighting a losing battle with a squirrel over their turf beneath one of Mom's bird feeders, despite additional air support being mounted by an angry blue jay. The squirrel would duck just in time with each swoop from the screeching dive bomber. The little varmint seemed to enjoy the sport of the whole affair as he gathered up the bird feed spilled from above. Just then the squirrel's brother leapt from a nearby limb onto the feeder causing two sparrows and a cardinal to join the battle. Dad laughed and took a sip of coffee.

"I get a real kick out of watching those critters," he said.

"Yeah, it is pretty entertaining I guess," I couldn't help smiling. It was nice to see him so relaxed. This was a real contrast to the busy career Air Force meteorologist I remembered. His job with the state allowed him a much more leisurely pace of life now. No more postings in northern Alaska or Reykjavik, Iceland; like he had been when I was born. Dad had packed Mom up and sent her home to

Raleigh to live with my grandparents. He insisted that I should be born here like they both were. Now they were back to stay.

Just then reinforcements showed up in the form of two more squirrels sending the pigeons into full retreat. The sparrows continued harassing the one on the feeder and the determined blue jay made a couple more passes at his foes on the ground before he packed it in and flew off in the direction the cardinal had left by a moment earlier.

Dad looked up at the clouds and pointed out something about their formation and the direction they were moving. Then he mentioned something about the movement of the Gulf Stream. This could go on for hours without pause. I've never known anyone else who actually talked about the weather and not be making idle chit chat.

"Dad?" I asked when he stopped for a breath.

"Yes?"

"Do you ever miss the Air Force?" Someone had asked me this recently and I had to admit that I didn't know. We never discussed such things. He was always either instructing or disciplining. Never did we share our feelings about anything. To him life was a series of choices. You made a choice, you adjusted to it and you moved on. Feelings were not relevant in his little ecosphere.

"Well..." he caught himself in the middle of rolling his eyes. Something in my grimace must have caused him to take this a bit more seriously. "Do I, hmm... Well sometimes I do."

"Why, you were either on some piece of tundra freezing your tail off or battling mosquitoes the size of bats in the tropics, what's to miss?"

"You have a point, but..." His eyes focused on the victorious squirrel on the bird feeder for a moment. The sparrows had given up the fight and flown off to join their less persistent brethren. "I guess it was the most significant thing I've ever done." He turned back and looked me straight in the eye. There was a certain something there I had not seen before. A personal warmth; maybe he had longed to talk about these things but didn't know how. I broke the gaze and looked down for a second.

"I see what you mean."

"Oh, other than you and your mother of course," he added eagerly.

"Of course," I grinned. "Dad," I looked back down. I needed to say it but couldn't really look directly at him. I didn't have much practice at this. "I love you… and I'm proud of you." The last part I barely croaked out. I felt his hand on my arm and I looked back up.

"I know son," I was unsure whose eyes were moister. We both choked back our tears, not willing to turn loose. That was just not how we did things. We sat there in silence the rest of the morning watching the squirrels play. It was nearly lunch time before we headed back into the house.

f f f

I had hugged them both warmly before going. I hadn't hugged my father since I was six years old. I reveled in their lingering warmth all the way back to Asheville. I was sure I wouldn't be able to go back to Raleigh very soon, but sometimes plans have a way of making themselves.

I knelt and picked out the best rose from each spray before walking back to my car. The passenger seat was the perfect spot—I thought—and rolled down the driver side window. I closed the door and leaned my head back against the headrest. It had turned warmer that day and the slight breeze did little to ease the heat. Everyone had left earlier and I had the cemetery to myself. I knuckled my eyes then reached out and turned the ignition. Lance had been right; I would be going back to his cabin. I had to.

f f f

I didn't bother going home to Asheville first. Instead, I sped on up along the winding Yancey County roads until I reached Lance's driveway. It was early evening by now. The bubbling of the stream seemed barely noticeable. The rich earthy fragrance hardly registered. As I opened the gate, a gaggle of geese annoyed me with their honking overhead. I drove on through and slammed the gate behind me.

I slipped and slid about the narrow gravel road until I pulled to a stop in front of the cabin. The old man leaned against the wooden rail on his front porch. My tears no longer flowed; they had been replaced by something harder and more determined. I climbed out of the car and glared up at him.

"I told you that you would be back." He said softly.

I walked across the yard and stopped at the front of the porch. I looked at him for an eternity without speaking. Finally I shook my head and asked, "Who are you?"

He walked down the steps and circled around me and headed out to the side of the house without answering. I shadowed him all the way to the chairs beside the woodpile.

"I'm sorry," he said after a moment. "House fires are a bitch… but they were asleep. There was no suffering."

"How do you know all this? How did you know this would happen? How…" I stammered, "Why… I mean… Did you have something to do with this?"

"No Howard," he shook his head, "I have no power over these things. I just know about them."

"How do you know? How do you know any of this? How do you know me for that matter?"

The old man grunted and let out a sigh, "I know all about you. I've known you for over twenty-five years." His piercing blue eyes gripped me.

"But…" my words were feeble, "but, I'm only twenty-four. Did you know my parents?"

"No, I didn't," he leaned forward, "The fact is I will know you for over twenty-five years… or at least I would have."

"I don't understand."

"Howard," he said softly, "I am from your future. You may not believe me now, but you will… in due time."

"So," I asked, "were we like buddies or something?"

"Yeah," he nodded, "pretty much."

"What are you doing here then?"

"Did you go see your folks?" he asked. I nodded. "Good," he smiled, "you always broke my heart any time I heard you talk about that; the deep regret. You would say, if only I had made time to see them…"

"So that's why you're here; to make me see my parents one last time?"

"No," he looked off toward the valley. "I have a much bigger reason."

"When are you going back?"

"I'm not."

"Why not," I leaned forward, "enjoying the good life in your mountain paradise too much?"

"Good life," he grunted, "I'm practically a prisoner here. Can you imagine how lonely it is being afraid to talk to anyone because you might screw something up?"

"Then why are you talking to me?"

"You will understand that," he shook his finger in the air letting it hang on the last word, "once you've heard why I'm here."

"I'm all ears," I said leaning forward. I widened my eyes emphasizing the point.

"Okay," he sat back and smiled. "It will all make sense; soon."

CHAPTER

4

"**E**VENTUALLY," the old man said, "There will be no America. It will just be another subject state to a global government. Everything is international law this and greater good that." He bobbed his head sideways as he said this. "In theory all this sounds alright," he held up a hand. "Everybody is taken care of, everyone is equal; the big old fat utopia." He laid his head back and sighed.

"But…" I offered.

He laughed, "I think you know how well this worked in practice. You see Howard; you were the only one of us that could see what a disaster this global village would become. You have foresight, you always did."

I'm sure I squirmed slightly. A crow landed on a limb above us and called out a few times before flying on. Lance sat and watched the crow sail away over the expanse. The sleek black bird dived into the valley below as a hawk flew from the distance and dove in after him.

"Anyway, the America you know will be gone," he stared out across the mountainside. "Even the greatly reduced freedom you've grown used to won't exist. There will be no president, just a North American governor who reports to the European government."

"So, you're here to fix it right?" I asked. "What do we do to prevent this?"

"Nothing," he smiled sadly.

"But," I said, "I can write about your experiences, get you on TV, something…"

He laughed softly and shook his head. "No, it's not that simple."

"But, we have to…"

"No Howard, no one would believe us anyway. Hell, you're not fully convinced yourself are you?"

I looked down and pulled out my notebook. This was unbelievable, but there had to be an explanation and I couldn't come up with a better one.

"You see," he said, "there are a lot of American's who think that this is a good thing. They don't want the responsibility of taking care of themselves. Sure they rave all the time about how much they love freedom, but when they have the opportunity…" his face took on a flustered look, "They don't even want their own money or property. They would rather give it to the government and trust that they will get some back. No my friend, they won't thirst for freedom before they drink from tyranny."

"So we're screwed? Is that why, you're here; to deliver hopelessness?" I stammered

"Not exactly," he smiled, "let me tell you the story."

I shrugged; there didn't seem to be many options, so I listened. Lance sat for a moment composing his thoughts staring out across the peaceful mountainside.

"A lot of folks around here think I'm from somewhere else because no one knows me," he smiled, "but I'm a North Carolina boy like you. I grew up in Alamance County; the first place where the people took a stand and told the British to take their taxes and shove them. Of course the Brit governor Tryon couldn't have this, so they killed a bunch of them and executed their leaders. That happened in a field beside Alamance Creek. They called it the Battle of Alamance. It wasn't much of a battle, more of a slaughter really; but it did serve to show all the colonies just what they were dealing with. There would be no redress of their grievances, no fair forum. Any complaints would fall on deaf ears and death to those who refuse to remember their place as subjects of the crown. The future leaders learned from this that if they laid it on the line they had better be prepared to back it up with hot lead and cold steel."

"Nice little history lesson," I said. "What does that have to do with the future?"

"The future is the same as the past," he leaned forward. "It always is. That's the reason governments don't encourage their people to learn about their past. Well... enough on that. About me, I was born in 1980. I was the captain of the football team at Burlington Central High School."

"You're the oldest looking twenty-one year old I have ever seen," I smirked. He laughed.

"I was fifty-six when I returned to this time. That was four years ago," Lance ran a hand through his thick salt and pepper hair. "I guess in reality I would be about sixty now." I had to admit that he was in very good shape for a sixty year old. He was a good sized man, just a little over six feet tall with a thick chest and broad shoulders. The mountain life kept him in good tone.

"Anyway," he continued, "I was a really good football player. I was all-state quarterback," he smiled. "Several schools, including UNC were offering me full scholarships. My future looked bright."

"Looked bright?" I had caught the nuance and he smiled that this hadn't slipped by unquestioned.

"Yes, looked. Well, Howard, our big rival was Durham and we had just beaten them. We were behind by three and it was third down on our four yard line. I barely managed to scramble away from their linebacker in my own end zone and there wide open was Larry Maddox. I sailed the ball right into his hands and he was off. He outran the only defender and it was green grass and blue skies all the way. We won, seventeen to thirteen."

He smiled and put his hands behind his head. The memory seemed to relax him then he sighed and the smile faded. "Well, we celebrated that night. There was a party at the Finches' cabin down at Lake Mackintosh." A scowl crossed his face, "Connor Finch was the backup quarterback. Quite a schmoozer; he could charm anybody, but very jealous of me. I was quite sleepy when I left the party and I fell asleep driving home along some back roads beside the lake."

In Due Time

Lance stood and walked over to the woodpile and picked up a stick of wood, then tossed it back onto the pile. He stood with his hands on his hips for a while. It almost seemed that he would not continue, and then he came back and sat down again.

"I had a brand new Mustang, boy it was pretty. Sleek, royal blue; I had just polished it. Of course I kept it that way," he scratched his chin then shook his head. "Oh yeah, anyway; it ran off the road and hit a culvert on the left side of the car. The floor area crumpled in and crushed my left foot and the car went into a spin. I knew I was in real trouble when I heard the splash. I had landed in a shallow inlet in a corner of the lake." He lowered his head and grunted, "It was just deep enough to cover my car. Only the top of the roof was sticking out. I had left the passenger window slightly ajar to let some air flow in; of course it also let the water flow in rather quickly. I was able to release the seat belt and work my foot out from where the dash had collapsed on it, but..." he seemed to have trouble looking directly at me. The lines in his face deepened, old pain etched in his brow. "Well, I couldn't get the door open and the electric windows wouldn't work. My foot was too messed up to let me crawl to the other side and I was in a panic."

"The water was up to my chin. I prayed out loud," he chuckled nervously. "I never did that. Don't get me wrong, I was always a believer, but sorry to say, I never was the praying type; especially out loud. So it was like the Lord's Prayer, the 23rd Psalm, singing Jesus Loves Me, whatever I could think of until the water got too high. Then it was just sputtering 'God help me' and 'Jesus save me' and such. The end was upon me and I was scared." His chest rose and fell. In his mind the water was all about him and he vainly searched for air.

"I remember the moon shining through the water about the front windshield. I would put my mouth up at the ceiling to get a breath of air and then settle back into the seat until the air was gone. I wasn't sure I could keep doing this much longer," his shoulders sagged a bit. "Then I heard a loud bang on the roof above me. A voice cried out for me to hold on, so I pushed up on the seat and the console and pulled in another lungful of air and heard something hit my window.

I looked over as it hit again. It looked like a metal tool of some kind. The water resistance was too great, he wasn't going to be able to break the window and I couldn't hold out. As I began to sink back into the seat, he had turned the tool; I was to later learn it was a tire tool that came to a point on one end. Well, he turned it around and made a stabbing motion with the pointed end into the water and it slammed into the window shattering it. The last bubbles escaped my mouth when I felt the hands under my shoulders."

The retelling seemed to tire him out. My own breathing had grown shallow and now I relaxed a bit. The edge of my seat dug into my rear.

"The next thing I remember I awoke on the side of the road. There was a young man, about my age," the old man smiled, "sitting beside me. I could hear a siren in the distance. The boy was vaguely familiar. The voice and face," he made a tapping motion in the air with his finger. "I had seen him but I couldn't place him. That would change."

"That's quite a tale," I said, "you were lucky."

"Luck had nothing to do with it."

"Well," I offered, "at least it has a happy ending."

"Ending hell," he pointed at me. "This is just the beginning."

CHAPTER
5

SOME days Joshua Lance wondered if survival had been worth it. Surgeries involving pins and rods, long periods in casts and grueling physical therapy wore him thin. The worst thing was watching from the sidelines while his team played without him. The wind sprints they ran now had been Josh's pride. He had been the quickest on the field since little league. Now walking was a challenge.

The one bright spot through this ordeal had been Artemis Pike. Since saving Josh from a watery grave, Art had been a faithful companion. During the weeks in the hospital, Art would be there every day after school, even driving down for an important operation that Josh had to have in Chapel Hill.

Josh hadn't known Art very well before that. In fact he had not even been able to recall his name. Artemis Pike was a lonely science geek about two-thirds Josh's size. There was little doubt that he was a genius, yet he came from a white trash background living in a mill village at the edge of town. Art's old man's drinking was legendary, according to Josh's father. His Dad felt rather sorry for the boy and encouraged his friendship with Art. Sometimes, folks say, that the apple falls far from the tree. In this case, it seemed to have been propelled several miles away by a tornado.

Connor Finch smirked over at Josh during a break in a throwing drill. Josh nodded in reply; wearing a smile he didn't feel. The team was in trouble. Finch had his days, but most often he choked under pressure. If only they had someone besides that creep to step into the spot, Josh sulked. Finch would forever be a bad memory for Josh. The last time he had felt normal was before Finch handed him his last drink of the night before he left the party.

"Thought I might find you here," the voice came from behind. Josh turned his head as Art stepped down and took the spot on the bleacher beside him.

"Hey man," Josh said and turned his head back to the field. They sat quietly for several minutes.

"Why do you torture yourself?"

"What," Josh turned his head to face Art.

"I mean…why do you come out here? You can't get out there with them." In the short time he had known him; this was the most assertive thing Art had said. It was good the boy was loosening up and speaking more freely.

"Where else would I be," Josh said. "I guess it's a habit by now." They sat in silence for the rest of the practice.

The remainder of the season had been touch and go as Josh expected. Still expectations were high the night the state playoffs opened. Burlington Central had been favored to storm into the finals and take it all. That was before the fateful night of the wreck. Wilmington was no pushover, but Josh had their defense figured out. He sailed past them in the regular season opener. Thursday afternoon, Josh had tried to work with Finch as the coach had asked him, but Finch seemed to resent the advice. Josh limped off to the side and watched the drills. Finch sent a receiver in his direction and overthrew him, firing the ball into Josh's left knee. Josh sat on the ground for several minutes gritting his teeth and rubbing his leg. Finch stood over him proclaiming that it was an accident. Accident my ass, Josh thought, hoping that he could hold back the tears. If Finch could hit his mark that well in the game the team would have it made.

Now the minutes were quickly fading away and Burlington Central was down by three. Their running backs had managed to work them down to Wilmington's thirty yard line. Todd Scott centered the ball into Finch's hands and Finch faded back. Larry

In Due Time

Maddox stood open in the end zone and Finch launched the ball in a high lobbing pass. The pass was coming up short and Larry struggled to reach it. A cry rang out from the crowd as the ball tipped off his fingers and right into the hands of a Wilmington cornerback. A roar rose from the other side of the field as the young Wilmington player dashed to the corner and up the sideline into the wide-open field. The only Burlington player remotely close was Finch and the boy easily outran him. A few plays later, the game was in the books; twenty to ten. Burlington Central was headed home; the whispers that this would not have happened had Josh been healthy didn't escape Finch's notice.

Throughout their senior year Artemis bloomed. Josh found himself increasingly amused by his quirky new friend. At first Josh had let him hang around out of obligation; he did owe Art his life, but the friendship developed. Josh had gotten to know the Pikes and shared his father's opinion of Mr. Pike. The man was a loudmouth dullard as well as a drunk and Josh was grateful that Art didn't insist on their spending much time at the home. Mrs. Pike's diminutive nature seldom gave away much in the way of independent thought, so Josh had no clue where Art's intelligence came from. He often joked that the Pikes had the world's smartest milkman. Knowing the old man, Josh wouldn't have blamed Mrs. Pike if that were true.

Art confided that he had called the police one night when his parents were fighting. The old man had slapped his wife so hard that Art thought she wouldn't get up and that was all he could stand. After he called the law, Art ran from the house and hid down the street after his father threatened his life. The police removed him from the house that night, but Mrs. Pike refused to press charges and he was back the next day.

Josh pushed his lunch tray to the side. Art sat across from him at one of the plastic picnic tables outside the gym. The young man still had little to say a full week after the incident. He was always more quiet than most, but this seemed to have pushed him further into his shell.

"What are you going to do next year?" Josh asked and bit into an apple.

"I don't know, sure as hell getting out of the house," Art said. Josh chewed his apple. Art's eyes were focused down at his tray.

"But what are you going to do?"

"Probably get a job and take some classes at the community college." Art propped his elbows on the table and set his chin in his hands.

"I've got an idea," Josh smiled. "Why don't you go to Chapel Hill with me; shoot, I need a roommate."

"Don't have the money," Art answered looking out toward the woods behind the gym.

"Money," Josh made a mock spitting motion. "Hell, they print more of it every day. My old man knows people; I'll bet we can get you a scholarship." A light seemed to return to Art's eyes and he looked directly at Josh for the first time.

"You think so?"

"Yeah, I do," Josh grinned, "but we don't have any time to waste. We'll go by after school and talk to him."

Art's mouth opened, but barely a sound came out. Josh thought he said, okay, but he wasn't sure. Instead, Art just smiled and nodded.

From that point on Art's disposition brightened. Once the scholarships proved to be more than a pipe dream, there was a layer of air beneath his feet. Nothing from home bothered him like it had. The fact that his mother refused to get out worried him, but at least he knew he had somewhere else to go.

The warmth of graduation day capped off their senior year. The surgeries and physical therapies were over. Josh no longer needed leg braces or even the cane he had used for a time. About the only thing he couldn't do was play football. The injury had taken the edge off his speed. There was also the issue of water; even getting too close to the edge of a pool made him break out in a sweat. He would have to overcome this phobia; Josh had always loved swimming before his near drowning. He reasoned with himself that the night in the car was unusual and he had nothing to fear, but he still had not progressed beyond being able to sit beside the pool. Putting his legs in the water was still too much to expect, but with bikini season here, he would try harder.

"Smile," the guys turned as the camera clicked. Josh's mother laughed and his father grinned. Mrs. Pike had been over to wish Josh well earlier, but old man Pike was nowhere to be seen. It didn't seem to bother Artemis that his father was not there instead he seemed to expect it. Josh began hamming it up as his mother continued to snap pictures as fast as the camera would take. He picked Art up and swung him around. His bad leg slipped on the wet grass and the two of them ended up in a heap on the ground laughing.

CHAPTER

6

JOSH marked his place in the book, set it beside the bed and closed his eyes. Joseph Conrad and other old English writers had that effect on him. Art on the other hand could pick up a book on any subject, British literature or a dry Physics text and become instantly engrossed. A couple hours later he would set it down; fully absorbed and never to be forgotten. Josh wished he had the same command of his memory.

His eyes had just closed when the snip-snip of scissors disturbed his nap. Josh turned his head and watched Art cutting from the Raleigh News and Observer. It was beginning to take on the appearance of a completely detonated minefield. The mutilated remains of the Charlotte Observer lay at the foot of the bed and the as yet untouched Atlanta Constitution and New York Times were neatly stacked at the head. Scrap booking! Josh shook his head; what on earth was so fascinating about the gazillion articles in the dozens of binders in the bookcase beside the bed? People he didn't know and places he'd never been. Art was hopelessly addicted. Everything from Creative Loafing to the Washington Post; Art could find something worth saving in it.

"Find some totally fascinating neighborhood watch meeting in the paper Art?" Josh chided. Art smiled and kept clipping.

"Go ahead and laugh, there's some good stuff in here," Art said without looking up. "You ought to read some of it."

"Oh, I have," Josh shot back, "didn't grab me. What I want to know is what is in the special book." Josh swung his legs to the floor, "The one you keep locked up."

"Nothing," Art stopped clipping for a few seconds. The muscles in his shoulders grew tense. Josh had asked once before with the same results. Once Art had been reading from it and set it down on his desk and walked across the room. Josh eased over and picked it up. Before he could open it, Art had grabbed the book from him and proceeded to lock it in the bottom drawer of his desk. Art relaxed and began clipping again. "Just personal stuff… that's all." Josh studied him. Art's eyes darted about and he pretended to not notice his watchfulness.

"Uh huh," Josh pulled his legs back onto the bed and rolled onto his side, turned his back to Art and was soon snoring.

♩ ♩ ♩

"Hey Josh, hold up!" Josh had tried to duck around a corner, but he had not moved fast enough. Now Finch was trotting up to him with a broad grin covering his face. Well, he couldn't avoid him forever. He did his best to put a pleasant expression on his own face

"What's up," Josh nodded.

"Been looking for you," Finch held out his hand. Josh reached out and gave it a quick shake.

"Oh yeah," Josh said with feigned interest. His eyes wandered up the street like he wished he could.

"Having a party Friday night at the lake and…" Finch tapped Josh on the chest with his forefinger, "you're invited." Josh smiled at this little bit of melodrama. If he hadn't seen it so many times before, he might have been impressed.

"Hmm, I don't know…"

"Oh come on," Finch waved his hands about. "Go to the football game then come down there afterward. Just like old times. Oh yeah, and bring your little friend along, what's his name…" Finch snapped his fingers twice, "Ernie, Bob…"

"Art," Josh glared at Finch.

"That's right, Artie…" Finch smiled. "Come on, you'll both have fun." Josh sighed and pulled his book bag higher on his shoulder.

"I'll ask him," without another word, Josh turned and headed up Franklin Street.

𝆑 𝆑 𝆑

"I've always wanted to go to one of his parties you know," Art gushed. Burlington Central had lost, but the new quarterback was a talented sophomore and next year looked promising. Josh nodded slightly as he pulled onto I-40 from Maple Street. "I mean, I know Connor is kind of a jerk," Art babbled on, "but I hear he has all the pretty girls there. His parties were all the talk…"

"Yeah," Josh grunted, "there is that." Now the mix was sure to include a number of college women as well. Josh didn't know if putting up with Finch was worth all that though, but he couldn't remember seeing Art this excited about anything before. Maybe it would be worthwhile after all.

Josh took his time on the dark country roads. The moonlight reflecting off the lake pulled at his gut. It had been nearly a year, but he could feel the cold water on his skin, smell the dampness inside the car. Art's hand on his shoulder brought him back to the present. He realized that his grip had tightened on the wheel and his breathing had grown shallow. Art was studying him with a look of concern. He nodded and smiled then focused back on the highway.

The party was in full production by the time they arrived. Josh introduced Art to different people, especially the young women. This didn't concern Josh so much. He had never appreciated his ease at attracting the opposite sex until he became so close to someone who didn't have that gift. Tonight his mission was Art. If he could get his buddy to loosen up and become more comfortable talking to the girls, his work would be done. There would be plenty of time for seeking relationships for himself on other nights. As the evening moved along, he sent Art off to work on newfound acquaintances. Art kept returning and Josh kept shoving him back out of the nest. Fly little birdie fly, Josh grinned. He was talking with, Steve, his running back from the previous year. They had been trading barbs because Steve had walked on at North Carolina State this year.

In Due Time

They would chat a bit then he would look over to check Art's progress. There was one little redhead in particular that Art seemed drawn to. Julie May, Josh remembered after struggling for the name at first. She was a year behind them, having entered her senior year at Burlington Central. Art had good tastes, Josh mused as he stood watching them talk. She was maybe an inch shorter than Art, about five foot six he guessed, and petite, but very well proportioned. She was surprisingly able to hold a conversation that didn't involve cars, shopping, makeup, or cell phones. Finding someone able to enjoy a deep discussion with Art could be a challenge. Julie brushed back a long strand of shiny red hair and laughed. Art beamed, his hands moving about with the exchange.

Josh caught a glimpse of Connor Finch out of the corner of his eye. Finch was whispering something to a buddy and pointing toward Artemis. Josh tensed up immediately. The other guy looked over at Art and they both laughed. Finch began making his way toward Art and Julie with an easy sneer twisting the corner of his mouth.

Finch stepped between them with his back to Art and started talking to Julie. She would periodically look around Finch and say something to Art, but Finch continued to ignore him. After a moment of staring down into his drink and smiling weakly every time Julie said something to him, Art turned and began to walk away. He looked up and caught Josh's glare. Josh shook his head and nodded back toward Julie with an arched eyebrow. Art looked back toward Finch and Julie, Finch now had an arm around the girl's shoulders twisting his fingers in her silky hair. Art shrugged helplessly. Josh glared harder and took a step forward shaking his head and pointed toward Julie. Art got the message this time. He turned back and tapped Finch on the shoulder. Finch ignored him. Art tugged at Finch's arm and was ignored again. Art looked back at Josh. Josh shot him a deep frown and Art turned and stepped around to the front of the two. In the process of doing this he bumped Finch's arm and knocked his glass out of his hand. The glass tumbled inward spilling straight down the front of his pants and soaking his crotch. Julie jumped back and let out a nervous laugh.

In one swift move, the back of Finch's fist landed against Art's cheek with a loud smack. Art's head snapped to the side and he staggered backward and landed on his butt on the floor. Finch was drawing his foot back to launch a kick into Art's side when Josh caught him by the arm. He snatched Finch around to face him. Finch's fist flew toward Josh, but he was too quick for the smaller man. He caught Finch's wrist with his left hand and seized him by the throat with his right. Josh drove his knee into Finch's gut and rammed him back into the wall and held him there.

The sound of running feet brought Josh around sideways. He lifted his left leg and caught Finch's buddy with a sidekick that sent the toady to the floor in a heap. He slammed Finch back into the wall and warned everyone else to stay back.

"You sorry sack of…" Josh screamed into Finch's face. Finch's eyes bugged in fear and he tried to plead with Josh, but a gurgling rasp was all that escaped his lips. Josh realized that he was clenching his throat too tightly and relaxed his grip. He spun Finch around and forced him face down onto the floor. With his knee in the middle of Finch's back he grabbed his hair and jerked. Finch let out a quick scream.

"Don't you have anything to say," Josh asked.

"Let me go you son of a…" Finch said. Josh jerked his hair again causing another anguished yelp.

"Wrong answer," Josh bore down harder with his knee bringing a groan.

"I'm sorry Josh," Finch said barely above a whisper.

"That's nice, but I'm not the one you need to apologize to," Josh forced his face down into the floor then yanked it back up.

"I'm sorry, uh…" Finch gasped, "Art."

"That's better," Josh said.

"Let me up Josh, please." Tears streamed down Finch's face. Josh pulled his knee off and got into a crouch beside Finch and yanked him up by the hair. He turned Finch around and shoved him in the chest causing him to land on his backside and slide a few feet. He glared down for a couple of seconds then gave a warning look around the room.

In Due Time

"We'd better leave," Josh half whispered to Art. He watched the room; no one else seemed likely to give him any trouble. Art nodded and looked over toward Julie. She had turned her back and was leaving with some other girls.

CHAPTER

7

"**I** SAW you go in," Josh turned his head at the sound of the voice. Finch leaned against the wall outside the library. Josh looked him over; a fight here would not be good. Both of them would probably be arrested and expelled. Finch was relaxed and looking down.

"Yeah," Josh said, keeping a step back. If Finch came after him, he would back off and deal with him when there were fewer eyes watching.

"Listen," Finch pushed away from the wall and took a pace forward. Josh eased away a step. Finch held up a hand, "I was all wrong, I'm sorry. Okay?"

"Okay," Josh said, the hesitance let the word hang in the air for several seconds. He squinted and cocked his head sideways, not taking this admission at face value. "And..."

"And nothing," Finch grinned, "I just lost my temper, that's all. I was wrong."

Josh said nothing. His eyes bore into Finch. Connor Finch had always been a slippery one, but could he be sincere? Impulse and bad judgment had been his calling card as long as Josh had known him. Josh finally gave a slow nod and began backing away.

"Whatever you say Finch," Josh nonchalantly waved and walked off toward the Pit.

$$ f f f $$

In Due Time

Josh flipped on the light as he walked into the room. He didn't recall where Art said he would be at that time of day. He grabbed his English book and flopped down in his chair. Josh let out a groan; his notebook lay across the room on the table beside Art's work area. It was there from earlier when he returned after class and headed out to the library. After grabbing the notebook, he turned to retrace his steps back to his chair and stopped. Something was out of place. Josh turned back and scanned the corner. There! What was that doing out in the open? Art had left his private scrapbook out on his desk. Josh had never seen him leave it out. Hell, Art would set a land speed record putting it away whenever someone else came into the room when he was looking at it. What did he keep in that thing, porn, something incriminating? What?

Josh smiled and eased into Art's desk chair. He looked around slowly and tapped lightly on the cover. No, he couldn't do this; it wasn't right. He braced and began pushing himself up. He had made it only a few inches before he settled back and flipped the book open. It contained more articles like the rest of the scrapbooks. What was different about this one?

Josh began to read and realized that the first story was about him; a profile about the football team with a whole section about his all-state selection the prior year. It gushed about the team's state championship hopes with him at the helm. He smiled recalling the times. The sun and wind on his face every afternoon, the bittersweet burn deep in his muscles after a hard practice and the thrill of a hard fought win. Some days he felt guilty for not having football practice. He turned the page and frowned. The next story was about him as well.

There was a picture of a wrecker pulling his car from Lake Mackintosh. The headline above it read, "Victory Marred by Tragedy." He did not recall this article. Josh was reading the opening sentence, "Burlington Central's brilliant victory over Durham, showcasing the outstanding abilities of quarterback Joshua Lance preceded the devastating tragedy later that night when…" He jumped from the chair and turned at the sound of the door. Art's face seemed drained of blood. He glanced down at the open book on the desk and back at Josh.

"What... uh, what are you doing?" Art asked.

"Um, well... nothing," Josh tried to smile. Oh man he knew Art would be upset with him. How could he do this? The guy valued that book like nothing else, but now he was more curious than ever. He half turned his head and shifted his eyes down at the book. Art practically lunged for the book, slamming it shut and shoving it into his special locking drawer. Josh hung his head and eased back over to his bed and sat down.

"Did you read it?" Art sputtered.

"Not really," Josh murmured.

"What did you read? What did you see?" Art squeaked out.

"Nothing, I had just opened it, really." Josh looked back up. A tear trickled down Art's cheek. "Really, I'm sorry, I didn't read anything." Art sniffed slightly and locked the drawer, then turned and hurried out into the hall to the bathroom. Josh sighed loudly and flopped back on his bed. Oh boy! He thought and covered his face with his hands.

$$fff$$

The rest of the year went by without further mention of the incident. Art was careful to not leave the scrapbook lying out and Josh resisted the urge to ask about it. None of it really made sense to Josh and he feared damaging their friendship if he pressed the matter. After all, Art did save his life.

Now it was fall again and they were in the third week of their sophomore year. They walked out of the bookstore into the common area known as The Pit. Art was looking down when Josh reached over and grabbed him by the shoulder.

"Hey man," Josh nodded over toward the student center. "Lookie there!"

"What," Art mumbled.

"Over there," Josh moved behind Art, grasped both shoulders and pointed him in the direction he had indicated. "You see?" Art stuttered out something Josh couldn't quite understand. Josh laughed, "Come on!" He stepped out front and motioned for Art to follow, "Hey Julie! Julie!" He cupped his hands around his mouth and looked back to where Art stood frozen; a deep frown lined his face. A quick glare and jerk of the head brought Art along behind him. The little redhead looked about puzzled and recognized the athletic young man trotting her way. A smile spread across her face and she came striding toward them.

"Hey," she squealed and leaped up hugging Josh and giving him a quick peck on the cheek. "How are ya'll doin?" Art was standing a few steps back, so she just nodded and smiled, "Art?"

"We're fine," Josh said as he reached back pulled Art forward. "I didn't know you were going here."

"Yes," she smiled. Her red hair gleamed softly spilling over the front of her sky blue Carolina tee-shirt. The soft waves danced about her firm shoulders as she nodded.

"Well, we're glad you did," Josh grinned then quickly looked down at his watch. "Oh man, I gotta get to class. Hang on one sec, Julie." He held up the index finger of his left hand and reached over, took Art by the arm and dragged him a few feet away with his right. "Listen Art," he said in a whisper, "you go over there and talk to that girl."

"What are we going to talk about?" Art's eyes widened pleadingly.

"I don't know, go get something to eat or drink. I don't care, but…" Josh shook his finger in warning, "I'd better not hear that you talked to her for five minutes and just walked away you hear!"

Art looked down, "Okay, I guess so."

"I mean it Art, if I hear that I'll take you out back of the dorm and slap you bald headed." Art looked back up, Josh was grinning down at him.

"Well, we wouldn't want that would we?" Art laughed nervously. Josh clapped him on shoulder.

"Julie," Josh stepped back over and raised his voice to a normal level, "I gotta run, but why don't you two get caught up. I'll see you around, alright?" He waited until he had gone around the corner of the bookstore before he looked back. Art had stepped up and was talking to her and pointed toward the student center and they turned and began walking that way. Good, Josh thought and headed up the street.

ƒ ƒ ƒ

"So," Art said taking a seat on a bench beside Julie. "Um," he half laughed, half grunted nervously. "Things got kind of crazy before." Julie tossed her head back and let out a soft giggle.

"Yes they did," she smiled, "Connor is such a jerk. I'm really sorry he hit you."

"Yeah," Art looked down for a second then asked, "Do you two have something going on?"

"What?" Julie's screwed her face into a tight grimace, "With Connor Finch? Hell no." She rolled her eyes and Art's face brightened. "What a jerk, I've never even been out with him, but he's still tried to put his hands more places that my doctor has." Art blushed and Julie let out a laugh and jerked her right hand up to cover her mouth. "Sorry," the fingers of her left hand brushed his forearm, "I didn't mean to embarrass you."

"You didn't," he shot back too quickly. "Um, not really… that is." Art smiled nervously and shifted about on the bench.

"Listen," she leaned in, a strand of her hair hung down and brushed against his arm. He drew in a deep breath. "I was really enjoying our conversation before all that happened."

"You were?" Art asked and Julie nodded. "Then why did you turn away and walk off?"

"I was embarrassed and a little scared." She leaned in further looking him in the eye, "And I guess," she sighed and leaned back. His heart skipped slightly at the feel of her warm breath. "Well, I guess I kind of felt like it was my fault."

"No," Art insisted, "like you said, Finch is a jerk." He was staring intensely at her now. She smiled.

"You know, that's what I liked so much…"

"What?" He asked.

"That," she pointed, "the way you have so much passion when you talk." Art's eyes widened at the word "passion," he had never thought of himself as passionate about anything. "I mean when you get to talking about science and mechanical things and the history of all that stuff, it's like… well, it's like you're in a zone or something… so focused." She placed her hands up beside her eyes like a horses blinders. "Most guys can't carry on that kind of conversation and you just get into it so much… and I find that fascinating."

"You do?" Art's brow knitted. He sat with his hands on his knees.

"Yes," she said, "I don't know a lot about that kind of stuff, but…" she reached out and placed her hand over the top of his. "I'd like to." She arched an eyebrow and pressed her lips together into a sly smile.

CHAPTER

8

JOSH sprawled back in a lounge chair. The sun glinted off the surface of the pool making him squint behind his sunglasses. He had still not ventured into water deeper than a bathtub since his accident, but now felt pretty proud that he managed to sit beside the pool with his legs dangling in the water. It had taken four years for this. The first time he tried it, he nearly fainted. Watching the young ladies emerge from the depths of the pool, the wetness of their bodies glowing under the glare of the yellow sun was enough for him.

Art and he had lived in these apartments during the six weeks since graduation. It was hard to believe that it had been four years since they first came here. It was even harder to believe that the pretty little redhead swimming laps about the pool was still around. When he had pushed Art to talk to her that day, he had no idea Julie would be on the scene three years later. Josh rose from the chair and plodded over to the edge of the pool where Art sat watching Julie swim. As he came closer, Josh felt himself swoon for a second with the moving water. He swallowed hard; half closed his eyes and sat down on the concrete. He scooted the last couple of feet and eased his legs down into the warm water.

"Quite a day, huh?" Josh smiled. Art nodded, but kept his head forward watching Julie gliding under the water; her hair streaming behind her like a windsock in a gale. She broke the surface and began bobbing up and down, breast stroking along. Josh had to admit that if Art was going to stick with the first girl to pay him any attention, he had made an excellent choice.

"Ready for grad school?" Josh asked.

"Looking forward to it," Art answered. Several schools had wanted him, but in the end Duke won out. So here they were, still living near Chapel Hill. Duke was only a few miles away, Art had argued so they could continue being roommates; but he didn't fool Josh. It was Julie who was keeping him near.

"Lucky dog," Josh gave Art a gentle shove on the shoulder. "You and Julie are playing the summer away while I'm a poor old working man." Julie had stopped on the opposite end of the pool and was standing in the shallow water wringing her hair out. She had her back arched and her head back working the water out with her hands behind her head, face glistening in the sun. She had excellent skin, she didn't freckle in the summer like most redheads; instead her skin turned a light golden brown.

"You're damn right I'm a lucky dog," Art grunted. "An ugly little geek like me scoring a woman like her."

"You're not ugly man," Josh turned to look at his friend. "You're just different."

"Humph! That's not what all the other kids told me all my life..." Art's eyes cast downward and his face screwed up mockingly, "You're ugly, you're a shrimp, you're stupid... Hell, even the girls used to beat me up."

"Oh come on," Josh forced a laugh. "You see, we know you're not stupid, so that invalidates their whole argument."

"Well... if I'm not ugly, then why..."

"Aw man!" Josh said, "Kids are just mean, you know that. You're not ugly, you're not a big strapping athlete, but we're not in high school anymore, so... well so what?" Josh paused, "You're different, but that's what makes you special... You are way too damned serious, but we can work on that." Josh punched him in the chest and grinned. "Hell boy, the proof's in the pudding, look over at what you've got going for you." They both turned and looked at Julie adjusting her suit, "Only the hottest girl in the whole pool." Art nodded.

"Yeah, and the best friend in the world," Art smiled.

"You'd better believe it," Josh laughed.

"And to think," Art continued, "it wouldn't have been, if I hadn't gone early…" Art stopped suddenly.

"Early for what?" Josh asked.

"Oh, uh," Artemis stammered, "I was just thinking about how close we came to losing you in that wreck. That's all. Something made me leave the house early."

"Where were you going anyway?"

Artemis quickly looked away. "I don't remember." Then he turned his head back and smiled, "But I'm glad I was."

"Yeah, me too," Josh stared down at the water feeling his breath quicken a bit. Julie came torpedoing under the water toward them suddenly, breaking the surface like a seal. She grabbed the side of the pool and hoisted herself out between Art and Josh, shouldering them to each side.

"The best seat in the house," she bubbled, "right between Duke's newest professor and researcher and the hottest young account executive at Rhynelow Chemicals."

"Graduate assistant," Art corrected.

"Well, you'll be the best they've ever had." Julie ducked her head, flipping her hair forward then slung it backward, drenching Art and Josh and raining water all about the pool deck behind them. She liked doing this; sometimes she would sneak up behind them and shake herself like a dog—slinging water everywhere—then run. She giggled and grabbed Josh by the arm and pulled him toward her. "I got you're part right at least didn't I?"

"You sure did," Josh said swaying toward her. He was surprised by her strength. His weight pushed her against Art, forcing him to catch himself to keep from toppling over. "Hey, I've got to go to Burlington tomorrow."

"What for?" She asked as she released her grip, allowing him to right himself.

"Finch Mills," Josh nodded.

"Really?" Julie said. Art's head turned at this too. "What do you sell them?"

"Flame retardant."

"Oh yeah," Julie said, Art usually went silent when she got on a tear. "Keep my drapes and jammies from burning?"

"Something like that," Josh laughed.

"Do you have to deal with Connor?" Art broke his silence. His lips cast into a frown.

"No, thank God, I'll be meeting with his father."

"That's bound to be better," Julie wrinkled her nose.

"Yep," Josh smacked the side of his head dislodging a drop of water that had tricked down into his ear from Julie's earlier water dance. "I have them in the morning, and then it's over to Durham to Nash Tool and Die Company."

"What do you do for them?" Julie asked.

"Lubricants."

"Oh yeah?" Julie smiled, "So you lube their tools?" She laughed and Art turned a deep red. Josh smirked and gave them both a quick nudge in turn with his fist as he climbed to his feet.

"Funny how much easier to embarrass Art is than you are," Josh grinned walked over to retrieve his towel.

$$fff$$

Josh walked through the door of Gordon Finch's office and sat down. Mr. Finch's grandfather had founded the mill eighty years before and Gordon Finch had been raised into it.

"Josh I know we've never really met," Finch sat down in his leather office chair behind his desk. "But I feel like I already know you. I've watched you play football from the time you boys were in middle school."

"Yes sir," Josh nodded.

"You were always a natural."

"Thank you," Josh smiled, "Of course, having a good backup like Connor helped."

"Humph," Finch mused. "Competent I guess, but good? I don't know…"

"Um, well…" Josh shifted in his chair. He fumbled about for the right thing to say, finally deciding that there wasn't a right thing to say. Thankfully Finch continued, sparing him.

"He had decent raw talent, but…" Finch grimaced, "the boy was always lazy. I'm afraid he's too much like my father in law, God rest his soul. Looks just like him, that's for sure, which is a good thing. Other than looks, I pray to God that he doesn't take after him; that man, Lord have mercy… don't get me wrong, he could be a decent sort, when he was sober that is…" Finch glanced at Josh and leaned back in his chair. "Sadly, that wasn't much of the time. And you want to talk about a mean drunk… Thank goodness, my wife takes after her mother; that was a truly lovely woman, inside and out."

Josh opened his mouth then realized he had nothing to add, so he nodded and smiled.

"Fortunately the old man drank himself to death not long after we married." Finch observed the frown on Josh's face and smiled sadly, "Oh I know that's a bad thing to say, and," he shook his finger gently at Josh with a grin, "if you tell my wife I said that you and me will have a big falling out. But you just can't imagine the family occasions that man ruined for us and his poor wife." He shook his head slowly, "Such a sweet and beautiful woman. I guess she married him for his looks… then again… he could be quite charming when he wanted to be. That just never lasted long. I actually had to throw him out of our house once. At least Connor got his looks from them and didn't end up with a mug like mine." Finch laughed. Josh smiled and shifted in his seat. "But as for the rest… well, we'll just have to work on that won't we?"

"Uh," Josh looked around, "yes sir."

𝆑𝆑𝆑

Josh zipped along on I-40, Gordon Finch had kept him long and he struggled to make up the time. Nash Tool and Die was not far off the interstate and Josh rolled into the parking lot shortly after reaching Research Triangle Park. He hopped from the car and dashed through the front door and strode into the lobby.

Josh fumbled with his notebook, thumbing through the pages as he walked up to the front desk. He set his briefcase on the floor and finally looked up.

In Due Time

The name on the desk read "Alice Birch," but all he could see was her face. The soft gentle eyes as deep and blue as the Caribbean Sea, the easy smile, framed by soft playful lips. He wondered how long words escaped him before regaining his composure. It must not have been too long, or at least Alice didn't seem to take note of it. Josh guessed this happened to her often.

"Ah, yes," Josh looked down finally reading the name. She was new since his last visit. "Joshua Lance to see Mr. Nash please." He looked back up, once again trying to not leer too blatantly; he reminded himself that he was here to do a job.

"Oh yes, Mr. Lance…"

"Josh…" he interrupted quickly, "Please," his tone softened.

"Okay… Josh," her lips curled up on one end. "He's been expecting you."

"Thank you," he said and turned toward the double doors leading back to Nash's office. About half way there, Josh glanced back, Alice Birch smiled and waved. Josh blushed at the thought of being caught looking.

His meeting with Nash was overdue and Nash had much to discuss. Josh tried to keep his head in the room and immersed in the lengthy agenda Mr. Nash laid out before him. He took notes and promised to follow up on the items that were troubling his customer. By the time the meeting was finished, Josh nearly bolted to the lobby. He pushed open the double doors and felt his heart sink. A quick glance at his watch told the tale, it was nearly 5:30 and her desk was empty. He dragged through the lobby and out the front door, sank into the seat of his car and let out a long frustrated sigh.

CHAPTER

9

JOSH couldn't come up with an excuse to visit Nash Tool and Die again so soon, so he did the next best thing. He began frequenting the restaurants nearby whenever he wasn't forced to be out of town. After a month Josh had about given up. It would likely be another three months before he would have a good reason to visit Nash, but he was realizing that he just may have to wait.

Josh's next visit brought more disappointment. He bounded through the front door, on top of the world. He would think of something, he knew it. As he walked across the lobby, he was greeted by a smiling pretty face. But it wasn't hers.

"Hi, I'm Joshua Lance. I'm here to see Mr. Nash." Josh tried to mask his dimmed enthusiasm.

"Yes, Mr. Lance. He's expecting you."

Josh took two steps and stopped. He turned and looked back at the receptionist. "Oh yeah, that other lady, um…" he pretended to stumble for the name, "Alice I think…"

"Yes, Alice is still around. She's just out today."

"Oh, okay." Josh stammered slightly, "That's good." He turned back toward the inner door.

"I'll tell her you asked about her." The blonde receptionist said. Josh turned back to see that she had a playful smile. He reddened slightly.

"Thanks."

ƒ ƒ ƒ

"You are not going to mope around this apartment another evening." Artemis said, "Do you hear me?"

"I'm not moping." Josh replied.

"Damn right you're not. You're coming out with us."

"Nah," Josh waved him off, "Haven't you heard, three's a crowd."

"Look. I get into the PhD program at Duke and my best friend isn't going to help us celebrate. I don't think so." Art turned at the sound of the door. He smiled as Julie walked into the room.

She jumped on Art playfully pushing him to the couch. They engaged in a brief tickle fight before tumbling to the floor laughing. They kissed then laughed some more.

"Good grief," Josh said, "see, you two can't keep your hands off each other. Go out and have fun."

"Mr. Lance there thinks he can get out of going to celebrate with us." Art said from the floor where Julie had him pinned.

"Is that so?" Julie climbed off Art and pointed at Josh, "You might as well go change clothes now, because you are coming."

"I'd be a fifth wheel. Ya'll go have fun."

"I'll call one of my friends, and then we'll have an even number. There's this one woman, I just know…"

"No. I'm not in the mood."

"In the mood or not doesn't matter Mr. Lance." Julie poked Josh in the chest, "The only question is do you want me to find a date for you or not."

"Alright, I'll go, but no date." Josh turned and disappeared into his room.

Josh attempted to be light hearted through supper. He pretended to not be bothered, but doubted that he was fooling anyone. Art and Julie seemingly didn't notice. Josh wondered if he could ever find anything as special as what they had. The idea startled him. He had never really thought in those terms. That's when he realized that he must be growing up. The thought of that nearly sent Josh into a panic.

Josh sat across the table from Art lost inside his own head. Julie had stepped away to the bathroom. Josh became aware that Art had stopped talking and was staring at him.

"I'm sorry, did you say something?" Josh looked up at Art.

"I've said a bunch. I just don't think you heard any of it." Art laughed.

"Sorry."

"Look," Art reached into his pocket. "I got this for Julie." He pulled out a small jewelry box and opened it. Inside a small diamond ring shined.

Josh studied it quietly. "Wow," he finally managed to say. "When are you planning to give that to her?"

"I don't know yet. It has to be sometime special."

"Are you ready for this?" Josh asked, "Is she?"

"I am!" Art eagerly responded and looked down. "And I think she is too," he smiled as he cut his eyes back up at Josh and darted a quick look toward the ladies room.

"What about school?"

"I'm still going to finish. We'll probably wait until I'm done."

Josh blinked and looked around. He blinked again hunting through his mind for the right words. Finally he simply said, "Good luck."

As they finished eating, Josh kept noticing the smiles. Art's look of contentment and long gazes at Julie pulled at his heart. Josh wondered if any particular woman could ever make him feel that way.

Art and Julie wanted to see a movie. Josh resisted at first and finally acceded. On the drive over, he sat in the back silently listening to them softly talking up front. Their manner was so easy; they seemed to have known one another forever. He had heard of people being "soul mates," but had never really believed it. Now he wondered if this was it.

The movie was mind numbing and Josh struggled with the point. At last he decided it was pointless to worry over. His mind was already too full. Art had asked if he enjoyed it and Josh said yes without elaborating.

In Due Time

It was in the lobby that Josh's eyes settled on the flowing black hair resting on the soft shoulders. The peach blouse framed the gentle lines of a torso that tapered into the waistband of a pair of Lee Jeans spreading over the firm curves of her hips. Beside her stood two small children, a boy and a girl; gesturing excitedly at a machine full of stuffed animals with a crane in the top.

"Allow me," Josh walked up to the machine and put the proper change into the slot. He carefully maneuvered the crane and retrieved a small pink teddy bear which he handed to the girl. The girl squealed and the woman smiled. He stared briefly at the soft pale lips resting under the pug nose. The lips had just a hint of color, not painted bright red. Josh decided that he preferred this.

"What about me? I want one too," the little boy insisted.

"Alex, don't be rude," the woman scolded. Josh smiled at the boy and turned back to the machine. It took three tries this time, but soon he turned to hand the little boy a red, white and blue stuffed dog that had been resting in the corner of the machine.

"Thank you Mr. Lance."

"It was my pleasure Ms. Birch," Josh smiled and gently shook a finger, "but please; call me Josh."

"Then you must call me Alice… Josh." The sound of his name had never pleased him more. It seemed to roll from her lips like butter melting over a hot biscuit. "Where are my manners," she gestured at the children, "these are my kids, Alex and Amanda."

Josh struggled to keep smiling. "You and your husband must be very proud."

"I am… and he was," she hesitated. "He died when Amanda was a baby."

"I'm sorry." Josh grimaced. The fleeting pain in her eyes made him want to pull her close. He felt a degree of shame at the realization that deep down he was pleased at the revelation.

"Thanks for the toys." Alice took the children by the hands and turned toward the exit.

"Alice?" Josh called.

She turned and smiled.

"Would you like to have lunch some time?"

Alice raised one eyebrow in a question.

"With me, I mean," Josh stammered.

She lowered her eyebrow and spread her lips into a coy smile. "I would love to. How about Tuesday? Meet me out front of my building at 12:00?"

Josh nodded eagerly. He thought he said yes, but later wasn't sure he managed to get any words past his drying lips. She smiled again; turning her mouth up in one corner then turned and walked out into the night.

CHAPTER

10

A HORDE of angry butterflies raged through Josh's gut. He had thought that Tuesday would never come, but here it was. He glanced at his watch again, 11:55; she should be coming out soon. It quickly occurred to him that he should get out and wait in front of his car. No, he thought, that would make him seem too eager. Ah shoot! He opened the door and walked around to the front and leaned on the hood.

All his life, Josh had his pick. He never worried about one getting away; he knew another just as good would be along shortly. Why was he so frantic over this woman? She had filled his dreams, he would close his eyes and imagine her voice in his ear; he had not stopped thinking about her at all. What was so special about this one? You're gonna get hurt, he warned himself. You finally care about a particular woman and she's going to break your heart.

He closed his eyes and smiled, remembering the dream he awoke to that morning. They were lying on the floor of a cabin in the mountains. A fire crackled in an oversized fireplace before them. Her head lay on his chest and he ran his fingers through her thick dark curls, enjoying her hot breath along the side of his chest and over his forearm. Her soft breasts pressed against his ribs and he could feel her heart beat against his belly.

Alice's emergence from the front door made Josh catch his breath. The gentle sway of her hips transfixed him as she glided along. She looked about, then saw him and smiled; he relaxed and hurried over to open the passenger door.

"Hello," she said. "You're on time... I like that." Josh nodded and shut her door once she was seated.

$$fff$$

Josh slid into the quiet corner booth. Alice smiled and Josh struggled for something brilliant to say. He feared that too much silence would sink this relationship before it started. Relationship; was that what he was seeking, he wondered. Finding the right thing to say was usually not so hard for him.

"How was your morning," Alice finally broke the ice. Smooth and assertive; he liked that. The words flowed over her tongue and past her lips like a refreshing breeze on a still day. Josh smiled.

"Fine," he rapped his fingers lightly on the table, "working up sales proposals."

"Ooh, sounds exciting," she leaned in placing her hands on the table before her.

"Not really, government stuff, pretty dry."

"Oh, I see," she leaned in further staring intently with a sly grin. "I suppose you could tell me but then you'd have to kill me."

He laughed, "There's probably something in the Patriot Act about it."

Alice chuckled, placing one hand over her mouth. "I wouldn't doubt it."

"You know, I read more stories about it being used to shut down strip joints or grab tax evaders than actual terrorists."

Alice smiled and nodded, still leaning forward on the table. Josh couldn't help noticing her chest resting on the edge. He realized that he was staring and diverted his gaze back up. She had that certain I-caught-you-looking twinkle in her eye. He smiled trying to hide his embarrassment.

"But, I digress," he said quickly, "I'm sure you didn't want to come here and talk about politics. I know I don't."

"What do you want to talk about?" She asked coyly. Her eyebrows arched slightly, making her eyes appear even larger. He took a breath, getting lost in her gaze. Those eyes reminded him of two pools of Caribbean water inviting him in for a swim. He leaned in and laid his right hand between her hands.

"I want to talk about how you are the most stunning woman I have ever seen," he couldn't believe he was saying this, but didn't want to stop, "and how you have the most dazzling blue eyes known to exist." She flushed a slightly deeper olive tone and ducked her head.

"Now you're embarrassing me," she looked back up and smiled.

"I'm being too forward, sorry."

"I didn't say that," she smiled again and ran her fingertips lightly over his hand looking down at it. She looked back up tilting her head slightly, "Thank you."

They both sat back abruptly as their food arrived. The waitress seemed embarrassed at interrupting them, barely looking up from the food. Alice giggled.

"Um, Alice," Josh said.

"Yes," she answered.

"Would you like to go to the movies or something Friday?"

"Well…" she dragged the word out and Josh's hopes sank.

"Oh, I guess you probably have plans."

"No," she said soberly. "But, I doubt I can get a sitter that quickly."

"Oh, that's fine," he said excitedly, "bring them along. There are a couple of good kid's movies out now. We'll let them pick."

"Okay…" she dragged this word out too. She paused considering it. Josh wondered if she felt it was too soon to bring him around the kids that much. Then she grinned. "You know Alex carries that little stuffed dog you got for him all over the place. He's turned it into some kind of flying super hero dog." She grinned putting her hands up in front of her in a pretend flying motion. "He takes it zooming all over the house, like Super Dog or something."

"They're good kids," Josh smiled.

"Yes," Alice sat back and nodded slowly, "They are aren't they? Hey, our food is getting cold."

"Yes," Josh nodded, "we'd better eat."

fff

Friday night was the first of many such outings. Things progressed over the next year and when Art announced he was marrying Julie that was all the prompting Josh needed. It surprised no one that there would be a double wedding. Young Alex and Amanda pulled double duty—Amanda as flower girl and Alex got to be best man for not one, but two grooms.

Josh and Alice settled into a small house a few miles north of Chapel Hill. Alex and Amanda each had a small room of their own. The "master" bedroom was not much larger. A tiny living room sat just off a square eat-in kitchen. Josh's father had offered to help them out with a better place, but Josh wanted to make it on his own. The lack of space didn't bother Josh, however; everything he really cared about was within arms reach.

The week after Artemis earned his PhD, he sat on Josh's back deck having a beer. He was silent for a moment after Josh's question as he took another sip. He sat studying the ice crystals melting and sweating on the outside of the bottle.

"I've done some looking around." Artemis said, "Still haven't decided if I want to teach or go to work in industry."

Josh nodded and leaned forward setting his bottle on the small table between them. He sat back and stared at a tree in the yard for a moment before drawing in a deep breath.

"I have an idea," Josh said. "I want you to think about."

"Okay, what?"

Josh smiled and leaned his head to one side. "Why don't we start our own company? You and I."

Artemis furrowed his brow; his face took on a pinched look. "What?"

"I mean it." Josh said, "You already have a half a dozen things you've been developing. Hell that compound that doubles the strength of body armor is priceless by itself." Josh picked up his bottle and ran a finger around the rim. "No sense in just giving any of that away to some ungrateful employer. Let's develop it ourselves." He raised the bottle and inclined it toward his friend.

In Due Time

Art's face relaxed and his mouth began to curl up at one corner. "That takes money. Where would we find it?"

"I know people. My father knows people." Josh enthused waving his free hand in the air. "I could have them lined up ready with their checkbooks before you know it."

Artemis smiled, "You might be on to something there." He reached out with his bottle and tapped it lightly against Josh's. "What the hell!"

Josh broke out into a broad smile, "You won't be sorry." He took a drink, swallowed and looked back at his friend, "This will make us both millionaires."

CHAPTER

11

THE company started out in an old decommissioned strip mall just south of Research Triangle Park. Artemis had fashioned a laboratory in the back of what had been a large drug store. It had been walled in complete with an airlock entrance into the lab area. The rest was mostly open with a few desks sitting around.

Just outside the laboratory entrance two cubicles shielded the desks from which Josh and Artemis handled the affairs of the company. At this point the company consisted of Josh, Artemis and a secretary.

Rice Oakland rolled up in his Ford Expedition and pulled into a space. He unconsciously looked down to see if he was within the lines then laughed. There were only two other cars in the entire lot. It was a few minutes after seven in the evening and what few people would normally be there were gone. A faint light spilled out from the back of the old store and softly glowed through the front glass. A large circle with crossed spears sat over the front door with the words, "Lance and Pike Enterprises" underneath.

Oakland drew in a deep breath and slowly stretched his immense frame. He rubbed his palm over his closely cropped hair and breathed out, counting to ten. Short hair was nothing new for him, but he had not jumped on the head-shaving trend that was the trend among other young black men. Well, might as well get this over with, he thought as he lifted his left leg out and stood. A slight twinge shot through his knee as his two hundred and sixty pounds pressed down on it. He would always clearly remember that day. In his junior year, a tackle from the University of Michigan landed squarely on it from the side, sending his body one direction and his lower leg in the opposite one. The crack still reverberated in his ear and churned his stomach. That's the day that Rice Oakland's football career at North Carolina State ended.

During his long convalescence, he had plenty of time to think. His NFL dreams flushed into the cesspool of broken dreams. He spent the first few days feeling sorry for himself, but the futility of that eventually set in and he began formulating a vision. He could either waste his life on "what-ifs" or he could rise above it. Oakland decided that the Physical Education degree he was working on was not in his best interest. When the pros were scouting him, it seemed irrelevant, but now...

The thoughts of being a teacher or even a coach didn't appeal to his vision. He began to realize that he had always had an interest in both Chemistry and Math, but football made such plans difficult. He reasoned that the same well ordered thought processes that helped him with these subjects were what also made him a standout in football. He could instantly read an offense and determine what it would likely do better than anyone on the field. The next month he changed his major to Chemistry. Good grades, hard work and a heaping helping of sympathy over his injury got him the grants, scholarships and loans he needed to finish his degree, but he wasn't stopping there. The day he walked away from campus with his PhD was a prouder day than his first on the football team.

The door was unlocked and Oakland eased inside. The building was dark except for the lonely lights spilling out from the cubes in the back. He stood waiting for his eyes to adjust. As Oakland was about to call out, the overhead lights came on. Joshua Lance stood against the back wall studying all six and a half feet of the small mountain before him. Lance had a somber look and gave a slight nod.

"You're late Oakland," Josh said. Oakland shrugged. Josh broke into a wide smile as he waved him toward his desk. Artemis emerged from his cubicle and met him half way across the floor with his hand extended.

"Dr. Oakland, pleasure to meet you."

"Dr. Pike." Oakland enveloped the smaller man's hand.

"You know Art," Josh began, "Oakie here was the only guy to sack me in my senior year. Only time I was sacked!"

"That's because we only played y'all once," Oakland laughed.

"Touché,"

"Josh tells me you're one of the best researchers at Rhynelow," Artemis said.

"Hardly," Oakland grunted, "you had all those guys been there over thirty years."

"Well, you would be," Josh put a hand on Oakland's back prodding him toward the cubicle on the left that had Art's name on it. "If they would give you the chance, that is." Josh waved Oakland into a chair and he took a seat on the corner of Art's desk. Art peered out from behind his desk and leaned forward with his elbows on the desk studying Oakland.

"We're not going to beat around the bush, Dr. Oakland," Art continued, "I'm going to need help in the lab if we are to make this company happen. How would you like to be our Director of Research?"

"Wow," Oakland said, "you get to the point. What makes you so certain I'm the right man?"

Art nodded toward the corner of the desk Josh was sitting on. "If Joshua Lance believes in you, so do I."

"Oakland," Josh clasped his hands together tenting his index fingers outward, stabbing the air. "We are breaking the mold here and there is no one I can think of that can help us do that better than you. You are exactly what we need here and we are exactly what you need." He paused to let the point hang for a moment, "You see, those old boys in the lab at Rhynelow will never let you do the kind of work you want to and are capable of. They are protecting those projects for themselves. I broke through and was promoted because money talks and in sales I had some serious leverage in Alamance and Guilford counties and Dr. Rhynelow knew it. Through my old man, I had an in into just about every company around there and I worked it. You on the other hand…" he waved his hand dismissively, "well, you don't have that kind of leverage and the fact that you are damned good only makes you a threat to the scientists above you. Here, with your help, we'll not only break the mold, we'll shatter it into microscopic bits."

"Um," Oakland tried to digest the rapid fire monologue, "how many accounts do you have here?"

Josh smiled and leaned back, "None." He put his hands on his knees and leaned forward his eyes bearing down on Oakland, "But we will. You see Oak, there are things on the horizon that I am not at liberty to tell you about, but they will come to pass and when they do…" He leaned back and held his hands up in a surrender type gesture and slowly shook his head, "then, watch out! There are going to be some really big things happening here."

"Wow," Oakland said looking back at Art. Art's somber veneer cracked slightly and he grinned and gave a quick nod.

"Oakland," Josh spoke again, "we need you here."

Oakland looked down at his manicured nails for a moment then looked between the two men. He drew in a breath and turned his head back toward Josh. "Can I think it over?"

"Take all the time you need, but…" Josh wagged his finger, "Don't let this pass you by."

$$fff$$

Artemis Pike and Rice Oakland had spent the prior three days organizing the expanded laboratory. The two scientists had immediately bonded over their projects. It had not taken Oakland long to decide and now here he was. The demolition and construction took out the wall separating the original space in the old drug store from the adjacent vacant clothing store had gone smoothly. There was now an archway leading from the existing lab to the other side that was dedicated to more lab space.

Art and Oakland had hired two interns to assist them, but the office part was still manned by Josh and one secretary who also served as the receptionist for the company. Each scientist now had his own space in a corner of the lab in addition to the common space for ongoing projects. They also maintained cubicles outside the airlock for the limited time they were not in the lab.

The two men were finishing up the list of projected materials needed for a large-scale production of the improved body armor when they heard a commotion. Art looked at the grinning Oakland and headed toward the exit of the lab for the main floor. Out in the main section Josh had the secretary out from her desk doing his best rendition of the Waltz across the floor. He gracefully left her with a quick twirl and grabbed Art in a bear hug and swung him around with a war-whoop before returning the shorter man to the floor.

Josh reached up and put his hands on Rice Oakland's broad shoulders. "Oakland, I would swing you around too if I could lift that much weight!" Oakland laughed.

"Josh, what?" Art demanded.

"It's a done deal; the Department of Defense is going to finance the project." Josh held out a piece of paper, "We have a signed contract."

Art looked upward and closed his eyes. He said a silent prayer, slapped his hands together and let out a loud whoop of his own.

"Let's go out and celebrate," Josh said.

"Celebrate? We've got too much to do. Details to attend to…"

"We can start on the details tomorrow."

"But…"

"Okay, we can talk about some of it over supper, but we are going to celebrate and that is all there is to it, now call home and have the womenfolk meet us there."

Art's shoulders slumped in resignation and he shrugged. "Okay. Can't argue with you." He smiled and headed for his phone.

CHAPTER

12

"**H**OWARD that was outstanding work you did for us on the Department of Defense project." Josh sat in his leather executive chair. A large wooden desk separated him from Howard Spence in the office in the back corner of the old retail outlet. The drywall was up now, but remained unpainted. The last time Howard had been here the two by four wooden studs were still exposed. Outside of the lab area and the restroom, this was the only actual walled room to be found in the building.

"Thank you," Howard smiled. It had been a good payday for his public relations consulting firm. Firm, hell, Howard thought, it was really just him. There was the occasional temp he would hire when he was on a deadline. Those had been few and far between. Until this job came in he wondered if he would be able to meet his utility bills for that month.

"That said," Josh rocked back in his chair slowly studying him. "I have a proposition I want to discuss with you."

Hot dog, Howard bubbled, more business. He wanted to shout; instead he maintained an even, but pleasant smile. Josh rose from his chair and walked around to the front and leaned against the desk.

"Howard, I am assembling a leadership team here at Lance and Pike and I want you to be a part of it."

"Uh…" Howard blinked and shifted in his chair, "You're offering me a job?"

"Yes," Josh grinned.

"Like a full time position…"

"That's right."

"Well…" Howard shuffled his feet searching for words. "I wasn't really looking for a job. I mean my firm…"

"How much are you bringing in over there?" Josh stared intently, "I'll bet we can beat it."

"Um… Well, I'm really not at liberty…"

"How about this Howard," Josh reached back and grabbed an envelope from his desk and handed it to Howard. "Here is a formal offer package extended to you for the position of Vice President and Chief Communications Officer."

Howard took the envelope and opened it. He quickly read through it, trying to keep his composure. He feared his poker face might fail him when he noticed the smirk on Joshua Lance's face. The offer was very good, over ninety thousand dollars a year more than he made at the newspaper and he had yet to bring in anywhere near his former salary since he had been on his own. His throat was suddenly very dry.

"I know you'll want to think this over Howard," Josh said. Howard nodded weakly.

Howard thought about it on the way home. The money was good, but he couldn't get past the whole working for someone else thing. Of course he wasn't likely to face the same dilemma he had at the newspaper. He shook his head and growled at just the thought of that situation. What a miserable mess it was and how he had to stand by and watch as they ruined a good man's life. Ruined, Hell, they might as well have killed the guy themselves. But what did that matter, it got reported on the Podunk community beat his moment in the sun; all the major newswires, syndicated columnists accepting his stories as gospel. No critical analysis, no fact checking; just swallowed it hook, line and sinker like good little fish.

It all culminated the morning the wife found her husband floating face down in the pool. Being called indefensible names to national audiences, the loss of his business and the impending foreclosure of his home was finally too much for him. And this bit of hack reporting had been too much for Howard. Without a clue as to what he would do next, Howard Spence hung up his dreams of changing the world with the truth. The carnage left by another reporter's lies was too repugnant to his sight.

He spent the next week sitting in his office working on short stories and sketching out fancy ideas to use in his next project; whenever that would be. One morning he sat behind his clean desk, reorganizing his workspace yet again. A crow landed in a tree outside his window. Its cawing drew his eyes. He rose and leaned against the windowsill looking down at the ground below; the trees filtered the sunshine giving the grass a dappled look. The crow cawed again and Howard looked him straight in his coal black eyes.

"Old buddy," he mumbled, "it looks like you're just as busy as I am today. Or for that matter," he shrugged; "you have as much purpose in life at the moment." He turned from the window and resumed his seat. Rocking back and forth slowly and making faces as he chased random thoughts about inside his head, he finally blew out a long sigh and sat back upright. After rapping his fingers on the desk for a moment, he reached for the phone.

$$\mathfrak{f}\,\mathfrak{f}\,\mathfrak{f}$$

"Getting settled in?" Howard looked up. Josh stood in the doorway of his new office cradling a coffee cup between his hands. The first week and they already had his nose to the grindstone. The new building stood four stories tall across the parking lot from the old strip mall they had previously occupied. Construction continued all around them even though Josh had been eager for them to move into the half of the fourth floor that was now complete. The banging and drilling was enough to drive Howard mad.

"Yeah," Howard half rose, but Josh waved him back into his chair. Josh strolled over and took the chair across from him.

"What do you think about the Finch Mills proposal?" Josh took a sip of coffee.

"Well," he cleared his throat, "they definitely are the lowest bid. And they've been around for quite a long time. Of course, they are a small company… are you sure they'll be able to deliver the materials?"

Josh nodded and set his cup on the desk. "I think it's a win-win proposition. I've dealt with Gordon Finch for several years. We'll be an important account for them. He'll address any problems delivering the vest materials immediately. I'm not sure we would get that kind of attention from a larger company."

"There is that other thing…" Howard did his best to smile. Josh nodded soberly. "Art's not thrilled about this you know…"

"Don't worry about that," Josh traced a trail along the edge of the desk with a finger. "We won't have to deal with Connor and Art won't have to deal with them at all. I'll handle them."

"Okay," Howard grinned and spread his hands palms out.

"Well," Josh's tone brightened, "have you had a chance to start working on the proposal for the Boston Police?"

"Yes," Howard reached over and grabbed a notepad from the far edge of his desk. "I was just starting to jot down some preliminary ideas." He ran a finger down the list, glancing at the paper. "Nothing concrete yet…"

"Fine, fine…" Josh grabbed his cup and headed toward the door. "We'll set up something tomorrow to do a little brainstorming."

"Sure thing," Howard smiled as Josh headed out the door. The sound of a circular saw echoed from the other end of the corridor.

CHAPTER

13

ALICE'S lips parted and a laugh tumbled out. Josh studied the contours of her face; the soft flutter of her eyelids enchanted him. She was smiling and pointing across the room, her eyes watching him sideways. He reached under the table, took her other hand and returned her smile. The firm warmth of her hand holding his; pressing it against the silky material of her skirt and the toned thighs encased beneath it made his heart skip. He had not been crazy about attending this reunion. Ten years out of high school, big deal! Only to her it was a big deal, she had insisted. It was a big part of his world and she wanted to see it. So here they were in the hotel ball room. For other occasions it might be a conference room or a lecture hall, but tonight it was a ball room.

The flurry of Julie dragging Art from his chair and toward the dance floor grabbed Josh's attention. Art looked like a child being marched into the bathroom for a dose of castor oil, but Julie would not be denied in her desire to dance. When Alice tugged on his hand, Josh smiled and went willingly. He almost laughed at Art's attempts to keep off Julie's feet. Her eyes were closed and her head lay on his shoulder; completely unbothered by the occasional intrusion on her toes.

Alice's lips curled bemusedly as he returned her gaze. The dark room glowed under a mix of colored lights. Alice's eyes sparkled. Josh bent down and lightly kissed her, parting his lips slightly. The sweet softness of her mouth made his stomach flutter. He slid his lips along her cheek and nuzzled into her dark curls, inhaling their fragrance. Her warm body rubbed against his; her breasts swayed against his chest and the rhythm of her breath on his neck buoyed him up as if they were dancing on a cloud. Josh closed his eyes and squeezed her tighter. He would be happiest if every moment of his life could consist of this. There he stayed until the music died and the lights rose again.

On the way back to their table, his eyes flitted over Stacy Baker... Stacy Finch, he corrected himself.

"I'll meet you back at the table," Josh said. Alice nodded and headed back. Josh eased over and stood there until Stacy looked up and he smiled. She grinned and met him halfway giving him a hug.

"Is everything alright?"

"Yeah," she nodded quickly, too quickly Josh thought.

"Finch treating you good?" he tilted his head to one side and peered through squinted eyes.

"Fine."

"Doesn't look like it from here," the bruise on her cheek was more obvious now. Josh nodded his head toward it.

"Oh, this," she touched her cheek lightly, "that was nothing. Just a misunderstanding, nothing really." Josh stared back in silence, "No big deal."

"You know, Stacy, you don't have to put up with that."

"It was my fault, really. He apologized, it's okay." Stacy fumbled with her words, her eyes wide, "He said he was sorry."

Josh blew out a loud sigh. Out of the corner of his eye he saw Connor Finch walking his way.

"How's tricks?" Finch slapped Josh on the back.

"Oh," Josh smiled weakly, "just fine."

"I was just talking to old Art," Finch smiled. "Sounds like it's getting real interesting over there."

"Sure is," Josh nodded, watching Stacy out of the corner of his eye. She looked away, mostly glancing between the wall and the floor. He remembered how vibrant she had once been. Smiley Stacy, she had been called. Now she bore the expression of someone who had been drinking drain cleaner.

"Well," Finch persisted, "your success is our success, so keep at it."

"Um, yeah…"

"Well, Finch Mills…" Finch started and Josh interrupted.

"Listen, I've got to get back…" Josh reached out and grabbed Connor Finch by the forearm. "And Finch…"

"Yes?" Finch looked down at his grasp then back up.

"You take good care of this girl…" Josh glared directly at Finch, "You hear?"

"Oh yeah," Finch nodded nervously, "Of course."

Josh let go and shot a quick glance back at Stacy then turned and walked away.

When he returned to the table, Art and Julie were talking quietly with Alice. Julie smiled and Art raised one eyebrow as Josh settled into his chair. He picked up his drink and cradled it between his hands.

"Have a nice talk?" Art asked in a hushed tone. The low growl in his voice was almost enough to make Josh smile… almost. The bluish tint around Stacy's eye lingered in his mind. He looked down and imagined Finch's face before him. The shaking of the glass and the rattling of the ice alerted him to how hard he was squeezing it. Thank God these glasses weren't cheap and thin. Josh looked up and saw the concerned looks.

"Yeah," he forced a grin. "We talked."

"What a creep," Art snorted.

"Yeah," Josh murmured. "He is that."

CHAPTER

14

"GO long Alex," Josh called as Alex Birch pumped his little legs and headed out across the yard. When he had run about twenty yards he looked over his left shoulder just like Josh had taught him. Josh launched the football into a tight spiral aimed about a step ahead of Alex. He leaned his small body forward and stretched his arms snatching the ball out of the air. After two steps he turned and ran toward Josh.

Josh marveled at the growth and increase in speed he had seen in the little boy. The ball was brand new; Josh had given it to Alex for his tenth birthday. As the boy drew near, Josh stepped to his left and swept him from his feet, swinging him around and then setting him down on his back in a mock tackle.

"Durn, you always catch me," Alex pouted. Josh laughed and tousled his step-son's hair.

"I won't be able to for much longer, if you keep improving like you have." Josh winked. Alex brightened and giggled. The two were soon in a wrestling match like the one they had watched that morning on TV. Josh nearly pinned Alex twice, but would let the boy flip him over each time. Finally with the boy sitting on his chest, Josh gave in. Alex pounded the ground three times and jumped up with his arms in the air and did a victory dance. Josh laid there smiling lazily.

"How about ice cream?"

"Yea!" Alex yelled.

"Go inside and tell your mother and see if your sister wants to go." The boy didn't have to be told twice and was off like a shot.

Josh was dusting himself off when Howard Spence pulled into the driveway. Josh waved and strolled over to Howard's Explorer.

"What brings you over on this fine Saturday, Howard?"

"I was working on the LAPD proposal and wanted to go over something with you."

"Okay," Josh looked back toward the house and saw Alex coming out the door with Amanda in tow. Josh smiled and looked back into the Explorer, "Come on, we can discuss it over ice cream." Howard opened his mouth to protest, but Josh had turned and was half way to his Four Runner where the kids waited. He reached out, opened the door and turned and motioned for Howard to follow. "Well, are you coming?"

Howard shrugged and opened the door to his Explorer. He locked it and climbed into the passenger seat of the Four Runner. He turned and watched as Alex helped buckle Amanda into her seat. The little girl looked up at Howard and smiled. He grinned back and reached for his own seatbelt.

"So what's on your mind Howard," Josh asked as he rolled up to the stop at the end of his street.

"Oh," Howard turned back to face Josh, "I, uh, think I'm finished, but I wanted you to look over some of the figures. You know, make sure they look alright to you."

"I can do that." Josh smiled as he looked about for oncoming traffic. His face became more serious as he pulled onto the main road. "I really appreciate your working so hard to get that done. It isn't absolutely necessary, but when I go out there Monday, it will be a huge help."

"No problem Josh." Howard murmured watching the houses and trees roll by. He sat listening to the children humming softly in the back seat. Howard tried to place the song, he thought he recognized it from his childhood, but he couldn't quite recall it. Then he remembered that it was a tune he had learned in Sunday school when he was a boy. The title still eluded him, though and he soon forgot it as Josh turned into the small strip mall and rolled up to the front door of the Ice Cream Palace. It wasn't much of a palace really. It barely had room for ten tables inside and a few of wrought iron on the sidewalk out front.

"Why don't you pick a table out front here and set up your papers." Josh looked down and smiled at the children, "And we'll go in and get the ice cream. So what are you having?"

"Oh, I wouldn't care for any."

"Oh, come on Howard, everyone loves ice cream." Josh held his hands out to his sides in mock exasperation. "I'm buying."

"Vanilla will be fine."

"Oh how completely boring."

"Chocolate then."

"Better, but still boring."

"Rocky Road?"

"Now you're talking!" Josh punctuated the air with his right forefinger in a stabbing gesture. "Come on kids."

Howard sat at the nearest table. The lime green paint was peeling off of the iron of the chairs. He sat staring across the parking lot waiting. He turned his head back at the sound of the door. Josh walked with a cone in each hand, the kids led the way; they had already started on theirs. Josh handed Howard his scoop of Rocky Road and Howard smirked as he stared at Josh's cone. It was two scoops, one chocolate and one vanilla.

Josh noticed Howard's mirth and shrugged, "Maybe I like being boring."

$$fff$$

Howard had thought he was just answering a question. He didn't understand that he was obligating himself to stay for supper that evening. Of course he could have done worse than hamburgers and hot dogs fresh from Josh's grill. Besides, all he was missing out on was an evening at home cuddling with the television remote.

"So, Howard," Josh was flipping hamburgers as Howard sat at the picnic table on the back deck. "What do you think about this new North American Union that is being proposed?"

Howard shrugged.

"Oh, come on Howard, I know you have an opinion. Spit it out man."

"Well," he sighed, "I can't see it going anywhere."

"I don't know. There's all kind of pressure to compete with the European Union. In fact I have heard that perhaps they might skip the NAU and go ahead and include Central and South America into one giant American Continents Union."

Howard studied the table with his lower lip poked out slightly as he considered this. Finally he shrugged again with his hands extended palms up.

"Howard, you don't have to be politically correct with me. What's on your mind, Hmmmm?" Josh laughed.

"I don't know Josh; I think it's a bad thing."

"Why? It would expand our markets," Josh tilted his head to one side as he began adding hot dogs to the grill. "Our weapons systems and body armor divisions could profit handsomely."

"Maybe so."

"You can't just clam up now, Howard; back up your reasons."

"Well," Howard hunched forward looking up at Josh, "it may be good for the company... for a while... but I don't believe it would be good for the American people to divest our sovereignty like that. It is never good to have that much power under one roof anyway. Hell Josh, one of the reasons this country became so strong was the division of powers among the states anyway. You know, the whole checks and balances thing. One state learns from how another does things and such."

Josh bobbled his head slightly for a few seconds, mulling this over. "Maybe... Of course money does talk. Do you really think that the unified government would mess with a system that is so profitable rather than learning from it?"

"Not everybody likes our system."

"Since Communism fell, doesn't that pretty much leave Capitalism?"

"Communism didn't fall everywhere and there are many pseudo Socialist societies Josh; some of them in the countries that would be part of this Union."

"You really think they would kill the goose that laid the golden egg?"

Howard rubbed his temples and sucked in a breath, "Remember Josh, even a pure Communist system is quite comfortable for those that are in charge."

"I see your point," Josh nodded, "heck, like you said, it probably won't happen anyway; fun to speculate on though." Josh grabbed a platter from the table and began shoveling burgers onto it.

CHAPTER
15

"**W**OW!**"** Art looked around after stepping into the foyer of Josh and Alice's new house; before him spread an open broad front hall with a staircase leading up the left side to a landing with a sitting area situated between living space on either side of the second story. A handful of people milled about the grand hall and the formal living room to the left. On the right the hall extended into an open sitting area with a couch and a pair of chairs around a coffee table. The hall and sitting area formed an L-shape with the door to Josh's study opening into the front sitting area. Art's eyes traveled the length of the floor to ceiling windows gleaming in the front corner.

"Do you like it?" Josh smiled.

Art nodded as his eyes roamed about the space.

"Oh, I just love it!" Julie gushed giving Josh a hug and a kiss on the cheek. "Give me the tour!" She said grabbing Alice.

Josh and Artemis headed into the living room where Rice Oakland and Howard Spence were engaged in a lively discussion.

"… I disagree, Howard," Oakland was saying, "having a more centralized government will make for a more stable political environment." Howard was about to counter when Josh raised his hands.

"Boys, this is not a night to discuss politics. Eat drink and be merry," he smiled, "for tomorrow we shall work."

𝆑 𝆑 𝆑

"And this is the master suite," Alice opened the door and motioned Julie in with a flourish.

"Wow," Julie looked around, "This is all so great." Alice smiled.

Alice led Julie into the bathroom, pointing out the two large walk-in closets on either side of the entrance. Inside she watched Julie run her fingers along the marble countertop at the lavatories. Julie paused at the double whirlpool tub.

"Double occupancy, hmm?" Julie arched an eyebrow and pursed her lips. They both laughed and Alice sat on the edge.

"We've wanted one of these for years." Alice smiled, "As well as the big one on the back deck."

"I'm happy for you," Julie patted Alice on the hand, sitting beside her; "Josh has done so much for Art and me. I mean, Art is talented, but without Josh's drive and business sense... well, we wouldn't have a portion of what we have. And you are so good for him. He loves you..." Julie let out a quick laugh. "Well, I don't have to tell you that."

Alice beamed, "It's still nice to hear it though. Oh, wait until you see the balcony. Josh likes to have breakfast out there."

𝆑 𝆑 𝆑

The four men were now gathered in Josh's new study. They sat in overstuffed chairs made of imported leather which surrounded a small coffee table in a corner opposite Josh's desk. The walls of that corner were lined with built in bookshelves which reached to the ceiling, populated with leather bound keepsake editions of classic novels; most of which Josh had never read.

"What do you think guys," Josh asked gazing out the bay window beside them which opened out between the bookshelves of that corner. All nodded or murmured their approval as they took in the fine wood paneling of the walls.

"I was thinking," Josh said, "we should discuss this proposed Union of American Continents that Howard is obsessed with." He winked at Howard who was scowling.

"You're damned right we should discuss it!" Howard's eyes were blazing as he spoke. "It would be a disaster for this country."

"Now Howard, calm down." Josh said, he heard Rice Oakland chuckle drawing another glare from Howard. "That's not what I'm talking about. Not everyone here is so sure it will be a disaster, but what we really need to talk about is what does this mean for us…" Josh looked around, "as a company, I mean. How can we profit from it."

"Profit?"

"Yes Howard, that's what we do — we're a company — we strive to make profits." Josh leaned forward, "So we need to weigh out the contingencies on this thing. It is looking more likely every day, so if it comes to pass, how are we going to make money from it?" Josh leaned back and looked around at his colleagues.

"I can't believe this," Howard threw up his hands, "our company could well be nationalized, then how are we going to make money."

"I doubt that Howard. In fact, I believe it will open more markets to our products. Body armor, weapons systems… a lot of stuff we are currently restricted in selling outside our borders."

"So, I know Oakland thinks it's a great idea; Josh is just concerned about turning a quick buck from it; what do you think Art?" Howard turned to face Artemis.

Art shrugged, "I'm not as hooked on politics and history as you are Howard. Things like that don't hold my interest, I'm a scientist. I trust Josh's judgment on such matters." He lifted his glass in a silent toast in Josh's direction.

"Josh is failing to see the big picture. He can't see beyond markets and dollar signs."

"Josh has made me a very wealthy man," Art said, "he's made us all wealthy… You included."

"This is not about money Art. This is about our country's sovereignty. We don't want to be subservient to a bunch of third world banana republics."

"Do you really think that will happen?" Oakland interjected, "I mean we are the dominant partner. Every country wants a piece of our pie. It would be an opportunity to make South America more like us, economically and politically."

"Don't be so hasty on that, Oak. Pandering to the whims of the developing nations," Howard made quotation signs in the air around the term, developing nations, "is bound to figure in."

"Of course there's also the need to compete with the European Union." Artemis offered, "Both economically and militarily."

"Are you kidding," Howard slapped his thighs, "the same people who are pushing for this will then want to become part of the EU. Can't you just see it? These two continents started out as a bunch of colonies to a handful of European countries and we'll just end up being one giant colony to one huge European nation!"

"Gentlemen," Josh was waving his hands gently, "let's not disintegrate into a political squabble. We are all free to hold our opinions and support whatever organizations pushing whatever points on this independently of this company. Instead, the point I wish to make is that this is either going to happen or not happen. What we have to do is figure out how to come out looking favorably to whichever side does prevail."

Artemis and Howard both settled back in their chairs. Oakland's amused countenance persisted. He winked and broke into a broad grin as Josh surveyed the group. Josh tented his fingers beneath his chin.

"Make no mistake guys, whatever the outcome; we've got to be prepared to capitalize on the results."

𝆑𝆑𝆑

Alice and Julie sat on the balcony outside the master suite. Perched on two padded chairs with a small breakfast table between them, Alice pointed out the view of the lake just beyond the screen of the trees behind the house. A neat wide trail led down to a covered dock. Julie could see why Josh would enjoy having his morning coffee out here. He had always been an outdoorsy type.

She could also appreciate the woman he had chosen to make his life with. Her even demeanor had a calming effect on those around her and she knew he drew strength from Alice's positive outlook. Nothing ever seemed to ruffle her feathers; Julie had never seen her without a smile. Not the silly toothy grin variety, but the small confident slightly curled lips type. The kind of smile that says I know something that you don't.

"I wonder what the men are doing." Alice inquired.

"Oh, probably talking business or debating something else stupid." Julie said. Alice laughed and brushed her dark hair back. Her hair was so dark that it seemed to draw the light out of other objects and radiate it back. Julie observed that the two could not be more different physically. Her long straight auburn hair and thin frame contrasted with Alice's petite but ample figure and curly jet-black hair. Their husbands couldn't be more different either, yet they couldn't have been closer if they were brothers and sisters.

$$fff$$

The sun was drawing low in the sky and the other guests had left. Josh, Artemis, Oakland and Howard all reclined on the back deck. Enjoying their drinks and studying the sunset.

"If you could do anything you wanted to, what would it be?" Josh inquired, "Howard?"

"I want to write novels."

"Really?" Josh leaned over and peered toward Howard. "Have you written any?"

"Just one. I just got an agent." Howard took a drink and swallowed and sighed, "He seems pretty hopeful."

"Wow," Josh murmured, "I don't think I could ever do that. What about you Art?"

"I want to pioneer time travel."

"What?" Josh exclaimed and Howard and Oakland snickered.

"Yeah."

"What makes you think that's even possible?"

"I have some ideas. Still in the planning stages." Artemis smiled and looked over at his friend.

"Oh right!" Josh pulled himself up on the arms of his lounge chair. "It may seem workable on paper, but even you my friend can't make that work for real."

"We'll see."

Hah!" Josh laughed, "Now, back from Fantasy Island! What about you Oakland?"

"I'm doing it right now baby!"

"What, you want to sit in a lounge chair the rest of your life?"

"Nah!" Oakland laughed, "I mean the company, the good life," Oakland lifted his glass in a silent toast, "all the women I can date."

"Yeah, I've been meaning to talk to you about that." Josh smirked, "When are you going to settle down?"

"Never man, never." Oakland laughed.

"Nice to have goals," Josh chided. "I guess with the exception of Buck Rogers here, we all enjoy living right now in the present." Josh tossed a glance over at Artemis who laughed and shrugged.

"Hey, I've got a joke for you," Howard blurted.

"We've heard it!" Josh groaned. Art rolled his eyes.

"I haven't," Oakland interjected.

"You don't want to hear it Oak," Josh laugh.

"Sure I do," Oakland said, "tell me."

"Okay, but it's really old and corny," Josh smirked. "Go ahead, tell him."

"Alright," Howard began, "there was this woman and she went car shopping. The car salesman takes her out for a test drive and says that he wants to drive to show her what it can do." Howard grinned and Oakland nodded that he was following. "So he takes off and gets the speed up to a hundred miles an hour and they're flying straight at this brick wall. Well the woman is about to freak and at the last moment he slams the brakes on and slides to a stop just inches from the wall, okay?" Howard smiles and puts his hands out, index fingers extended like a conductor keeping time with his own words, "So the guy says, 'Do you smell that? That's the smell of burning rubber, that's how powerful these brakes are.' So the woman takes the car home and takes her husband out for a drive and gets the speed up over a hundred and her husband is telling her to slow down and she tells him to just chill out and watch. So the same brick wall looms into sight and she slams on the brakes just in time like the salesman did and sure enough slides to a stop with a couple of inches to spare. She looks at her husband and says, 'Do you smell that?' He looks back and says, 'I ought to, I'm sitting in it!'" Howard and Oakland both roared while Josh and Art groaned.

"That's pretty good!" Oakland said.

"I can't believe you never heard that one!" Josh scoffed.

"Yeah," Howard said, "that was one of my Dad's favorites. He would tell it to everybody."

"Do tell," Josh said in a sing song voice.

"Yep, that was about the only thing we connected over," Howard quieted, "... jokes. After a certain age, we just didn't seem to have that much in common, but speaking of time machines," Howard said, "there is one other thing."

"What's that?" Josh cocked his head to one side.

"If I could, I would get in that time machine and go see my folks one last time." Howard stared up into the clouds, not focusing on anything particular. "Or at least I would tell my younger self to get his lazy ass over there and see them like he... I... should have in the first place."

"Yeah?" Josh narrowed an eye. The others sat in silence. Howard's eyes misted slightly.

"I was a busy man," Howard grimaced, "or at least that's what I told myself. Hell, I could have made time if I wanted to... I just didn't want to..." His voice cracked a bit, "Who would have thought, they were only in their fifties, but... well, the fire department put the fire out, but the smoke..." Howard looked down, a tear rolled down his cheek, "I was told they didn't suffer... In fact they probably never even woke up, so they didn't even know... and I wasn't there. I hadn't been in over a year."

"Damn man," Josh got up and slapped Howard on the shoulder, "you're gonna make me cry. I'll get us another beer."

"No thanks," Howard said, "I think I've had enough."

CHAPTER
16

EARL Harper waved from his boat in the middle of the lake. Harper's rambling house was the envy of most on the lake. Josh wondered who the tall stranger was beside Harper. He seemed familiar, but Josh couldn't place him. Perhaps he had seen him coming and going from Harper's house on the cove opposite his. Josh knew he would find out soon. The boat was headed straight for his dock.

"Ahoy Josh," Harper called.

"Earl," Josh responded, climbing to his feet so he could help Harper tie up to his dock.

"Josh, this is an old friend of mine, Wesley Stein."

"Pleased to meet you," Josh reached over the side to shake Stein's hand. Harper was one of the largest insurance brokers in the area with ten agencies.

"Wes here is in the paper business."

"You fellows want something to drink?" Josh nodded toward a set of Adirondack chairs on the shore with a large cooler sitting beside it. Harper and Stein climbed onto the dock and followed.

"What are y'all up to Earl?"

"Not much, just cruising the lake and saw you out." Harper said. "Thought you might like to meet Wesley. He likes to argue as much as you do, so I thought I would bring him over."

"That so?" Josh looked toward Stein who nodded and smiled. "You're a debater?"

Stein smiled and nodded enthusiastically.

"Well, some friends of mine are meeting up tonight. We usually have some pretty lively discussions, want to come?"

"Fine with me, Earl?" Stein spoke up.

$$fff$$

Josh looked around the room. They were gathered in a sitting room in the basement of Art's house. The sound proofed room was the lair of Art's prized home theatre system, which he had lovingly collected and wired up himself. The television and sound system were the envy of all who saw it and they had spent the early part of the evening being impressed by it. Now they sat drinking and talking.

They ranted about everything from skateboard laws to tax policy. Things they wouldn't normally have time to discuss during the day. For some time whenever they would gather for a dinner out or a party, the men would soon be heavily involved in the subject of the day. The women would complain and suggest that they should go off to themselves somewhere and "save the world." So they did and here they were.

A variety of views, each ready to make his case; Wesley Stein fit right in. Earl Harper mostly listened. Howard Spence and Rice Oakland book-ended the extremes of most arguments; Josh, ever the businessman, often played devil's advocate but always arrived back at the financial angle of everything and Artemis would usually support his position with technical data.

Josh relished in this; sipping wine and pretending to have all the answers. All of life's comforts, holding influence over the movers and shakers. He had never been really poor, but life had never been nearly as good as this. He sunk back into the deep cushions and smiled.

It was then that it was suggested that this should become a regular activity. Yes, a debate club, someone offered. No, a debate society, another amended. Better yet, a secret debate society, what happens here stays here, a place where we can tell all our secrets and concerns with no worries!

What shall we call ourselves? The question was presented. How about the council of the Ox? Someone suggested in honor of the man who had first encouraged the meeting. Only one objected, the one who had related how he had briefly been known as "the Ox" years ago and how the name came about. All the others found this hilarious and quickly overruled him, thus the Council of the Ox was born.

$$fff$$

Alice had put the kids to bed some time before and she was propped up against her pillows reading when Josh came in. He settled on the edge of the bed and reached for her hand, he pulled the delicate fingers to him and kissed them softly. There was a stirring down low in his body as he continued kissing his way up her smooth arm. Alice giggled softly causing him to grin as he approached her shoulder.

At the nape of her neck, she met him half way parting her lips and kissing him deeply. Josh took her cheeks in his hands and slid his tongue between her soft lips. Alice's hands were around his back, tugging his shirt up to his shoulders. He leaned back and she pulled it over his head. She traced her way down his neck to his chest with her lips and tongue as her hand slid slowly up his thigh.

Josh laid back and blew out a long sigh. The warmth spread through his body as he casually stroked her hair. He really loved its texture. The course curls slipped along his fingers and palms. He closed his eyes and drifted along with the feeling and sounds that surrounded him.

When she crawled back up beside him, he kissed her tenderly and pulled her gown from her shoulders. Alice stood letting it drop to the floor and they slipped between the covers. He held her tight, enraptured by the warmth of her body against his, breathing in the faint scent of her perfume and nuzzling into her hair. We each have our own unique smells and how he loved hers. Josh raised his head up and placed his lips against Alice's again and kissed her softly then reached over and turned out the light.

CHAPTER
17

GORDON Finch's office was a virtual shrine to the University of North Carolina and especially the football team. He and Joshua Lance would often spend hours on the subject. Josh never minded this, looking around the weathered oak paneling of the walls of Finch's office. The boards were polished to a high gloss and he breathed in the fine wooden smell that permeated the room.

Josh sat across the desk in a high backed leather chair with his legs crossed chatting idly with Finch who looked rather comfy leaning back in his desk chair, also covered with fine leather. Beside Josh sat a framed print of Kenan Stadium, the home field of the North Carolina Tar Heels, that Finch had just given him and on the desk a coffee cup which matched Finch's own Tar Heel cup. Josh already had a place in mind for the print, right behind his desk in his office. He made a notation in his notebook as Finch absently pushed an ink pen about his desk top with one finger.

"So, you feel confident that your plant can handle the increased output on the fabric for those vests for this order." Josh looked up expectantly. Several major police departments had committed to outfitting their officers with Lance & Pike's new line of body armor.

"You bet." Finch picked up the pen he had been playing with and tossed it in the air, catching it with the other hand.

Josh looked up and studied the older man for a moment. "You alright?"

Finch set the pen down and leaned forward on the desk, blowing out a breath. "I'm fine. It's just... well its Connor." Finch leaned back and waved like he was swatting a fly.

"What's happened?"

"Nothing I care to go into; let's just say that the boy has no moral fiber." Finch studied the ceiling briefly then returned his gaze to Josh. "Josh you know I wouldn't talk about any of this with most folks, but you're like one of my own. You know how he is." Josh nodded and grimaced, but Finch didn't notice. "Thank God that boy of his, Hampton, doesn't take after him. He's more like me than Connor, but then again, he spends most of his time at my house anyway." Finch ran a hand through his thinning gray hair. "Connor's wife doesn't trust him; hell, she's scared of him. I don't know why she stays, but she does. He's a poor businessman and now he's running around with a bunch of young tarts at some of these parties they have. Rants, craves, raves or some stuff like that. God knows if they are even legal age."

Josh shifted in his chair, he wanted to break off this discussion, but didn't know a graceful way. He had long held Connor Finch in contempt, but sitting here listening to the man's own father talk this way unnerved him.

"I just hope," Finch sighed, "that I can hold out until Hampton is old enough to take over here, then I can bypass Connor altogether." Finch's face brightened slightly, "Ah, hell, you don't want to listen to all this. I guess I just needed to vent to someone."

"Oh, it's OK; it'll all work out." Josh said with little conviction.

"What do you think about this new treaty or union or whatever it is that they just voted in?"

"It seems to be much more than that. They're planning to consolidate the command structure of the armies of all the nations into one." The Council of the Ox had discussed this at great length the night before. As usual, Howard was outraged and ranted for several minutes without taking a breath. Rice Oakland argued that if handled correctly, this could prove to make our country stronger as part of a bigger whole and Josh ignored the gnawing in his gut and focused on the financial aspects.

"Really?" Finch raised an eyebrow, "The news makes it sound like just another mutual defense treaty or something, kind of like NATO."

"Well, the protocol they ratified actually outlines plans to consolidate the governments and draft a new constitution and everything."

"Hmm!" Finch frowned, "Do you think that will work?"

"I don't know. A lot of folks think that we will essentially be running this new government, so not much will change. Others are really ticked off over this and scream that the sky is falling." Josh shrugged, "I guess we'll see."

Finch laughed, "Yes, I suppose we will."

𝆑 𝆑 𝆑

Josh walked from the Finch Mills building and climbed into his car. He decided that he wanted to go for a drive around Burlington before heading home. He soon found himself rolling to a stop beside Lake Mackintosh. Gazing out over the calm of the water, Josh found his mind dragging his body down in the shallow edge of the lake he now watched. It was quite peaceful now, but on that one fateful night, he believed he would never escape it.

This talk about Connor Finch carried him back. There was something about that drink Finch had given him that always nagged at him. The sleepy and unsteady feeling had moved upon him rather swiftly after drinking it, but he always dismissed the notion. As much of a creep as Connor Finch was, Josh never believed he would intentionally spike his drink.

Josh climbed out of his car and walked over beside the bank. He swooned as he got near the water and stooped down. Everything had changed right here. His life nearly ended, his football career was over, and Artemis Pike had entered his life. Art, a young man he barely knew and would not likely have ever given the time of day to, suddenly became an integral part of his entire destiny. That night as the grim reaper closed his boney fingers about his throat; Artemis Pike reached in and snatched him from death's grip.

A smooth rock lay on the ground beside his foot. Josh picked it up. He rolled it over in his hands for a moment then looked again across the water. A slight wind sent minor ripples over the lake. He stood again and sent the rock skipping along the surface. Josh scanned the woods for a moment. Across the road a trail led through the woods to an old house all the kids thought was haunted. He laughed remembering nights they had gone there looking for ghosts. He shook his head and returned to his car.

The afternoon sun filtered through the hard woods lining the road. He cut into a neighborhood and cruised along admiring the quaint older homes then drove along highway 87 until he pulled up beside the old courthouse in Graham. The quiet little town had often been a source of peaceful reflection for Josh. Not much happened here and he hoped that wouldn't change.

On the far side the square a car pulled into a space. Josh felt his stomach tighten. Connor Finch didn't get out of the car, but Josh could see him clearly. Finch's back was to Josh. After a few minutes another car pulled in beside Finch's. A young woman climbed out and walked over and opened the passenger door to Finch's car and climbed in. Josh couldn't see her clearly, but she was pretty, slim and had straight dark hair which reached to the small of her back. The girl didn't appear to be past her late teens… if that.

With one foot still on the ground outside the car, the girl leaned over and kissed Finch. Then she lifted her foot in and closed the door. Josh gritted his teeth as Finch backed the car out and drove away.

CHAPTER
18

MORE than a year had passed since the command structure of the military for the American Union had been implemented. There had been a loose knit consolidation of political authority as well. The leaders of the largest countries were assembled into a council, but currently the Congress still exercised power so not much had changed for the common citizen. The time was drawing near, however; for the drafting of a new central constitution.

After a brief period of excitement, the American people had settled back into their sleepy daily routines. Football, music and Hollywood once again demanded most of the focus of their free time. A small portion of the population, Howard Spence for one, continued to scream about these events and the news media scoffed at and ignored their concerns. Joshua Lance mostly focused on making inroads toward brokering influence with the new military and civil authorities so Lance & Pike would continue to take in a lion's share of the military and police contracts.

Josh looked up from his desk as Gen. Botero entered his office. He closed the door behind him as Josh rose to greet him. The Columbian general had relocated to the Pentagon where he served as a senior advisor on military contracts, and Josh's main government contact.

"To what do I owe the pleasure General?"

"I wish to speak to you about one of your people, Mr. Lance."

Josh cocked his head slightly, but maintained his smile. "Yes?"

"Normally, this would be handled by a lower ranking staff member, but due to the esteem your company is held in…"

"What concern would the central command have with any of my people?"

"Mr. Lance, you do realize that there is about to be a new constitution drafted." Botero nodded and Josh returned the gesture, "Well, we must take pains to assure that this process is not hindered by any malcontents. This is very important."

"I'm not sure I understand what you are saying General."

"Your Mr. Spence has written, um stories, no… uh, editorials… in your newspapers against the consolidation of power."

Josh struggled to maintain his smile, "So? That's just his opinion. No harm in that, right?"

"Oh, but there is," Botero leaned forward placing his hands on Josh's desk. "This is a very important event. We cannot allow this kind of public undermining of our efforts."

Josh realized that his mouth was slightly open and closed it. "Listen, General, Howard is free to say whatever he wants. He's not threatened anybody, hasn't screamed 'fire' in a crowded theater, so to speak, so this should be no concern of the government or the military."

"Oh, but it is Mr. Lance."

"What? What about free speech? You know, the First Amendment?"

"That is suspended pending the formulation of the new constitution. Your old constitution no longer exists. It will not be in the best interest of the people of the new Union for anyone to interfere with the process and it will not be permitted."

"Howard's very law abiding; he will not cause any problems. He has simply expressed his preferences and opinions. Once this is all done, he will accept it as law and that will be that."

"Mr. Lance, we know of his leanings from the books he has published as well as the articles he has written." Gen. Botero raised his eyebrows. "I am paying this courtesy call for your sake. Take him in hand, Mr. Lance. We do not want any trouble." Botero rose with a nod.

Josh stood, "I'll talk to him."

"See that you do. Please handle it, Mr. Lance." Botero smiled in a way that made Josh almost cringe, "Handle it, or we shall." Botero closed the door as he left. Josh sagged back against his desk and stared at the door for several minutes.

f f f

Gordon Finch was pulling the tennis ball from the mouth of his Labrador retriever, Beau, when Connor's car pulled into the driveway. Hampton scrambled out and scurried over to his grandfather who wrapped him up in a massive hug. Beau bounded over and the boy scratched the broad head and began stroking the dog's shiny black coat.

"Connor," Gordon Finch acknowledged his son with a quick wave.

"Dad," Connor responded flatly.

"Are you going in to finish those production reports you've been promising me?" There was an edge to his voice. Connor had been growing increasingly tardy in producing the management reports his job required. If this had been any other executive, Gordon Finch would have fired him ages ago, but this was not any other executive; this was his son. So he went on needling, harassing and cajoling; whatever it took and Connor Finch continued bearing the title of senior vice-president.

"I was just headed there now Dad."

"Good," Gordon shot him a glare. "You're already a week and a half late."

"Don't worry Dad, they'll be done." Connor climbed back into his car. Gordon waved again half-heartedly and turned back to the boy and the dog.

He paid little attention as the car roared to life behind him. Gordon's focus was now on happier things. Hampton was holding the tennis ball aloft laughing as Beau jumped for it. The boy was getting taller, still not much meat on him, but his shoulders were broadening out some. It was hard to believe he was nearly twelve.

It seemed not long ago that he was a baby. Then he was toddling around in this yard, all knees and elbows, chasing after Beau. The boy had this idea about wanting to ride the poor dog. Gordon grinned and shook his head at the thought.

Hampton drew back and launched the ball across the yard. Beau zipped after it, catching it on the first bounce. Beau brought it back and dropped it at the boy's feet. A couple of tosses later, the dog danced away from Hampton when he tried to retrieve the ball and brought it to Gordon. Gordon reached down and picked it up and sent Beau dashing across the yard again. He was beginning to feel a little warm so he sat down in the iron yard chair and watched as the boy caught Beau and wrestled him to the ground. Boy and dog rolled around in glee, Hampton laughing loudly. He rolled away, grabbed the ball and sent the dog running again.

Gordon rubbed his jaw gently. He must be tense, his neck felt stiff and his jaw was getting sore. Beau trotted back and dropped the ball at his feet. He reached for the ball with his left hand. He could feel a stinging in his shoulder, extending to just below his shoulder blade. He would have to spend some time in his hot tub getting the kinks worked out. Transferring the ball to his right hand, he let it fly across the yard. It was hotter now, a bead of sweat rolled down the side of Gordon's face. He didn't think it was supposed to be this warm today, but it seemed to be getting worse. He needed some air conditioning.

Then Gordon felt the clamping sensation deep in his chest. His jaw throbbed now and the searing pain extended from the middle of his back all the way to his left elbow. Oh no, he panicked, his mouth grew dry, he struggled to look up. Hampton was several feet away with his back to him, watching Beau chase after the ball. He opened his mouth to call to him, but only made a rasping sound. Gordon reached for the chair and sunk to his knees. He struggled to yell, but only a gurgling noise came out. He was watching as the boy turned, his eyes going wide. Gordon realized that he was now on his side looking up.

Help me, he tried to cry, but his lips just slightly quivered. The boy's face was becoming less distinct now and the trees began to swim about in his vision. Gordon felt himself being drawn backwards. He tried to reach up for Hampton, but his hand barely fluttered. A dense fog seemed to be closing in around him. Goodbye Hampton… goodbye.

CHAPTER
19

THE high gloss of the mahogany casket shone in the mid-day sun from the sea of flowers all about it. Josh believed it was one of the heaviest things he had ever lifted as he helped carry it from the hearse and set it on its perch. The grave yawned expectantly beneath it. He leaned over and kissed his wife and daughter on their foreheads then pulled them toward the end of the procession of mourners parading past the Finches. Alex walked up beside him and put his arm around him. Josh squeezed his son's shoulder in return.

He hugged Mrs. Finch warmly then worked his way down the line, mumbling some meaningless but expected words. He crouched down in front of Hampton Finch and placed both hands on the boy's shoulders. Josh stared at the young Finch for several seconds then told him that his grandpa was the best. He moved on and saw Alex shake the boy's hand and say, "Very sorry."

Josh waited on the other side for his crowd to get through. He had noticed Art with his usual uncomfortable look as he shook Connor Finch's hand. Art would shake with one hand while tugging at his collar with the other. His posture was slightly leaned backward and his torso bore the tension of someone who was about to break into a run at any instant.

"Why don't y'all wait in the car?" Artemis said to the rest as he motioned for Josh to follow him. The two walked away from the grave site and Art sat on a large black granite marker bearing the name Smith. Josh eased down beside his friend.

"What are we gonna do?"

"What do you mean?" Josh responded.

"I mean, is he going to be running the mill now?"

"Connor?"

"Yes," Art said impatiently.

"I'm sure he will. It's a private company," Josh kept his voice low. "It belongs to him and his momma now. You don't expect that she's going to toss him over do you?"

"I don't like it."

"It'll be alright."

"We should find someone else to do the work."

"I said it will be alright!" Josh sighed, "Besides, we have a contract with them. Let me worry about it. Once the contract is up, we'll see how they're doing and review it." Josh shrugged, nodding slightly toward Art.

"I still don't like it." Art shifted his weight on the stone and kicked against a tuft of grass. "I don't want to have to deal with that man."

"You won't have to, I will. Listen, don't worry about it, he's my problem, not yours. Besides, the old man's barely cold. There's time for this later."

Art frowned, his lower lip protruding noticeably, "Fine, it's your problem. Just keep that jerk away from me."

"Deal," Josh clapped Art on the back and headed toward the car.

$$fff$$

The office of Robert Cloud was small by congressional standards, but Cloud was never given the best of anything. He had made too many enemies. The chair Josh sat in was comfortable, but then he supposed that Cloud himself got to select the furniture. This was an informal stop on a formal trip. Cloud had held his seat for years by catering to his constituents rather than the power brokers in Washington. Every attempt had been made to remove Cloud from the district neighboring the one Josh lived in now because he refused to "play ball" with everyone from the leadership to the lobbyists.

Despite their best efforts and money, twelve years later he was still there.

"So, Bob, how did all this happen?" Josh asked between sips of the drink the congressman had handed him.

"Well," Cloud crossed his legs and leaned back in his chair. As usual, Cloud occupied the chair beside his guest's rather than putting his desk between them. "The Senate ratified it. It wasn't hard, despite all of our protestations here in the House. The President was in favor of it, quietly of course. For all his ramblings about keeping America strong, he's really one-worlder under it all. After you've been president what's left to do? As you know, he will be named as the provisional prime minister of the new government under this half-baked constitution they came up with. What you probably don't know is that he was promised this as a carrot for his support.

"The Senate leadership was mostly on board from the start. All they had to do was get Senator Sparks out of the way--he could have killed it--so they did. That campaign finance conspiracy charge holds no water at all, but they shopped it to grand juries until they found one that just plain didn't like him and returned an indictment." Cloud smiled sadly, "It probably won't even come to trial, but it's done its real job. It got him out of the way."

"How will all this work?" Josh leaned forward, resting his elbows on his knees.

Cloud took his glasses off and rubbed his eyes then returned them to his nose. "Each legislative body in each country will be accorded one vote as a body and each chief executive will also have one vote. All of this will be tallied by the Secretary of the Union, kind of like the Secretary of State here." Cloud chuckled, "Now that's where the real power rests. If he wants a vote to turn out a certain way and the prime minister and other cabinet ministers see things the same way, what's to stop him from implementing it as he sees fit, like with the 16th and 17th Amendments."

Josh shifted nervously in his chair. "What do the people think about this? Folks I know aren't too crazy about any of it."

"Oh, they're screaming bloody murder, every representative's phone bank and email box is flooded, but it's a little late now. A few of us here challenged their authority to do this, but they did it anyway. No one could stop them; I damned sure couldn't." Cloud blew a deep breath out, "No that horse is already out of the barn. All we can do now is sit back and watch."

CHAPTER

20

THE sun sparkled off the rippling water like tiny diamonds rolling along a conveyer belt. It filtered through the red and golden leaves warming Wesley Stein in his heavy sweater. The autumn breeze gave the lake a steady chop and prevented the day from being reasonably warm for the time of year. Josh lazed back in the Adirondack chair opposite Stein. Wesley had become a frequent visitor to this side of the lake since their first meeting. The boat dock bobbed along with the gentle cadence of the water. Josh's eyes followed the hypnotic rhythm. The conversation had lulled. Football had been discussed to their satisfaction and the current television season held little charm.

"So is your family native to this area Wes?" Josh asked. He reached into his cooler and pulled a Coke out and popped the tab.

"My mother is," Stein said, "my father is from New York originally, but I grew up here."

"How did your dad get here?"

"He came here to work at the paper company, that was after he got out of the army... well actually after he got back from Israel."

"Israel?"

"Yes," Stein said, "he was a World War II vet, Ranger at Normandy. In '47 he decided to explore his Jewish roots and joined the Israeli army. He was there for a few years. He was in their war for independence in '48."

"Really?"

"Uh huh," Stein scratched his head absently, studying a falling leaf. "After a couple of years he grew homesick for America and got a job working at the paper company here. After a few years the owner was ready to retire, so Dad bought it from him. Built it into the company it is today."

"Wow," Josh said.

"Yes… wow," Stein smiled. "He was older by the time I came along, my mother was younger than he was, but we were best pals. He taught me all about business, politics, war, fighting…"

"I bet he knew some tricks," Josh leaned forward. Stein smiled and nodded.

"One thing he told me was that fighting was as much a mental game as a physical one."

"How so?"

"For instance, you should always try to appear calmer and more confident than your opponent. He's less likely to attack someone who is ready. If you look worried, he thinks he's got it made."

Josh nodded thoughtfully.

"You might be able to avoid the fight altogether that way, but…" Stein leaned forward tapping the air with his index finger. "If you can't calm him down or discourage him with your own resolve, sometimes it is better to make him angrier."

"Why would you want to anger a man who is already likely to attack you?" Josh furrowed his brow.

"Because an angry man doesn't think clearly," Stein sat back. "You hurl an insult, the more personal the better. You want him distracted, but you want to keep your own focus. That's how you win."

"Interesting," Josh murmured.

$$fff$$

"You seem rather pensive tonight Oakland," Josh quipped. The lounge area of Art's basement adjoining his home theatre had become the most common gathering place of the Council of the Ox. About every month or two they would meet at another member's home just to mix it up some.

"Why's that?" Oakland responded lackadaisically.

"I dunno," Josh shrugged. "You just seem quiet. What are your thoughts on how the new government is going?" Oakland was hardly alone; emotions were at best now mixed on the subject of the American Union. The former U. S. president was now installed as the provisional prime minister and settling into the new capital in Panama City, Panama.

"Good question," Oakland grunted.

"What?" Howard chimed in, "The brave new world losing its allure?"

"Don't gloat Spence," Oakland warned. "I'm not ready to declare that you were right, but... I'm starting to wonder." He added softly.

"I'm not gloating," Howard's mouth twisted into a sour grin. "I really didn't want to be right about this."

"Well," Josh said, "I guess there are going to be growing pains with anything of this magnitude, but..." Josh dragged out the last word, "With all the additional territories and government units, it is benefiting our business."

"Business, hell!" Earl Harper spat.

"What's the matter Earl?" Josh cocked his head. Earl waved a hand and said nothing.

"The government has nationalized his industry." Wesley Stein added soberly. Wes, like Earl had not shared much this evening. Now Josh knew why. After parting that afternoon, Wes had gone back home and picked up Earl on the way over.

"Nationalized?" Josh asked.

"Yeah," Earl's mouth twisted as he said this. "All insurance will henceforth be administered by the central government."

"You've got a pretty good operation built up, what now? Will the government buy you out?"

"Are you kiddin'?"

"No?"

"No," Earl said sharply.

"Are you going to sell your assets and retire then?" Josh asked. The others watched in silence from the edge of their seats.

"Retire! Hah!" Earl half shouted, "I'm leveraged up to my ass!

I'll be lucky if I come close to breaking even."

"Well, what are you going to do?"

"I dunno, they said I'll probably be hired on by the Central Bureau of Insurance." Earl threw his hands up, "Probably at about a tenth of what I was pulling down."

"You must have put some away though."

"I was going to, but... well, I had just expanded and bought more agencies about a year ago, so I was still plowing it all back into the business, but now..."

"Damn," Josh murmured.

"Yes... damn," Earl sighed.

CHAPTER
21

EARL took one last look around what had been their happy home for several years. Now that his business was gone and he was a simple government employee, he could no longer afford the house. He had transferred ownership that morning to the AU as government housing. He understood that the regional director of the Bureau of Land Allocation would be assigned this house. He would be moving into government housing too, but as a low level supervisor, he certainly didn't rate this. Earl Harper had managed thirty highly motivated agents in his business. They were productive because they all prospered together. Now he had four government bureaucrats who cared about little beyond making it through the day.

Earl had squirmed quietly in the Home Dreams office that morning. He waited for the Land Reclamation specialist for forty-five minutes. Finally a woman in her early fifties strode into the office and took her seat behind the desk. Her dark blue suit, white blouse and dark brown hair, dyed Earl guessed, matched the iciness of her impersonal stare. Earl's temples throbbed slightly.

"Mr. Harper, thank you for coming." She said perfunctorily then pulled the paperwork from a folder and began paging through it. "I believe we'll be able to put this property to good use."

"It was already being put to good use," Earl grumbled.

"Yes," she glared up, "so it was, but now it will serve the greater good."

"Greater good," Earl sputtered. "Good grief!" He noticed the woman was watching him with an amused grin.

"You seem unhappy about this Mr. Harper."

"Unhappy? I guess you could say that," Earl sniffed, "This was our dream home. I had it all, I had worked years to build up this business; the best was ahead and then the government just slams the door on it, like that." He snapped his fingers, "It's not fair."

"Well Mr. Harper," she slid her chair back, her lip curled up at one corner. "It seems you've managed to work the capitalist system and ride pretty high for years upon the backs of others… Is that fair?"

Earl stared in disbelief for several seconds then closed his eyes and laid his head back. As he massaged his temples he could hear a muffled snicker from across the desk.

𝆑 𝆑 𝆑

More than eighteen months had passed since the United States became part of the AU before the big news broke. Seasons would pass by in a blur since then, but Josh would always remember that day. The Council of the Ox continued their meetings, reveling in their farcical "secret society" status; and Josh had managed to keep his company on the good side of the new government. The contracts and the money continued to flow. This was no minor feat; this new mega government was as demanding as it was disorganized. It strongly discouraged dissent. The news media was not controlled, but the paper and television outlets soon learned what to avoid saying in order to avoid unscheduled visits from people they would rather not see.

On this particular spring day, Josh had been doing what he now enjoyed least; visiting the Finch Mills offices. This business relationship had become increasingly hands on in the time since Gordon Finch's death. Shipments were often late, Connor Finch was away from the office much of the time, and was a poor delegator. One day things came to a screeching halt when Lance & Pike was forced to delay an important shipment because Connor Finch had failed to order enough raw materials for the covers needed to complete an order.

Josh wondered why he still tolerated this behavior. Was it loyalty to the Finch family or was he just ashamed to admit that Art had been right. At any rate that event had forced him to form backup relationships with another manufacturer that had been courting their business for some time. He was still sending eighty percent of the business to Finch, but the message was clear; Finch could be replaced.

Josh had climbed into his car, preparing to leave the Finch parking lot. He adjusted the mirror to check out his image. He straightened his tie and was combing through his hair when the news came on. He had not believed Howard when he made the prediction, but here it was. The AU and the European Union had reached a preliminary agreement to form a new International Union. If ratified, the American states would be represented in the European parliament, with one prime minister overseeing all three continents involved.

Josh opened his cell phone and dialed in Howard's number. He stared at the display with his finger poised over the send button. After several seconds, he hit cancel and put the phone away. Some things were better discussed in person without your opinions flowing across the air waves and bouncing through towers and switching stations. He cranked the car and drove away.

𝆑 𝆑 𝆑

Josh reined Howard in with great effort and focused his attentions on the business side of the equation. Lance & Pike managed to ingratiate itself with the new International Union that now governed them. Josh's wealth along with that of his colleagues flourished, but life was changing in many other ways that Josh liked less.

Taxation and fees grew as did government scrutiny of the daily life of the people. No one dared to be caught without the new International ID card, lest they be checked. This carried a nominal fine and likely confinement until the subject's identity could be verified. In reality, this only took moments using fingerprints scanned into the portable computers each International Security

In Due Time

Police car was equipped with, but the police often took the person down to the station for several hours of lockup before getting around to the verification process. They laughed about this being to "teach them a lesson." If the detainee complained too loudly, the police would find themselves swamped with administrative tasks and the detention could stretch into several days.

Now Josh sat at the kitchen table. Alice was across from him and Alex sat to his side. The letter lay open in the middle of the table. Its demands were exactly what the news reports had said they would be. Josh had faithfully registered the one shotgun and one pistol he owned as had been required by law. Now a new law called for him to surrender them both at the local police weapons collection site.

"I don't like it; you're not going to do this are you?" Alice said.

"What choice do we have? Got to." Josh shrugged.

"We're getting more gangs all the time and break-ins are becoming common, besides, your father gave you those guns."

"They know we have them," Josh frowned, "They'll come get them if I don't. Besides, we have a security system, we'll be fine."

"I still don't like it. Our guns aren't a threat to anybody, unless they're up to no good."

"Well, I guess it makes it easier for the police to know who the bad guys are." Josh said with little feeling.

"Tell them we lost them."

"That won't work. It's not a big deal anyway, right?"

Alice sat staring at her husband, her lips pursed and her arms folded. Alex was holding his breath and shifting his gaze nervously between the two. Josh looked down at the table to avoid her glare. After a moment, she blew out a loud sigh and threw up her arms. "Fine!"

"We've really got no choice honey."

"Whatever."

"Okay," Josh rose and walked off toward the bedroom.

Josh opened the closet and turned on the light. He reached into the back and took out the 20 gauge pump shotgun his father had given him as a boy. After pumping the action a couple of times to assure himself that it was unloaded, he tossed it on the bed. He could still remember the day he got it. It was Christmas, was he fourteen or thirteen? He wasn't sure, but Dad and he had spent a lot of time together. Dad had drilled him on the safety rules until he knew them in his sleep.

He stared at it a moment and felt himself sniff suddenly. It had been several years now, but he still missed his dad. Josh turned back into the closet and reached up to take the .38 special revolver off the top shelf. He opened the action and emptied the shells into his hand. He inspected the old Colt for a moment. Dad had given him this not long before he died. It had been a gift to Granny from Grandpa. He remembered how she slept with it under her pillow. Josh smiled sadly and walked over and laid it beside the shotgun on the bed.

He stared at them lying side by side. The guns were something he didn't give much thought to; they were really just objects to him. Josh hadn't fired either one in years, but at the moment he felt a little nostalgic. Finally he wrapped them in a blanket and headed towards the stairs. He supposed the authorities were right. It was probably best to leave these things up to the police.

CHAPTER

22

CONNOR Finch sat behind his desk thumbing through reports looking out his door occasionally. He stopped to watch Ellen Marist walk to the filing cabinet, his eyes following the sway of her hips. He glanced down quickly when she turned to return to her desk that sat sideways to his office door. Ellen had been his father's secretary for years, now she worked for him.

He set the papers down when he saw Ellen's daughter, Lynda, came in to her mother's office. He always enjoyed watching the two of them side by side. They looked more like sisters than mother and daughter, despite the twenty year age difference. Ellen didn't look her thirty-five years and Lynda looked older than her fifteen. He allowed himself to dream for a moment, watching the blonde hair flow over Lynda's shoulders. Finch leaned back placing his hands behind his head. The lively interaction between them always brought a light feeling in his chest. If only… He let the thought hang for several seconds before he rose.

"Ellen," Finch walked into the outer office with some papers in his hand. He had been holding these for the right time. "Oh, hi Lynda. I didn't see you come in."

"Hi," Lynda smiled. His eyes met hers and stayed for a few seconds.

"Yes?" Ellen said. Finch quickly diverted his gaze down to the papers he held and handed them to Ellen.

"Oh… uh, yes. Could you revise these?"

"Of course."

"Done with school for the day, huh." Finch commented looking back to Lynda.

"Yes sir."

"Well, nice to see you." Finch nodded and spun back toward his office. He sat behind his desk and pretended to be busy as he watched over his paper work. Ellen and Lynda continued talking for several minutes. Finch took in every movement and shift in posture. Finally Lynda rose and kissed her mother on the cheek then turned to leave. She hesitated for a moment with her back to Ellen and peered into the office seeing Finch studying her. She gave a half smile, her mouth curving up on one corner and her lips barely parted. Then she was gone.

Finch walked over and closed the door to his office. Before sitting back down at his desk, he strolled to the credenza behind the desk and filled a glass from the decanter of bourbon on the shelf. Easing down in his chair, he sipped from the glass and stared out the window for several minutes. He checked the clock on the wall and took another drink. Each tick seemed an eternity as he waited. Finally, he tossed down the remnants from the glass and looked back at the clock. A smile spread across his face; long enough. He set the glass down on the desk and grabbed his coat.

He felt the sunshine warming his skin and the fresh air cleansed his nostrils as he opened the door to his Lexus. He settled into the leather seat and inserted the key in the ignition. The car roared to life. He had told Ellen that he needed to go out for the rest of the afternoon as he often did at this time of day.

He gunned the engine as he wheeled into traffic. Finch enjoyed the freedom of being the boss; telling others what to do, holding their fate in his hands and letting them know that he did, and most of all, coming and going as he damned well pleased. He laid his head back on the head-rest of the seat and exhaled contentedly. About a mile from the mill, he turned onto a dead-end side road and drove to the end. Finch rolled down the passenger window as he turned around then he drove about a hundred feet back up the street and pulled to the side.

Lynda Marist walked from the edge of the woods and leaned in the window of the car. "Going my way mister?"

"You bet," Finch smiled and Lynda climbed in.

"Nice day," Finch observed as he began to roll down the street again. He looked over at Lynda and she smiled and nodded.

"It's about to get a lot nicer," she said putting her hand on his thigh and letting out a light giggle.

"Just hang on until we get to the lake darlin'," Finch grunted with a look of mischief in his eyes. Lynda laughed as Finch guided the car back onto the main road and raced away toward the country.

ƒ ƒ ƒ

Josh's Four Runner glided along the mountain road. This was a long straight stretch before what Alice termed the "gosh-awful winding part." Alex and Amanda were at the Pikes' for the weekend.

Dad! We're big enough to stay by ourselves, Alex had pleaded. Josh wasn't buying it; he told Alex that he didn't want to come home to a scene out of "Risky Business." Alex had pouted briefly, Josh kept his humor about it and in the end they went cheerfully. Despite their chagrin at "being treated like children," Alex and Amanda both enjoyed visiting Art and Julie. Amanda especially enjoyed chasing the Pikes' baby around. Josh shook his head at having thought the word baby. His namesake, Lance Pike, was hardly a baby anymore. He was a four year old spark plug with the wildest red hair known to humanity.

He began to slow down and rolled on up to the end of the line of cars. The wait was not bad, fewer than ten cars, but Josh didn't expect that he would ever become accustomed to the checkpoints which were so common now. The black clad soldier, part of the security police branch of the new IU military, stood casually checking the ID of the driver at the head of the line. His sub-machinegun shifted as he leaned down to compare the face with the picture. After looking several times, he pocketed the ID and motioned to a space on the shoulder of the road. His other hand rested lightly on the Glock pistol at his side.

Josh continued to watch the show as he moved on up in the line. The next several were routine and now, he and Alice were next. Over on the side a soldier was shining a facial recognition scanner into the man's face. Josh handed his International ID card out the window to the waiting soldier.

"Nature of your travel?" The security policeman asked in broken English as he reached for the ID.

"Vacation," Josh answered. The soldier glanced down at the ID then quickly looked back up, the scowl now replaced with a warm smile.

"Monsieur Lance, you may proceed. Have a pleasant trip."

"See, you're an important man honey," Alice said as they passed out of earshot. "Or should I call you, Monsieur Honey?" Josh looked over trying to give her a reproachful glare, but failed when he caught sight of her grin. Alice laughed then looked back at the man sitting in the car still pulled to the side. A senior officer was tapping something into a computer and talking into a radio a few feet away from the car while one of the soldiers stood to the rear watching its occupant. "I wonder how long that poor soul will be stuck there." She mused.

"Probably for life," Josh grunted then tried to wipe the thought from his mind. These days, he was never sure when his jokes might prove to be all too true.

CHAPTER

23

ALICE settled into a rocking chair on the wide porch of the log chalet. The weathered pine planks were cool under her bare feet. Her white cloth sneakers lay to one side. She drew in deeply the earthy fragrance filtering through the trees on the afternoon breeze and opened the book. The latest Howard Spence novel was toned down from his earlier work, which had nearly landed him in a reeducation program. Such books were no longer available on the open market and all libraries had been ordered to destroy any outstanding copies in their inventory.

Howard had been reluctant to bend to the will of the government at first, but Josh had convinced him that complying was the prudent choice. Josh had expended a lot of political capital keeping Howard a free man. Even with the increased censorship of his works, Howard was living the life he wanted. He had tried to resign from Lance and Pike, but Josh was having none of that. Josh convinced him to stay, saying that his knowledge and skills were too valuable to the business. He now worked a part-time schedule and spent the rest of his time writing.

Josh bounded through the door toting a table top camping grill that he set up on the picnic table in the yard. He popped back inside then reappeared with a small platter bearing a pair of rib eyes and commenced to preparing the grill. Josh turned the flame up and began scraping the grill with a wire brush. Alice watched this over the top of her book for a moment, following the tensing and relaxing of the muscles of his arms and back. His broad shoulders peeked out each side of a thin blue tank top. She decided it was too early to turn her mind to such things and returned to her reading.

The moral points in this book were carefully watered down to avoid controversy, but they were still present. She wondered how long before even that would be deemed too much. Alice found herself on page fifty when the aroma of the searing steaks worked its way to her nose. She carefully laid the bookmark in place and eased her head back, enjoying the smells and sounds. The sounds of birds chirping and squirrels scampering through the leaves on the forest floor tickled her ears.

She went inside and made salads and they ate out under the trees. Afterward they walked hand in hand along a trail through the woods. About a half-mile down the trail the trees opened into a sprawling vista overlooking the mountain. They took a seat on an old log that had been shaved smooth and well worn by others who had enjoyed its hospitality before them.

She clasped her hands around Josh's arm and snuggled up against his side. After David Birch had died, she never believed that there would be anyone else. She had believed that it was just the kids and her from then on, but lightening had struck twice for Alice. Josh was staring out across the mountain side; the great valley spread out before them. His look of total contentment warmed her and she leaned in and kissed his cheek. She wasn't sure how long they sat there enjoying the sights, sounds and smells of the hills as well as each other, but all too soon the sun was hovering just over the next mountain.

"We'd best be getting back," Josh rose and reached for her hand. "We wouldn't want to get eaten by a bear."

"Ah pooh, we just have black bears in these hills and they don't eat people."

"All the same, I'd rather not be wandering around the mountain in the dark." Josh smiled. Alice laughed and took his hand. They walked back to the chalet arm in arm. The autumn evening was growing crisp, but he felt warm against her. She beamed and tugged him closer.

The next morning Josh sat on the porch reading from a newspaper he had ridden into town for. He was frowning as he read. Alice sat across from him with her feet in his lap.

"Can you believe this?" He looked over his paper at her.

"Oh Josh, it's our anniversary, can't you give the news a rest just for one weekend?"

"Okay," Josh folded the paper up and laid it beside his chair. "No news, just me and the most beautiful woman in the world on our tenth anniversary."

"How do you know I'm the most beautiful woman in the world? Have you met every woman in the world?"

"Okay, so you're just the most beautiful woman I know."

Alice giggled, rubbing his thigh with her foot. He was leaning back, returning her gaze. There seemed to be a glow connecting them, like a thread of light. She could see his thoughts and feel his feelings. She knew he was still itching to tell her about the paper.

"Alright, what did the paper say?" Her lips curled up at one end and she slid her foot further up his thigh, dropping her toes down slightly. He laughed and retrieved it from the floor.

Alice yawned; he was always obsessing over these stories. Josh would simply have to learn that most of this didn't affect them. If you weren't doing anything wrong, you had nothing to worry about. When he reached the part about the new law governing religious speech, however; her eyes opened wider.

"What?" She cocked her head to one side, her eyes barely a slit.

"Yes, that's right. They passed a law mandating that Christian churches must give equal time to other religions in their services in order to maintain their tax status and they are no longer allowed to preach anything against homosexuality or... about other faiths not going to Heaven. It's now classified as hate-speech." Josh made mock quotation marks in the air around the words.

"You'd best be careful saying homosexual out loud, dear... excuse me, I mean the H-word. That could get you a hate speech fine if the wrong person hears."

"Oh, I'm so scared," Josh put his hands on his cheeks and threw his mouth open wide. "I am getting sick of these ridiculous new laws." He tossed the paper aside.

"Careful sweetie," Alice warned, "now you're being subversive. That'll land you in jail."

"Ahhh..." Josh growled, rubbing his eyes, "What happened to the America we grew up in?"

"I dunno... gone I guess." Alice put her hands on the armrests of the chair and shrugged. "Let's face it, there's nothing you can do about it. You're an important man, though, so as long as you don't say or do anything too drastic, they won't bother us."

"True," Josh smiled sadly shaking his head, "I guess we'll just have to be content, but I do wonder how the poor people will cope with it."

CHAPTER

24

WESLEY Stein stood outside the community theatre waiting for Rachael to emerge with the twin boys. Benjamin and Abraham Stein were now eight years old and having a little culture forced upon them. Ballet had been their mother's idea; given their druthers the boys would have preferred a movie. Even so, Wesley had been surprised at how well they had behaved through the performance.

"Ready?" Rachael sidled up to where he leaned against the wall; the twins ambled along behind her.

"Of course," he grinned, pulling himself upright and pointed like a wagon-master directing his team. They wandered down the street, the boys close behind. Wesley slid his arm around Rachael, a smile spread across his face. He hesitated at the end of an alley and tapped his chin then pointed.

"Want to take a short-cut?"

"What, down there?" Rachael asked. She peered down the narrow dark corridor, and then looked back, her brow knitted questioningly.

"Sure, the parking deck is straight through there. Beats going all the way around the block," Wesley's eyebrows bounced twice and he smiled.

Rachael laughed nervously and shrugged. She peered around the corner and down to the end of the alley like she expected a goblin to emerge. Wesley snickered and took her by the hand and motioned the boys to follow. About half way along a mouse scurried in front of them and skittered away. Rachael jumped and gasped, then clasped her hand over her mouth as she suppressed a laugh.

"Voila," Wesley made a grand gesture toward the parking deck as they exited the alley.

"You're a regular Daniel Boone," she smirked.

He laughed and said, "Come along boys." The twins came trotting after their parents as they worked their way to the lower level toward the car. Wesley jumped and Rachael let out a gasp when a car squealed around the corner and screeched to a halt behind theirs, blocking them in. Two young men jumped out, the shiny blades in their hands gleamed in contrast to their dark skin. Wesley yelled to his sons to run and dashed to place himself between the young toughs and his wife. The closer one grabbed Rachael and raised the knife menacingly.

"Chill, or she's gonna get hurt."

"Okay, be cool," Wesley raised his hands carefully taking a step closer. The driver stepped around the car, pointing his knife toward Wesley. Wesley stopped.

"Just give us your money and nobody gets hurt."

"Fine," Wesley reached into his back pocket. The driver pressed his knife against Wesley's throat forcing him to slow his motion and ease the wallet out. The goon shoved him against the car and took the wallet from his hand. The other snatched Rachael's purse and threw it in the back seat.

"There, you got what you want, just let us go." Wesley said.

"Almost," the man holding his wife said. He looked Rachael over and grinned. Wesley felt his stomach sink when he noticed the trunk lid was ajar. The bile rose in his throat when the young punk pulled the trunk open and pushed Rachael toward it.

Wesley grabbed the wrist of the driver and swung around in one swift motion. He twisted the arm out straight and struck the extended elbow with the palm of his hand with all the force he could muster. The driver screeched in pain. Wesley drove his shoulder into the middle of the driver's back sending him head first into the side of the car window then he dashed toward the other tough.

In Due Time

The young man jabbed toward Wesley with the knife. Wesley rolled with the blow, but felt the sting as the blade caught the top of his shoulder. Wesley spun around, flipping his attacker in the process, putting himself between the man and Rachael. The young gang-member hit the concrete and rolled then bounded to his feet with the knife out in front of him.

"You're a big man, aren't you? Picking on a woman," Wesley nodded toward him and snorted, "You're not a man; you're a punk boy."

"I'm gonna cut your head off!" The punk screamed. Wesley noticed that several people had gathered at the garage exit and stood watching. Surely the police would be here soon.

"Bring it on boy," Wesley tensed preparing for the attack. The punk's face contorted in rage and he let out a snarl as he lunged toward Wesley. Wesley ducked the knife and dodged under the blow, came up at the man's side and slapped him on the ear with all his might. The punk yelped and staggered sideways, his hands going to his head. Wesley jumped forward with a sidekick into the hoodlum's ribs sending him to his back. That was when he saw the blue lights flashing through the deck and knew it was over.

$$fff$$

Wesley rolled over the next morning. The sun was just beginning to peek through the blinds. Last night seemed like a distant nightmare, but his shoulder throbbed to remind him it was all too real. He tried to focus, coming awake slowly. He rubbed his eyes, there it was again.

"Doorbell honey," Rachael grumbled.

"Yeah," he reached for his robe. Who could this be? Wesley nearly groaned at the thought. He really wanted to sleep some more.

"Coming," he shouted as he left the bedroom. Looking through the blinds beside the door, he saw the detectives from the night before standing outside. Wesley opened the door, "May I help you detective?"

"Could we speak with you out here?"

"Why don't you come in?" Wesley yawned.

"We'd rather you step out," the detective said in a heavy German accent.

Wesley narrowed his eyes as he pulled his robe together and tied it in the front and stepped just outside the door. "Could you give me a chance to get dressed?"

"Just step out here, please." The detective, Mueller, Wesley thought his name was, reached behind his back and pulled his handcuffs out.

"What's this about?"

"Place your hands against the wall."

"What?"

"Just do it, Herr Stein, don't make this hard."

He handcuffed Wesley and shoved him toward the car. A uniformed officer took him by the arm and dragged him along. Detective Mueller pulled out his notebook and studied it for a moment, when he finished he looked back at Wesley.

"Herr Stein, the men that attacked you have been charged for their crimes, however; those will at least be mitigated by your provocative words which we will be addressing today. Due to the racial nature of your verbal assault on them, we will be charging you with a hate language violation under the hate crimes statutes, now if you will be so kind." Mueller opened the back door to the car and motioned Wesley to get in.

"What?" Wesley half shouted, "I'm being charged?"

"Ja," Mueller grumped.

"Their charges mitigated?"

"Ja," Mueller nodded, "In fact I would not be surprised if he gets immunity since his testimony against you will be necessary. Of course if you confess..." The German detective grinned.

"How in the hell do you justify giving him immunity?" Wesley huffed.

"We must take these things seriously Stein," Mueller glared, "Especially with the war we are in with terrorists."

"The war on terror?"

"Ja, you know, the bombings like the one last week in New York. The kidnappings and beheadings..."

"What does this have to do with terrorism?"

"Herr Stein, you must understand that such inconsiderate words as yours inflame their passions and is the root cause of these actions."

"No, these things happen here because we allow it," Wesley's voice rose. "We cut and ran..."

"Enough Stein!" Mueller screamed and drew nearly nose to nose with Wesley. "The illegal American imperialist war... The unconscionable actions of your people against the Palestinian freedom fighters..." Mueller gritted his teeth and continued more quietly, "Americans and Jews, Herr Stein, they caused this." He nodded at Wesley, "Now it is time to pay for it."

Rachael came out and was watching from the front door. She had tried to come down to where Wesley was beside the car, but had been warned back by another security policeman. Wesley looked up toward her and shouted. "Call Josh." Then he climbed into the car.

CHAPTER
25

WESLEY fidgeted as he sat in the sterile conference room, waiting for his lawyer. Jay Van Story had long been one of the best attorneys in North Carolina. Joshua Lance called him as soon as he heard from Rachael Stein. Van Story circulated in Josh's social circle and was waiting at the police station when the detectives brought Wesley in.

Wesley noted the sour look on Van Story's face as he walked through the door. Van Story eased his lanky frame into the chair across from Wesley. The lawyer took his glasses off, set them on the table and rubbed his graying temples. Wesley fidgeted in his chair. The suspense gripped him, but he was not sure he really wanted to know. After a few seconds, Van Story put his glasses back on and sat watching Wesley.

"Well," he began, "the news is not the best."

Wesley's face sagged, "What?"

"They are willing to accept a plea of Second Degree Hate Speech. I thought I could get them to go for Inappropriate Language, but they wouldn't consider it."

"What would the sentence be?"

Van Story looked down and sighed before looking up, "Two years."

"Probation?"

"No," Van Story shook his head, "prison."

"No way! We'll fight it." Wesley slapped his palm on the table.

Van Story smiled sadly and held up a hand, "One thing you should know first."

"What?"

"In the police questioning, Rachael said that she didn't hear what you said, even though three witnesses—standing farther away—said that they did." Van Story paused watching Wesley, "They don't believe her and plan to charge her with obstruction."

"That's outrageous," Wesley was half out of his chair, "she was under stress so she probably didn't hear what was said. Besides, a wife doesn't have to testify..." Van Story held up a hand.

"My friend," Van Story cut him off. "You are under the impression that you still have rights... you don't! You are a citizen of the world now, not the good old US of A."

"Well, it's still not right," Wesley grumbled.

"All the same," Van Story motioned him back down, "that's the card they hold and if this goes to trial, they plan to put her and your kids on the stand and tear them apart. When she tells the same story under oath, they will then add perjury to the charges." He paused to let that sink in, "Then after all that, we'll lose."

"We'll lose?"

"Yes, we'll lose. They have an open and shut case. Three witnesses heard you."

"But," Wesley protested, "surely a jury..."

Van Story held up his hands, "There won't be a jury. You'll be tried in front of a three judge panel."

"No jury," Wesley squawked, "Can't we demand one?"

Van Story was already shaking his head, "No."

"But, the Constitution guarantees..."

"Not this one," Van Story's gaze was steady. "Different constitution now buddy, this one has no such guarantee. When they framed it, the argument was that juries slowed things down too much and that the common people didn't have enough knowledge of the law, besides... With the way judges steered trials... they only let juries hear what they wanted them to hear anyway and the time honored practice of jury nullification, well... that was long gone." He swatted the air.

Wesley stared up into a corner of the ceiling, trying to control his breathing. "And if I accept the plea?"

"They'll drop the charges against Rachael." Van Story lifted his palms off the table, turning them over in a shrugging motion.

"All this over one poorly chosen word?" Wesley shook his head ruefully, "I didn't even mean it in a racial context."

"I know."

"Even if I did, what about freedom of speech, what about the First Amendment?"

"Were you listening?" Van Story grumbled, "There is no First Amendment now."

"How did it come to this? How did we lose our country Jay?" Wesley's voice shook slightly.

Van Story sighed, "We didn't lose it buddy. We gave it away."

𝆑𝆑𝆑

Wesley Stein had just arrived at the upstate New York prison the day before. A guard walked up to the door of his cell and stood looking down at him.

"Stein, come with me."

"Where are we going?"

The guard didn't answer; instead he just gave Wesley a shove forward. After a while they passed through a set of double doors into the cafeteria area. Other prisoners sat about the room and the warden stood on a stage at one end.

The guard was joined by a second who grabbed Wesley by the arm and pulled him up the steps onto the stage. The warden stood staring up at Wesley. His eyes formed small circles that were set apart by a broad flat nose, set above a bushy walrus mustache which spilled over the front, obscuring his mouth.

"What's this about, Warden?" Wesley looked down at the broad little bulldog.

"This is a unique opportunity, son." The warden said through the blonde mustache which was generously speckled with gray. "You have the chance to set everything right." Wesley squinted against the glare shining off the nearly bare head. The warden grabbed Wesley by the arm and pulled him forward as he stepped to the microphone. That's when Wesley noticed that the only white people in the room were on or around the stage.

"Folks," the warden held up his hands for quiet, "I would like to introduce you to Mr. Stein, a new resident here," the warden looked over at Wesley and grinned, even though Wesley couldn't see his teeth from the mustache. "He is here because he spouted some rather hateful things about you people. Confession is good for the soul, so we want to give him the chance to apologize to you fellas and explain just why he seems to hate you guys so much. Mr. Stein?" The warden stepped back and gestured toward the microphone. He nodded to Wesley, his eyebrows raised in a deep arch.

Wesley looked around the room. All eyes were now on him, he felt his pulse racing and his face flush. The warden reached out and pulled him by the arm over to the microphone.

CHAPTER
26

JOSHUA Lance sat in his office staring down at the headline, "Local Businessman Arrested." The subheading continued, "Connor Finch Charged for Sexual Misconduct With Minor." Josh had read the story three times and still had trouble believing it, even out of Connor Finch. The fifteen year old daughter of one of his employees was pregnant and her parents had filed a civil suit on top of the criminal charges.

He rubbed his eyes and looked up to see Art standing in the doorway. Josh waved him in and pointed toward the chair opposite his.

"I see you've read it too."

Josh nodded with a grimace. He folded the paper and set it to the side then leaned back letting out a loud groan. Lacing his fingers behind his head, he stared at the ceiling for a moment.

"We've got to do something about him."

"I know," Josh mumbled.

"I tried to tell you, it was no good doing business with that piece of..." Art started.

Josh sat forward and held up one hand. He hung his head slightly and nodded feebly. He looked back up and the two sat staring at one another in silence. Josh attempted to speak a couple of times, but ended up just nodding and diverting his eyes down. Finally he managed, "You're right."

Art smiled sadly for a moment then asked, "What are you going to do?"

"I don't know," Josh shook his head, "but I'll handle it." He blew out a long sigh and turned to the side, "Lord knows we can't have this."

The two old friends sat quietly thinking that would be the worst news of the day, then Howard Spence plodded into the office with Rice Oakland in tow.

"I'm glad you're both here," Howard said.

Josh looked up with a frown, "We already know about Finch, Howard."

"Yes, that doesn't look good for us, but that's not why I'm here."

Josh sat back, his eyebrows furrowed. Art settled back in the chair he had half risen from before.

"What's this about?" Art asked looking at Oakland.

"Don't ask me, he said he would tell me when we got here."

"Sit," Howard patted Oakland on the shoulder and nodded toward an empty chair. He then pulled a chair from the corner of the office and sat down beside them.

"Look," Howard began, "I just got a call…" He swallowed and adjusted his position in the chair, "Uh, well there's no good way to say this. It's about Wes Stein." He looked around the room slowly.

Josh leaned forward, he felt his breath grow shallow and a hollow ache spread across the pit of his stomach. He gestured with his hand for Howard to spit it out. He knew he wasn't going to like this, but he had to hear it.

"He's dead," a tear trickled down the side of Howard's face. Everyone sat silently with their mouths hanging agape.

"Oh God," Josh stammered, "how?"

"Stabbed in the shower," Howard wiped the moisture from his face.

"Oh dear Lord," Josh said, "Oh God." He placed his face in his hands.

$$fff$$

That evening as he walked through the front door at home, Josh could feel the tension in his shoulders. His temples throbbed slightly with each heartbeat. Alice met him in the entryway and wrapped her arms around him. When he had called her earlier, Josh could barely manage his way through the whole story. Now Alice kissed him softly and whispered, "I'm sorry," into his ear. He stood there swaying slightly, enjoying her warmth against him.

He looked up to see Alex standing beside them. Josh reached over and grabbed the boy by the shoulder and pulled him into them. The fourteen year old slowly joined his parents' embrace. Josh could feel the tension easing here in the comfort of his family's arms.

"Daddy," Josh looked over to see Amanda standing a few feet away, "I baked some cookies for you." Josh laughed softly and reached out and gave his daughter a big bear hug.

"That sounds great sweetheart," Josh released her, "As long as I have y'all, I can get through anything." Alice smiled and they walked toward the dining room where supper awaited. Later, Josh retreated to the sitting area of their bedroom upstairs and put on his robe.

He was lounging in his recliner re-reading Howard's first book, "Studies in Tyranny" when Alice came up. It was one of Howard's finest historical works, to Josh's way of thinking and had long since been banned. He knew he would probably be fined if the wrong people knew he still had it, that's why he kept it hidden from public sight. Alice handed him a glass of tea and he took a long sip.

"That robe looks comfortable," she said, "think I'll put mine on." She glanced at him playfully as she slid her pants to the floor and began unbuttoning her shirt. She slid the blouse from her shoulders and winked as she bent to pick up her pants. She set them on a cedar chest and pranced toward the bathroom relieving herself of her under garments on the way. Alice retrieved her robe from a hook on the back of the bathroom door and looked back at him smiling.

"Show's over," she laughed sliding into her robe then settled into the chair opposite his and put her feet up. Josh set the book down and Alice graced him with one of her sweet smiles. The kind where her mouth curved at each end and her lips barely parted. He always felt the warmth radiating toward him.

Josh smiled back and took another sip of tea. He set the glass down on the side table and grimaced slightly. "I feel responsible for this, you know."

"Why?" Alice cocked her head slightly; the dark curls glimmered in the soft lamp light.

"Well, I hired Van Story for him…"

She was shaking her head, "That's not your fault and it's not Van Story's fault. He did all he could. Neither of you let him down; the stupid law let him down." She inclined her head a bit forward and sat with her eyes peering up through a strand of hair that hung down over her face.

"I know, but it still feels like I let him down."

She shrugged, "I guess that's natural. You were a good friend to him and he knew that."

Josh laid his head back and sighed, "Thank you."

"You're welcome," Alice stood and walked over to his recliner and climbed onto it beside him. She laid her head on his shoulder. The feel of her breath against his chest buoyed him; he often said that the heat was warming his heart. He stroked her hair and lightly tangled his fingers in it. He kissed the back of her head and felt the moisture creeping down his cheeks. She kissed his chest and reached up and stroked his cheek, pressing his face deeper into her hair. He breathed in the scent of her thick mane and smiled in spite of the tears.

Alice moved her hand from his face and looked up into his eyes. She smiled then kissed him and again stroked his cheek.

"Don't worry honey. You did everything you could."

He nodded, knowing that she was right. She usually was and he was glad for that. The world had changed so much from his early youth and despite the wealth that insulated him from much of the madness, he was still troubled by it. She was his safe harbor that allowed him to push forward, knowing that at the end of the day, everything would once again be alright. Josh pulled her face back and kissed her gently, then laid his head against the chair. He was feeling very tired and was soon asleep with her warming his side.

CHAPTER

27

"**M**R. Finch to see you," the speaker boomed. Josh felt a knot deep in his gut at the mention of the name. He had been in his office less than an hour. Connor Finch was wasting no time getting around to damage control. If only he had been this efficient with the rest of his life, maybe he wouldn't be in this mess. Well, he knew he was going to have to deal with this sooner or later. Josh took a deep breath and wiped his palms on his pants.

"Send him in," Josh sat down and tugged at his tie.

Finch ambled into the office; his uneven tie and wrinkled shirt matched the bags under his eyes. Josh stood and took his extended hand and motioned toward a chair. The two sat for a moment, Finch seemed as uncertain of how to begin as Josh was. Josh kept his peace deciding to let him sweat a bit.

"Well," Finch said, "I'm sure you've seen the news."

Josh nodded, but stayed silent. Finch was having trouble looking him in the eye. He would make contact then divert his gaze to the wall. Josh finally just cleared his throat then nodded.

"Yeah," Finch rubbed his nose and brought his eyes back to Josh, "well, it isn't as bad as it was made to look. I've got this under control and it won't impact our deliveries for Lance & Pike."

"How's that?" Josh leaned forward giving Finch a steady stare.

"What?" Finch stammered.

"How's it not as bad as it sounds?"

"Listen," Finch slapped his knees lightly, "I've contacted the right officials, made the appropriate contributions and such." He ran a hand through his hair.

"So you've paid people off," Josh said with a slight edge. Finch shrugged, looking down at his shoes. "What about the girl?"

"Oh, I've settled with her family and they're quite happy with the agreement. Her mother won't have to work any time soon. Kind of a shame really, she's a damned good secretary, but... still, it's taken care of." Finch's eyes seemed hollow.

"So, you just spread some money around and everything is fine now," Josh's voice rose slightly as he talked. "You can buy your way out of anything then?"

"It wasn't just some money, it was actually quite a bit," Finch pleaded, "Listen Josh, this won't interfere with our business arrangements."

"What about your wife?"

"Oh," Finch once again studied his shoes, "well... she was pretty upset."

"I'll bet," Josh remembered Stacy Baker as the perky teenager she was before she married Finch and his fingers involuntarily flexed into a fist.

"We'll work this out, though. She said so," Finch smiled sadly, "she told me that as long as the money was there, she would somehow put up with me, otherwise there was no reason to." He looked up at Josh and raised an eyebrow; "All I can say is thank God for our business relationship it keeps me afloat."

Josh was now finding it difficult to look Finch in the eye. Who the Hell was he to come here and use this kind of emotional blackmail! Well it wasn't going to work; not this time. Josh found himself staring out the window off to his side and was glad that it didn't open. That was probably the only thing saving Finch from taking an impromptu flying lesson.

Josh managed to quiet his anger and muster his courage, and then he looked Finch in the eye. "I want you to listen and listen closely Finch. There is no more business relationship." Josh arched his eyebrows and nodded his head to punctuate his point.

"What?" Finch stammered feebly.

"I mean, that's it, we're done, finis, no more Lance & Pike orders for Finch Mills."

"You can't do this."

"I just did."

"Listen Josh, we've focused our attention entirely on filling your orders for years now, without your account, I'm finished."

Josh chewed on his upper lip and stared at Finch, whose eyes had grown wide, "Maybe you should have focused on growing your business to include other clients then."

"I'm not going to let you do this Josh," Finch pointed his finger at Josh and rose from his chair, "I'll go to your board, I'll…"

"My board!" Josh stood half way resting his palms on his desk, "I've been the only person in the company keeping the board from taking our business elsewhere!" Josh banged his fist on the desk and glared back at Finch. Then he sat back down and lowered his voice, "Listen Finch, you've been unreliable for years, but we stayed with you out of respect for your father," he glanced down at his hands resting on his knees, "but no more. I'm not putting up with this."

Finch paced toward the door of the office, his breath coming in snorts like a rutting buck. He turned and sneered in Josh's direction and blurted, "You son of a bitch, I should have fed you something stronger that night back in high school and killed you outright. I couldn't even count on you to kill yourself on the way home like you were supposed to."

Josh's head jerked up and Finch's face froze and his eyelid twitched slightly. A deep frown marked his face. The two stood staring. The widening eyes of a man who knew he had said too much met Josh's look of anger and disbelief.

"What?"

"Nothing," Finch looked down at his left shoe, "uh… nothing, I was just mad, I didn't mean anything."

"Get out," Josh pointed to the door.

Finch walked slowly over to the desk and reached down and picked up Josh's Tar Heel mug, full of coffee and flung it into the framed print of Kenan Stadium. The glass covering the print shattered and the mug broke as it dug into the print and drenched it in coffee. Josh had taken no time to think, he just realized that he now stood with his left hand on Finch's coat and his other had a letter opener pressed to Finch's throat.

"Go ahead," Finch rasped, "You've taken everything else from me, you might as well kill me."

Josh's hand trembled and pressed the point of the opener against Finch's jugular then suddenly let it go and shoved Finch back toward the wall. The opener clattered on the desktop as Josh punched the call button on his phone.

"Call security."

"I already have," was the shaky reply from Josh's assistant.

Finch turned and opened the door as two security guards passed through the outer office. They asked Josh if he wanted them to call the police. Josh shook his head.

"Just make sure he leaves and doesn't come back." Josh met Finch's cold glare. He watched him walk out between the two guards went over to his window and leaned against the sill.

CHAPTER
28

ALICE lounged on the settee facing the French doors leading out to their balcony. She wished everything was as pleasant as the day seemed outside her door. Poor Josh; she had spent half the morning praying for him. He was such a loyal man, even to those who didn't deserve it. Well, this time it came back to bite him. A gust of wind swayed the tall pine off the edge of the balcony. Alice stood up, yawned and stretched. She hadn't realized the tension she was carrying in her back and chest until she began working her shoulders back and forth. A good walk about the yard was what she needed.

Soon all this would be an unpleasant memory; it would have to be she decided as she headed down the stairs. The house was quiet, but the kids would be home soon enough and that would be that for her solitude. She reminded herself to not wish these times away. They were hardly little kids anymore; Alex and Amanda were growing up so fast. Before long they would be gone and it would just be Josh and her in this big old house. There were worse things, certainly, she knew reaching for the front door handle.

It was bright outside, but the small front porch shielded the sun quite nicely. She loved porches. This front one was much too small, but the sprawling screened back porch more than made up for it. Sunlight glinted off something at the end of the driveway. What was that? She wondered. A car; now who could that be? She leaned against the railing watching for a moment then heard an engine start and the car backed down the driveway and left. Must have just been turning around, she thought, stretching down to touch her toes.

$$\textit{f f f}$$

Look at all this he has, Connor Finch thought. He had been sitting at the crest of the hill near the end of Josh's driveway for several minutes. He pulled a vial out of his pocket and tapped it over a piece of paper he had set on the console of his car. A fine white powder spilled out and he smoothed it out into a line with his finger. He put the dollar bill he had rolled up to his nose and soon his nerves were much steadier.

That scumbag was able to build all this because of me Finch sulked. If it hadn't been for all the help he got from Finch Mills through the years, Lance would be nothing and now he just craps all over me. Finch slapped the steering wheel. He had never actually been invited into this house, no Lance was too high and mighty to condescend to let the likes lowly old Connor Finch into his palace, but he had been all over the grounds anyway. When he knew no one was home, Finch had come out and walked all around. The swimming pool, the swing sets, the garden, the bird houses… He had seen it all and he had looked in all the windows.

Mr. Goody Two Shoes and his creepy little buddy had always thought they were better than Connor. Their high-brow talking, using big words, trying to sound so smart; well by the time it's all over… And that damned little slut. What was she thinking getting herself pregnant… And her momma; after all he had done for Ellen over these years, who did she think she was calling the cops on him. Hell, he would have paid them whatever they wanted to keep this quiet. Finch hit the steering wheel again.

The front door opened and he saw her step out. That little wild cat Lance married; that's something else he doesn't deserve. He knew just how he would bring her down to size too Finch smirked. She stopped and seemed to be looking his way. I'd better go, knowing that little hellion I might get shot, he thought. No, he shook his head; Lance wouldn't do anything as bold as have an illegal gun in his house. As deep as he had his snout in the government trough, there was no way he would risk getting caught with one. Only an actual government official could get away with that. Still, he thought, it wouldn't do for the police to drive up and catch him here. A drug bust on top of his other troubles sure wouldn't help. No, he needed to go somewhere and think all this over.

The drive home was a blur. He tried to think of somewhere to go, but in the end, there's no place like home; at least while it still lasted...

The tires of the Lexus screeched as he slid to a halt outside his house. He squinted against the early afternoon sun as he climbed from the car. His eyes were quite red from the cocaine, but he didn't care; he had to have it. He slammed the door and kicked it letting a few select words fly as he did. The curtains parted slightly and he could see Stacy peering out at him. She barely reacted to this kind of display anymore. She knew better.

Finch stumbled up the steps and pushed the door open. The small bar area beside the kitchen seemed to beckon him. Pouring himself a glass of whiskey, he turned to see Stacy standing there watching him. Her hands were on her hips as he took a swallow. Glaring back he finished the glass in a second gulp and set it down with a rap.

"Can you believe it?" Finch asked with a rueful laugh.

"Believe what?"

"Lance!" Finch turned and filled the glass again, "After all I've done for him."

Stacy shrugged her shoulders and sat down.

"He wants to throw our business deals away over this little matter." He paced back and forth in front of the bar taking quick nervous sips. The glass shook in his hand sloshing the liquid about.

"This little matter?" Stacy asked, her voice rising. "This little MATTER!"

"Yes, it's no big deal. I've taken care of it and you wouldn't miss a single hair appointment or tennis lesson." Finch's voice rising slightly with each word, "It was taken care of, but no," he dragged the oh sound out, "Mr. high and mighty has to make a big deal out of it."

"What are you going to do?"

In Due Time

"I don't know," Finch's voice was a high whine; "I'm ruined."
He slammed his fist down on the bar, rattling the bottles.

"Why don't you find new customers?" Stacy asked. "That's
what your father would do."

"My father," Finch yelled, "Oh my sainted father. Everybody
thinks he was so perfect; well let me tell you…" Finch stamped
his foot. "He wouldn't be able to do any better than I can." His
breath came in heaves now, "It's that damned Lance's fault. He's
wasted my time all these years, when I could have been getting other
business, now it's too late."

"What are you talking about, it's not Josh's fault."

"Oh sure, take his side." Finch shook his finger toward his wife,
"You always had a thing for him anyway. Well he's not so perfect
either."

"Well, he was busy building his business and taking care of his
family. Not out chasing the tart of the week."

"Shut up," Finch screamed, "he's no better than I am!" He
slammed his fist down again and leaned against the bar, cradling his
head in his arms.

Stacy walked up closer behind him as he sobbed. "Maybe I
should have pursued him. He didn't have the kind of money you did,
but at least my husband would be at home instead of out ruining my
life."

"So you admit it, he's the one you really wanted," Finch had
stood back up and was leaning against his hands on the bar with his
back to her.

"You may have thrown better parties back in high school, but he's
twice the man you are in every way." The defiant tone of her voice
was thick. Finch turned and swung with the back of his fist. She
dodged as she had become quite practiced at doing. Her foot slipped
and she tumbled backwards.

Finch descended onto her and jerked her up by her arm. He spun
her around and dragged her to the door. Snatching it open, he threw
her out into the front yard. Stacy's feet hit the ground and her knees
buckled under her, sending her tumbling face first into the grass. She
rolled over onto her back and rested on her elbows as she let out a

moan.

"Get out," he screamed, "go over to the school and pick up that stinking brat and just leave. Go to your dad's, go live under a bridge like the troll you are, I don't care, just get out of here."

Stacy crawled backwards for several feet before climbing up and running away. Finch slammed the door and went back to the bar. One way or another, he would see to it that Joshua Lance paid for this.

$$fff$$

Josh watched the sun set from his dock that evening. The water was still on the lake, occasionally a fish would jump and send rings radiating outward. The frogs began to sing mournfully. The darkness was thick and heavy, he felt he could reach out and touch it. The sight of Howard Spence strolling down the path seemed to ease the gloom that had been closing in.

"Understand you had a rough morning."

"I've had better," Josh answered. They both laughed.

"Your old buddy Finch is a nasty one, I hear."

"Always was," Josh sat musing. "You know, it just gets me."

"What's that?" Howard sat down beside him.

"A jerk like Finch gives booze and drugs to teenage girls and knocks one up…" Josh snapped his fingers, "Just buys his way out of it." He turned to look at Howard, "A good man like Wesley offends some creep who's trying to kill him and now he's dead."

Howard grunted and reached down in Josh's cooler for a beer. He popped it open and took a sip.

"How do you figure that," Josh looked back out over the lake.

"There is no figuring it," Howard stared out into the dark water, like Josh as if it held some answer.

"Well, it's not right," Josh pushed at a splinter sticking up from the dock with his shoe. "I wish there were something we could do about it."

"Yes," Howard said, "seems like there should be something."
The two sat watching the occasional fish jump in the otherwise quiet lake.

CHAPTER
29

ONE o'clock the next day found the Finch living room quiet. Connor Finch should have been in his office recruiting new customers and seeking financing. Instead he was face down on the couch. An empty bottle was on the floor beside it. The bottle shared the floor with an overturned glass, a dark stain radiated outward. Several brightly colored pills and a just a hint of some fine white powder littered the coffee table.

It had been six hours since he finally collapsed there and he was just now beginning to stir. He reached out and grabbed a hold of the coffee table. Finch tried to place one foot on the floor and raise himself from the couch, but he lost his hold and tumbled onto his side. He let out a loud grunt as the bottle and glass dug into his back. An angry toss sent it crashing into the wall. He was trying to clear his head as he sat on the floor; finally Finch rolled onto his knees and crawled to the bathroom.

Bloodshot eyes stared back from the mirror, perched above dark circles and hollow cheeks. Finch splashed cold water in his face. It didn't do much. The drugs and the liquor only helped for a while. He knew he would have to go in and face his employees sooner or later; or at least he should. Though, doing what he should had never been his strong point. No, he would do what he did best, hide from the problem and let someone else handle it. What did it matter, the situation was beyond saving anyway. He walked back into his kitchen and got a glass of water.

Finch spotted a cardboard box peeking from the edge of the pantry. He bent down and dragged it out. With one swift motion he tore a side away, then retrieved a butcher knife from the counter and sliced it into a square. Maybe he would make a sign, use it to picket in front of Lance & Pike, or just write bad things about Joshua Lance and plaster it on the light poles near his house. He was sure he would come up with some use for the cardboard. There would definitely be something he could do with it.

$$fff$$

While Finch rambled about in a haze, Joshua Lance sat in his office. He knew he was doing the right thing. Everyone had told him so and had urged him to dump Finch for years now, but still… He mainly felt guilty about those who worked at Finch Mills. They would almost certainly be looking for new jobs. Finch was too much of an idiot to be able to attract new accounts. He knew it, and even Finch himself knew it. It couldn't be helped though.

Josh turned his thoughts to the meeting with the Council of the Ox that night. That should bring him some relief. He would have fun and could discuss this matter. The validation would do him good. In the meantime, he decided that he would check in with Artemis. Art's office occupied the opposite corner in the same wing as Josh's office. They had allowed Art extra space so he could have a small private lab directly off of his office.

Josh strode up to the open door and stood watching Art peering silently through a magnifying glass at a belt like contraption. In the center of the belt was a thick round shield like apparatus with wires radiating out. Each wire was terminated with an electrode pad. Art turned a screw then stared some more, oblivious to Josh's presence. Soon Josh grew weary of watching the spectacle and lightly rapped on the door. Art looked up from his work and urged his friend in. Josh walked over and sat in a high backed leather chair across from him.

"What's this?" Josh pointed at the device. Art got up and walked over to the door. He looked around outside then closed it.

"Nothing yet," Art said as he returned to his seat. "One day though, it will stand the scientific world on its head."

"Sounds rather ominous," Josh smirked.

"Oh you laugh…" Art shot Josh a sharp glare.

"So, what is it?"

Art looked smugly back at Josh for a moment. "This will allow you to alter your place in time."

"A time machine? Really?"

"Yes really."

"I always thought you were joking." Josh grinned.

"Well, it's not a reality yet. This is just a prototype," Art grimaced, "it could be months or years even before I attempt a test."

"Why so long?"

"You have to be real sure before you go messing around with something like this." Art sat back and folded his hands in his lap.

"Why don't you just send an object, like an apple or something…?"

"Well, that's pretty much what I would do. Send something that I can't kill if things go wrong ahead like fifteen minutes, okay, but…" Art held up one finger, "I have to also send the device with it. If my estimates are off even a little bit, then you've sent your time device off to God knows where."

"I see your point," Josh leaned forward against Art's desk, "but that raises some questions. First, should you even be messing with this?"

"I am exercising the utmost caution. I won't try anything unless I am absolutely confident of the outcome." Art nodded and leaned forward holding his palms up in a show of confidence.

"Okay, what makes you so sure that this is even possible?"

Art chuckled softly, "Well, let's just say, that I have reason to believe that it can be done."

"Reason to believe? Like what?"

"I just do!" Art snapped, "That's all I'm saying. Now, if you don't mind," Art pointed to the door.

"Okay, okay," Josh waved his hands in a conciliatory gesture as he got up and headed toward the doorway. He opened the door half way and stopped. "Just make sure you don't beam yourself to the moon or something."

CHAPTER

30

INCH'S Lexus moved down the interstate quietly as the sun sank lower in the sky. He loved his car, but wondered how much longer he could hold onto it. His cell phone rang several times during the day; Finch ignored it. There could be nothing he wanted to hear right now. The square cardboard cutout sat on the passenger seat and the butcher knife lay in the floor. An ethereal feeling permeated his being; he was up and moving now and feeling no pain. Since last night he had switched from cocaine to meth. His pain and worries were temporarily gone. Now the only thing that occupied his mind was vengeance.

The exit that would take him to Lance & Pike loomed on his right. It triggered a stream of obscenities that lasted for several miles. He had to stop and gather his wits. A motel near Durham had served his needs during past excursions, so he exited and headed there.

He checked in and parked in front of the room. This place had pleasant memories for him, hours of enjoyment; but today was different. Now he needed to think. He had come over here not really knowing what he would do, but he had to do something. He took off his shirt and threw it over a chair then dove face first onto the bed. His mind once again drifted to past pleasures here and in other places like it. His life so far had been all about fun. Was that so wrong? Should he have listened to those who told him to shape up and pay attention to the things he considered mundane? Maybe so; one thing was certain, the fun had ended now. Everything was gone. Finch felt himself drifting and sleep soon overcame him.

What? He jerked awake. A nightmare, it was just a nightmare; maybe it all was. Sweat covered him and tears filled his eyes. He flipped himself onto his back and banged his head against the headboard. Jumping from the bed, he squared off and drove his fist into the wall. The sheetrock ruptured leaving a nice round hole. He struck again, this time his fist connected with a wall stud. He felt the impact and a slight throbbing in his hand, but strangely no pain. Finch held his hand up and noticed that two of the knuckles were red and beginning to swell.

He grabbed his shirt from the chair and put it back on. He moseyed outside and retrieved the cardboard and a magic marker from his car and sat at the table beside the bed. Finch sat thinking for a while then took the top off the marker and began to write.

$$fff$$

Josh helped Alice clear the table. Supper had been early this evening as it usually was on nights he had a meeting with the Council of the Ox. He sometimes laughed at their play pretend secret society hokum, but the ability to vent without penalty also kept him sane, as it did for the others too. The tension of the last few days had radiated out to his home life. He decided to bring up a happier subject.

"That's great news about Oakland and Alisa, huh!" He glided up behind Alice as she stood at the sink, slid his hands around her waist and kissed her on the side of the neck.

"Umm," she purred at the kiss, "yeah, I didn't think I would live long enough to see Rice Oakland settle down."

"She must be one hell of a woman to saddle that old boy down."

"I expect she is," Alice turned around and put her hands on Josh's shoulders, "I just hope they can be as happy as we are."

Josh looked down into his wife's eyes; they sparkled in their deep blueness up at him. He pulled her hips against him and kissed her lightly, "I don't think that's possible."

"You'd better be going. You'll be late." She giggled and kissed him back.

"Yes, I guess so. Y'all be okay here?"

"Sure," she smiled, "the kids have homework to do and I'll find something."

Josh hugged her tight then let go and walked to the door. He yelled his goodbyes and headed out to his Four Runner. Backing out of the drive, he felt hopeful about the release of the pent up feelings that the meetings usually brought. In a way he worried about Finch. This had to be quite a blow to him, but Josh had needed to do this for some time. He couldn't look the other way forever.

f f f

Connor Finch was sitting in his car off to the side of the road. His Lexus was partially obscured by a large bush, so he knew that it was unlikely that Josh had seen him as the Four Runner turned the opposite direction onto the highway. His breathing increased and his heart palpitated. He gripped the steering wheel trying to hold onto his composure. He had to be calm and sure of himself. Finch knew that he must not falter in his next moves or his best efforts would be for naught, but it was not easy knowing what he had planned.

He watched the Four Runner go out of sight over the hill. His gut churned, the feelings alternated between dread and euphoria. Finch sat for a few more minutes then started his car and pulled it onto the highway. No one was in sight as he rolled to a near stop; then turned up the Lance driveway.

As he pulled to a stop near the end of the long driveway, he felt a rush of nerves. The what-ifs flooded his brain. No, he had considered all the contingencies. Joshua Lance was known to spend Thursday evenings out, so he wouldn't be back soon, or at least he hoped not. Finch reassured himself as he put one foot on the concrete drive. He stood and eased the door shut, making sure to not slam it.

He couldn't waste time worrying, Finch told himself. No other houses had a line of sight on Lance's yard. No backing out now, he thought as he climbed the front steps. Connor Finch took a deep breath as he stood on the front stoop then rang the doorbell.

CHAPTER
31

"**N**ONE of this is right, it's not fair," Josh slammed his fist on the table. The meeting had started off with a bang and grew more boisterous.

"Since when is anything fair?" Howard groused.

"Well, something has to change," Oakland chimed in.

"Things have already changed," Howard said, "and they're only going to get worse. As I recall, you were all in favor of it too."

"I was not in favor of this and you know it," Oakland shouted, shaking his finger at Howard.

"Well, I tried to tell you this was the kind of thing that would happen, but you wouldn't listen."

"Well, what was I supposed to do about it?" Oakland jumped from his chair. He stood leaning forward against his fists on the table glaring down at Howard. Howard's eyes burned defiantly back up at Oakland, his lips drawn thin.

"Guys," Josh waved his hands, "time out. None of us did this, just chill out." Oakland sat back down, the two men relaxed a bit, but held onto an uncomfortable stare.

"Well," Earl Harper stuttered, "we should do something."

"Like what?"

"I, uh, don't know, but we should…"

"What are we going to do, Earl?" Oakland growled, "Invade?"

"Ha!" Howard mocked, "Now that would be a sight, it would be like attacking a tank with a BB gun."

"That's not what I'm saying," Earl said timidly, "but there should be... uh, well... something."

"Yes," Howard's tone softened, "there should be."

Josh knew that he had no answers. He was no longer certain that he understood all of the questions. The venting that he had longed for brought no relief, it only brought frustration. When the meeting was finished, Howard followed him to his vehicle. They stood chatting idly for several minutes. Josh sensed that Howard had something on his mind, but he didn't ask.

"You know, I've been considering something," Howard said finally.

"What's that?"

"I think I'm going to write some more books like what I used to write."

"How are you going to do that?" Josh cocked his head to one side, "All of your earlier books are banned and you'll never get any more like them published. Besides, they'll lock you away for it."

Howard nodded then held up one hand, "I know... but I think I may have found a way."

"How?"

"Under an assumed name, of course."

"Fine, but no one would publish it," Josh furrowed his brows.

"There are companies based in Africa and the Middle East that are out of reach of the International Union. Publishing companies, internet companies, you name it... anything for a buck." Howard smiled, "All run by American and European refugees."

"Good luck," Josh said as he climbed into his Four Runner.

Josh rolled down Interstate 40 lost in thought. He impulsively exited and headed toward his office. He strolled across the marble lobby and waved to the security guard. The elevator whisked him up to his floor and soon, he was unlocking his office. The lights flickered on and Josh strode to his desk and sat down.

The framed print of Kenan Stadium sat on the floor where he had set it after Finch had smashed his cup on it. The glass had been swept up and the remnants of the coffee mug sat in a bowl on the credenza behind his desk. Josh reached into the bowl and picked up a large chunk of the ceramic. This piece had part of a ram's horn on it. He turned it over in his hand and set it back in the bowl.

Josh rocked back and forth gently staring at the long gash in the print of the football stadium. It was probably futile to repair the mug and the picture, but Josh had not given up on the idea yet. He could always replace these with new items; however, Josh mused, those would not have been given to him by Gordon Finch. He remembered the conversation they had the day Gordon gave these to him. The deep disappointment and concerns about Connor's future. Well, his fears had proven correct, but Josh had always known that they would.

He knew that he should be getting home. Alice would be waiting for him and he didn't like to make her wait. He walked to the door, turned and took one last look at the torn and stained print then turned out the light and shut the door.

The highway was dark as Josh drove along toward home. A thick gloom drifted in about him. He was growing weary of all this and longed to climb into his bed and sleep beside his wife. If only he could awake in Alice's arms and discover that all this had simply been a bad dream. He knew this wouldn't be and he began feeling unsettled as he neared his driveway.

Something didn't feel right as Josh drove down the long drive. Just over the hill where the house came into view, his headlights glinted off something. A car, it was a Lexus, Finch's Lexus. He really didn't want to go through this again with Finch. Couldn't he get it though his head? Their business was concluded, if he were any kind of businessman, Connor Finch would find other customers and just move on. But Connor Finch was not any kind of businessman. That Josh knew. So, here he was, everything would have to be explained to him again. Josh would be firm. Finch had to be convinced that he was not going to change his mind.

Butterflies gnawed at Josh's stomach as he marched up the steps to his porch. That's when he noticed there was mud or something dark on the front door handle and the door was slightly ajar. He pushed it open and stepped into the foyer. The house was silent.

His belly felt like lead and his heart was pumping like a racehorse's. Josh called out… no answer. He nearly lost his breath as he stepped into the living room.

A rope was slung from the top post of the stair case leading to the second floor. At the other end of the rope was Connor Finch. His head was down and a rudimentary knot rested against the back of his neck. Josh held his breath as he stepped closer. Finch's mouth hung open and his deeply bloodshot eyes bulged. A large piece of cardboard was taped to his chest with some kind of transparent box tape. Large black letters on the crude sign said: "You ruined my life. Now we're even."

Josh felt his heart jump and he slowly turned and looked around. There were dark rust colored stains on the stairs. At the bottom a wide swath of this same color streaked across the hardwood floor of the living room and led to his study. At the door of the study, two other trails merged with the first. Josh's throat constricted as he took a step forward. His knees wobbled with each step. The study suddenly seemed miles away. He reached the corner beside the door and paused, not wanting to go any further.

Josh stepped around the corner and into the doorway. His head swam and he sank to his knees. He tried to speak, but words wouldn't come. Instead he emitted a low guttural noise that rose to a screech like that of a wounded animal. Long sobs beginning deep in his gut poured out and he sagged sideways, striking his shoulder then his cheek against the door of the study. As his face slid down the door, streaking it with his tears, the image before him burned itself forever into his very soul.

CHAPTER
32

JOSHUA Lance sat on the granite bench he had put at the foot of the graves. For the first several months he had come here every evening. His friends had finally persuaded him that this was not healthy. Now he only came on Wednesdays. Today was Tuesday so normally he wouldn't be here this afternoon, but today was an exception. This was the fifteenth anniversary of their deaths.

Earlier, he had made his annual pilgrimage to the cemetery in Burlington to visit the Finch family plot. Like the years before, he laid a wreath at the grave of Gordon Finch and knelt in prayer. He then rose, took several steps to the left, unzipped his pants and pissed on Connor's grave. He always drank several bottles of water before going there. When he finished he stood for several seconds watching the wet stain spread on the headstone.

"See ya' next year, you son of a bitch," Josh walked away and climbed into the Ford pickup he had bought several years back and drove back here.

That night all those years ago, still rested just below the surface with him. Detectives swarmed over the house as he sat outside on a brick wall surrounding a raised plant bed with a maple tree in the center. He had already cried his weight in tears and there was no moisture left to weep, but an involuntary sob would heave in his chest now and then. A detective Josh knew sat down beside him. Another he didn't know stood nearby making notes in a handheld computer.

"How are you doing?" Detective Schlegel asked. Josh didn't respond he just stared blankly back. Schlegel nodded and looked down. "I know, dumb question."

"You know," Josh began, "if I had kept one of the guns rather than turning them all in…"

"What?" Schlegel's head snapped upright.

"She wanted me to," Josh nodded toward the house, "If I had, it could be a different scene in there."

"That would be a serious violation of the law, Mr. Lance?" Schlegel asked. The other detective had stopped his note taking and was now staring toward Josh too.

"Why not," Josh asked through gritted teeth, "With my money, I could have pulled it off. I just didn't. Besides, I'm just talking."

The other detective took a step in Josh's direction. Schlegel held up a hand and shook his head. The other detective stopped. Schlegel studied Josh for a moment then stood.

"Walk with me Mr. Lance," Schlegel motioned for Josh to follow. Josh tagged along until they were out of earshot of the others. Schlegel reached out and placed a hand on Josh's shoulder and ducked his head slightly angling his eyes up to meet Josh's stare. "Mr. Lance I understand your grief, but you can't say things like that."

"Why not? It's true!"

"That's irrelevant."

"What is? The truth?" Josh shot back. Schlegel ignored the question.

"Look, in the interest of an orderly society and its proper governance, it is not in the public's best interest for individuals to possess firearms."

"Don't you mean that it's not in the government's best interest?" Schlegel ignored this question also.

"Besides," Schlegel let go of Josh's shoulder and made a sweeping motion with his hand, "if she had shot Finch, your wife would be spending the rest of her life in prison and your kids would be growing up without their mother. Would that really be better?"

"Would that be better?" Josh's voice rose slightly. "Would that be better! Do you mean would it be better for my children to be alive?" Schlegel made a smoothing motion with his hand.

"What I'm saying is private gun ownership upsets the societal order," Schlegel said sharply. "No one person's, or three for that matter, lives are worth that. You must understand."

"So... if my wife could have defended her life it would have destroyed civilization?" Josh couldn't believe Schlegel was keeping a straight face, but he could see that the detective was serious.

"No! But the best defense is to run away," Schlegel stabbed the palm of his hand with one finger, "You have to understand, killing someone with a gun is murder no matter what the reason. Zero tolerance," Schlegel opened his eyes wide and threw a quick nod toward Josh. "Can't be allowed; that's the way it has to be. Guns are not conducive for good societal order."

"Don't you mean strong government rule?" Josh snarled.

"Look, Mr. Lance," Schlegel looked down and spoke more quietly, "To speak of the desire to violate a law fundamental to keeping the people safe is a crime and to speak of your government in such a manner is sedition. Either of which would land you in a lot of trouble, but..." Schlegel let it hang in the air for several seconds, "I am taking into account your grief as well as your service to your government through your company. No action need be taken on this conversation. Find a good outlet for your grief, but I suggest you keep any such disruptive speech to yourself."

"So you can defend yourself as long as it's not with a gun or any other unapproved weapon?" Josh's question hung sarcastically in the air for several seconds. He knew he was on shaky ground, but he was not yet prepared to let this go. The two men glared at one another.

"That's right," Schlegel finally answered.

"That's not the way it's supposed to be."

"But that's the way it is," Schlegel shrugged, "It's the law."

Josh drew in a deep breath and tried to control his trembling. "The law should be interested in right and wrong."

"Right and wrong are irrelevant."

Josh stood stunned for several seconds. "If right and wrong are irrelevant, then what is relevant?"

Schlegel smiled, "The law... the people... the state."

Josh looked down and said no more.

$$fff$$

Josh was still sitting on the bench at the foot of the graves when Rice Oakland climbed out of the car. Alisa waved to Josh then drove away. Oakland walked over and sat down beside him. No words passed for several minutes. Finally Josh acknowledged Oakland with a nod.

"Thought I might find you here," Oakland said. Josh grunted. "Catch a ride to the meeting?"

"Sure," he looked away from the markers then rose from the bench. "You ready?" He was already half way to the truck before the question was finished. Oakland followed and climbed into the passenger's seat.

"You know Oak," Josh turned the key and started the truck, "When we started Lance & Pike, I believed as CEO that I owed something to my people. In order to get loyalty you must first give it." Oakland nodded. "But, none of that seems to matter anymore. Everything is nationalized; the government takes a huge chunk of their paychecks then heavily subsidizes the 'necessities' of life they can no longer afford due to their tax bill."

"That's true."

"Our middle managers get hit the hardest. They get paid more than they need," the sarcasm in the word need was obvious. "So the government takes most of their pay, then gives them back what some bureaucrats deem *is* needed. They make enough to get screwed but not enough to hire people to find ways around it."

"Thank God we have people to find ways around it." Oakland leaned in and nodded.

"True, but don't you believe for a minute that if we stop towing the line that it won't all be taken away tomorrow." Josh snorted and looked over at Oakland, "You can count on that."

CHAPTER

33

JOSH and Oakland left the meeting that night in silence. Everyone was silent by then.

"I still don't know about this Josh," Oakland said once they rolled away.

"Yeah, I know," Josh said.

"I mean, this whole Ox thing has just been for fun, but now…"

"Yeah," Josh looked at Oakland and nodded.

"Dear lord, what he's proposing…"

"Yep," Josh muttered.

"I mean, can this really work?" Oakland rambled, "Do we want it to?"

"I don't know," Josh's voice sounded stronger now, "but consider this. So much has happened to all of us that we aren't happy with… and we're some of the lucky ones."

Oakland nodded nervously. They rode along in silence for a few miles.

"Hey, isn't that your church," Oakland broke the silence.

"Yeah, sort of," Josh said. He was still a member there. It had been ages since he had attended though. There was an underground, "home church" that he often attended. These were quite illegal, but the government usually left them alone. As long as they avoided doing any real missionary work that is. Visitation and any form of recruitment was a fast path to a prison cell. Informants were everywhere these days. The younger generation had been taught a strong disdain for traditional religion, especially Judeo-Christian, in the public schools. There had been a boom in the early years of home schooling due to this. It had flourished for several years, until it was outlawed.

Josh and Alice had been Methodists during their years together. A few years after her death, the church had given in to IU government demands in order to keep their tax status and began granting "equal time" to other religions on their podium. He had left in favor of the Presbyterian Church at that point. The Presbyterians and the Baptists were the lone holdouts by then, but that didn't last long. They were soon shut down, one by one, for failure to pay the excessive taxes. Eventually even the ones that managed to pay were taken over for some imagined tax violation. The government would then install a hand-picked set of elders or deacons, usually members of the town council, to "reorganize" the church and bring it into compliance with tax code. The former minister of Josh's church had been charged with treason for publicly speaking against this practice during the take over. He was now serving a life sentence in a French prison. The worst dissidents were almost always sent to Europe to serve their sentences. Josh's blood ran hot thinking of this.

"I think we should do it," he turned and looked at Oakland whose mouth fell open.

"I don't know," Oakland said, "sounds like a fast path to prison to me."

"Not if we really keep ourselves secret."

"Maybe…"

"Think about it Oak," Josh's voice rose a bit, "we gather information on things the government is doing, then write it up and distribute it through African and Middle Eastern websites. As long as we're paying, they're asking no questions and they are out of reach of the IU."

"But they'll block them…"

"People have been finding ways around the blocked sites for years. Once they know about this, they'll find it."

"But…"

In Due Time

"You heard him, the underground churches and other such dissident groups will find out—we'll make sure they do—and they will do the rest to spread the word." Josh looked over at Oakland, "Oak, we know things that go on, inside scoop that the common folk don't. If these things are held under their noses…"

"I still don't know, I think this being the 'Ox' has gone to his head."

"Oak…"

"Okay," Oakland shook his head, "if you think it will work… well, I'm with you."

$$fff$$

The sun was peeking through the blinds of the bedroom the next morning when the alarm buzzed. Josh reached for his robe and slid into his slippers as he walked to the stairs leading down to his kitchen. He had been comfortable living in this condo these recent years, but it would never feel like home; then again, neither had the house during the weeks following the murders. He knew he couldn't stay there and unloaded it for a fraction of its worth. This was cozy and it was all he needed.

The smell of the coffee wafted to his nose as he wandered into the kitchen. His coffee maker had a timer so it would be waiting for him each morning. Once he had his cup prepared to his liking, Josh wandered over and flopped down on the cushions covering the window seat peering through the broad bay window facing out the back of his place. He sipped from the cup and stared over the steep forested hill that funneled down to a good-sized pond. A pair of ducks rose off the water and circled the trees then glided to a stop on the surface again. Great circles radiated out from where they landed. He drank down the rest of his coffee and walked up to his room to get dressed.

$$fff$$

Josh was reviewing a set of production reports when his phone buzzed. "Mr. Lance?"

"Yes?"

"There is a General LaVail here to see you."

"Send him up," LaVail, Josh thought. Oh yes, the new commander of the Middle Atlantic military district.

Major General Samuel LaVail was a compact man just a few years younger than Josh. His dark slicked back hair was showing considerable signs of graying on the sides, just at the roots. Beyond the roots was jet black. LaVail's hat was under his left arm as he extended his right hand to Josh.

"General, to what do I owe this pleasure?"

"Well Mr. Lance, as the new military commander in this district, it behooves me to get to know one of our largest suppliers." LaVail's smile was smooth. Josh had seen his kind before. All of his gestures, right down to his facial expressions, were rehearsed.

"You're American, aren't you?"

"I was born in the former United States, so I guess you could call me that if it makes you comfortable. I personally don't like labels," LaVail bobbed his head forward and arched an eyebrow, "it is one world now you know."

"Yes," Josh hesitated slightly, "so it is. It's just unusual to see an officer of your rank that was American born. Please have a seat." Josh motioned for the general to follow him to a corner nook with a mahogany table and a set of chairs. He buzzed his secretary and told her to have some coffee and pastries sent up.

"You know, Mr. Lance, I am one of the few generals who were born over here. Most of the experienced military men my age," Josh guessed that he was about forty-five, "from here were too shackled to out dated ideas about national sovereignty," LaVail waved his arms in a mocking gesture as he said those last two words and rolled his eyes at the same time. "Well, needless to say, this didn't make them very good candidates for such command."

"Yes, I see." Josh looked up as a pot of coffee and platter of pastries were laid out on the table. The two men sat smiling quietly until the door was closed again. He looked back at LaVail, "Considering that, general, what made you suitable for high command?" LaVail's smile faded for a second. Josh quickly realized that this might be a bad question and added, "If I might be so bold."

"Oh sure," LaVail swatted the concern away, the smile quickly returned, just as plastic as it had been before. "My parents had long been dedicated to the cause of social justice, going all the way back to the sixties and they always did their best to impart those values to me."

"What did your father do?" Josh asked, "For a living I mean."

"He was a lawyer at a big think tank out in San Francisco. Anyway, the defining moment for me came in college at Berkeley. I was at a protest and it hit me." LaVail theatrically imitated a slapping movement against his forehead. Josh marveled at how the sudden motion failed to disturb a single hair on his head. LaVail leaned in and said, "If I was to really be of service to the cause of helping the world come together to break the shackles of capitalist tyranny, the place to be was Europe. So, I went to France."

"Wow," Josh tried to look impressed, "quite a move."

"Yes," the façade seemed to fade for a moment and LaVail's face grew dreamy. "Those were some days back then. Tactics training, the riots around Paris..." LaVail leaned forward on the table. His face grew animated, now the smile seemed genuine. "You know we brought the French government to its knees, by god." He lightly slapped the table. "Soon they were singing our tune."

"Hmm," Josh poked out his lower lip thoughtfully, "I thought that was mainly Northern African Muslims."

"Well..." LaVail leaned back and gave a dismissive wave, "You use whatever means you can to accomplish a positive outcome."

The rest of the meeting was idle chit chat between mouthfuls of Danishes and doughnuts. When LaVail stood to leave, he shook Josh's hand warmly and assured him that he would stay in close touch. Josh smiled and nodded then subconsciously counted his fingers once LaVail unclasped his hand.

CHAPTER
34

TIME seemed to creep along for Joshua Lance. The absence of anything to look forward to left him with little reason to hurry home. His days were deliberately long in his office so his evenings alone would be short. In the months that had passed, he had grown more acquainted with General LaVail than he liked. LaVail's pride in things Josh loathed seemed endless. In the end though, Josh's acting skills and diplomacy were flawless.

As LaVail became more comfortable and candid, Josh had little doubt that LaVail had no clue how he really felt. To LaVail, Josh was just another greedy businessman who cared not what system he lived under as long as he could work that system to his advantage. In short, just the way Josh once was.

LaVail's world view was a pragmatic one. He knew that no government exerted its will without the backing of power and wealth. Of course Josh understood that the wealth and power of the individual was at the pleasure of the government. If he displeased them, he would be crushed without a single feather being ruffled amongst others of high standing.

Today was not a day to worry about this, today was a day to celebrate, or so he had been told. Josh shuffled his papers and picked through reports just like most days. To him, no day was cause for undue celebration. Not anymore, at least.

"Smile, old man, it's your birthday!" Art beamed as he stood in the doorway. Josh glowered back and nodded. He harrumphed and cracked a small grin.

"Thank you for sparing me the black balloons."

"Hey," Artemis spread his arms in front, "Howard and Oakland wanted to, but I know better." He chuckled, "I almost didn't stop them though, it's not every day a man turns fifty."

"Thanks for reminding me," Josh arched an eyebrow, "besides, you're not that far behind me."

"Way too true for comfort, buddy," Art responded, "Funny, I don't feel that old though. Of course Julie keeps me young. I'm lucky to have a good woman along for the ride. Oh," he stopped. Josh was staring down at his desk. "I'm sorry, Josh."

Josh nodded slowly, he still looked down but his gaze went miles beyond the desk. "It's okay." He finally said.

"Um, you are still coming over tonight," Art asked quietly, "right?"

Josh looked up and studied his friend for a moment. He had always prided himself on hiding his emotions, but he could see his pain mirrored in Art's face. This was a time he had expected to be happy. What was it he had joked about those years ago? He had seen his first sign of gray in the mirror and remarked that he was getting old, although he was only in his early thirties at the time. He had remarked to Alice that she would be trading him in on a younger man by the time he was fifty. Alice had put her arms around him and said that she was going to throw the biggest party he had ever seen when he was fifty and spoil him like no man had ever been spoiled. He had laughed and said he was looking forward to it.

Josh had expected to have grandchildren to bounce on his knee by now, maybe a grandson to teach football to like he had Alex. He had looked forward to being spoiled rotten by his beautiful wife. It hadn't turned out that way. Josh wasn't spoiled, only his life was.

Josh smiled back at Artemis, "I'll be there."

$$fff$$

After supper, Julie Pike lit the candles on a large cake. Blue icing against a white background depicted a ram wearing Carolina blue throwing a football. Two large candles, one in the shape of a "5" and the other in the shape of a "0" sat in the center. Josh was grateful that she had not actually put fifty candles on the cake. Even his athletic lungs would be taxed trying to blow that out.

Later they sat in Art's great room sipping coffee. Josh stared out the large windows that formed most of the wall at the back of the room as Artemis and Julie talked quietly. Josh had picked up Art's latest scrapbook. He flipped through the pages of clippings from various sources. Every newspaper within easy reach was represented along with special interest journals and newsletters, history and science on parade.

"You like all these scrapbooks Julie," Josh held the book up. Julie rolled her eyes and Art smirked.

"Has he ever let you see his 'special' scrapbook?"

"Hell no!" Julie shouted. Art began to squirm, the smile had left his face now.

"Hey," Art jumped up, "you want more coffee?"

"No, I'm fine." Josh responded and looked back at Julie, "So, he hasn't even let you…"

"How about you honey," Art's voice roared out in quick spurts.

"No, I'm fine too dear," Julie responded looking down at her half full cup then back at Josh. "Would you believe…"

"Hey," Art interjected again, "want to watch a movie or something?"

"Nahh," Josh said, "not tonight." He decided to let the matter drop. Art shifted his weight from one side to the other and smiled nervously. What are you hiding buddy? "Why don't we just sit here and relax a bit?" Josh sipped his coffee and let his mind roam.

"What?" Josh looked over. He had just realized that Julie was talking to him. His thoughts had wandered back to a weekend he had spent in the mountains with Alice. It seemed like a lifetime ago now. Rain awakened them in the wee hours of the morning beating on the tin roof of the rented house. He got up and renewed the fire in the huge fireplace then settled back beside her. He laid his head on her bare chest, reached up and stroked her hair as he listened to the rhythm of her heart. Each beat warmed and reassured him.

In Due Time

Whenever he felt cold and alone that was the memory he called up.

"I asked what you were thinking about. You were a million miles away." Julie smiled. Her hair was still red with a hint of silver here and there. She had cut it short several years before.

"Oh, nothing really," Josh smiled.

"Why are you such a closed book Josh? You need to open up and let the people who love you in."

"Julie," Art warned.

"No, I mean it!" Julie said, "You know how much we love you Josh. If it weren't for you Art and I wouldn't have ever been together. It's time for you to take off the sack cloth and climb out of the ashes."

"Oh God," Art muttered. Josh smiled sadly. Most people could never get away with saying that to him, but he never had the heart to be angry with Julie. He had often joked, referring to her as a sugar coated sparkplug. She was both the sweetest and toughest woman he had ever known. Josh knew what she said was true. She and Artemis had led a happy life because of each other. Josh owed his life to Art, but Art owed his happiness to Josh.

"I'm sorry Josh," she smiled. Julie had taken on a more mature look, but had managed to keep much the same shape she had always maintained. She leaned forward, "but you know I'm right. There is someone out there who can make you happy again."

"Thank you," Josh replied softly, "but I doubt it." He swallowed the rest of his coffee and set the cup down. "I really should be going."

He stood and slapped Art on the shoulder warmly. Julie smiled in a sedate manner and walked over and rose up on her toes. She hugged him and kissed his cheek.

"Julie May Pike," Josh grinned, "you are as lovely now as you always have been and I dearly love you and your husband." He looked over her and winked at Art, "Even when you are telling me things I don't want to hear. Good night."

CHAPTER 35

"**H**OW'RE things going at headquarters, General?" Josh asked. General LaVail studied the chess board. Josh shifted in his chair as LaVail would first pick up one piece and set it back down then another. Slick—as Josh had started privately calling LaVail—had arrived unannounced as usual. Josh had been reviewing his notes for the new weapons guidance system. He and Howard would be leaving in two days to do a slide show on the latest enhancements.

"Fine," LaVail shrugged. "The usual, small bands of guerillas; they pop up and make a show of things, get everybody stirred up. Then we put them down. In the end they always end up face down in the streets, thinking they've accomplished something. We win, they lose." He smiled smugly at Josh then his face turned more serious. "There is the one…" LaVail snorted, "jerk, calls himself the Ox, making things much too interesting."

Josh blinked twice, "Ox? Who?"

LaVail laughed and pointed at Josh, "He's nobody… just some guy, who calls himself Ox. He's writing lies and spreading them about. Gets all the nut cases upset, making things more dangerous." He waved a hand dismissively, "In the end we always win. The worthless little scum he stokes up eventually find themselves under our boots. And so will he, I'm going to enjoy catching this Ox."

"So you know who he is?"

"Not yet, but we think he could be in this part of the country, so it will look very bad for me if I don't get him."

"I see." Josh said, "So General, are you going to make a move or just play with the pieces?" LaVail grunted and smiled. He looked down again studying the board.

"Do you believe in God, or at least the Christian concept of a god?" LaVail asked. He kept his head down, but watched Josh's reaction out of the corner of his eye.

"Why don't you tell me?" Josh replied. "I'm sure you already know."

"How would I know that?"

"Who do you think you're playing with General? I know what kind of access you have."

LaVail smiled, "Well, I do know you belong to a church. Presbyterian, I believe, and you changed congregations from Methodist I understand."

"You know a lot."

"That still doesn't answer the question. Congregations are full of people who are there for the right reasons. A large percentage of them don't really buy that Christ hogwash." LaVail was looking straight at Josh now. His eyes were cold, but the smile remained.

Josh wondered if LaVail noticed the grimace on his face. He knew that would be hard to hide.

"So Mr. Lance, do you believe in all those Jesus fairy tales?"

"I do." Josh returned the stare. His mouth was set and his teeth gritted.

LaVail laughed and sat back. "Religion is the opiate of the masses. Isn't that what they say?" Josh gave a slight smile. "You know, Mr. Lance, I experimented with religion when I was younger. I just couldn't find one that suited me." He picked up a chess piece and rolled it between his thumb and forefinger. "I finally resolved that if there is a god, it is in all of us. Besides, all those holy rollers gave me the willies."

"Do I give you the willies General?"

LaVail laughed again and set the chess piece back in place. "No Mr. Lance, you don't. I think you are a smart enough man to balance your duty to your government with your belief in those myths."

"Humph," Josh grunted, "Myths."

"Yes, myths," LaVail's eyes bored into Josh, "I understand how those old timers raised in the so-called Bible belt might find it comforting to believe in your god. That's all well and good, as long as they can keep their proper loyalties straight, but so many can't. You see, Mr. Lance, you can believe in any tripe you want to, but in the end there is only one thing that matters. That is your duty to the common good." He leaned up and placed his arms on each side of the chessboard, "And that is best served by our government, one that serves the common good of all people all over the world. Not in just one region. Of course, it will all work itself out in time. The proper education of the children in our schools will lessen this need to depend on these legends and dogma over time. Another generation or two, we'll have them trained right."

Josh nodded and LaVail sat back and smiled.

"I know you understand that," LaVail leaned up and moved a knight across the board, "I believe that is check mate, Mr. Lance."

f f f

"So Howard, when we get back we need to really concentrate on the white paper on the new armor piercing ammo." Josh and Howard were walking toward the safety checkpoints in the concourse. Josh's throat was scratchy and his sinuses were stuffed. He was afraid it would get worse and had warned Howard that he might be giving this presentation. They were early for the flight, but Josh always liked to allow extra time.

"Got it, I've already started looking at it." Howard said, "Oh man, look at that line."

"You see! That's why I always insist on being early. You can never tell about this." Josh looked toward the check point and watched as two guards walked up and took a man by the shoulders and dragged him into a problem room and shut the door. The threat assessment board above the checkpoints changed color. Oh great, Josh thought, now they'll go over everyone with a fine toothed comb.

Three people ahead of them a man began to breathe heavily. His face was red and sweat trickled down the side of his face. He frantically rifled through his pockets. Josh heard him comment to the man beside him about leaving his inhaler in the car. He stepped out of line and began to trot toward the exit. The sudden motion caught the attention of a guard at the check point.

"You, halt!" The guard yelled and trained his Uzi toward the man.

"For God's sake stop," Josh said as the man came up beside him.

"Halt! Everybody down," the guard shouted. Oh no, Josh thought, they're going to shoot. Everyone around him dropped to the floor. Howard was squatting beside him.

"No! He's sick," Josh cried and reached for the man who had stumbled past him. He heard the bolt slide on the Uzi. His heart pounded in his ear and he felt a pressure on his legs as he crashed to the floor. Josh was stunned and looking up at the running man when the burst of gunfire echoed through the concourse. Blood splattered from the neck of the man and he crumpled to the floor. He tried to crawl back and died with his eyes staring straight at Josh. Josh reached out to the man.

"For Christ's sake come back here, you can't help him," Howard said in a loud whisper. Josh looked back to see Howard with his arms around Josh's calves trying to drag him back away from the carnage. Josh noticed the blood specks on Howard's face and realized that he had been sprayed also. He looked back to the wide open eyes of the dead man. His mouth hung open and his lips contorted as if he were trying to say something to Josh. The guard walked up to the man and placed a heavy boot on his shoulder. He laughed and rolled the body over onto its back with a quick shove from his toe.

CHAPTER
36

WORLD Unity Gratitude Day (3rd Thursday in November) – Five Years Later:

The gathering in Raleigh was large. Josh could still remember this being called Thanksgiving, but he knew it would not take many years for the younger generation to forget it ever existed. The government had decreed that the only thing to be thankful for was the unification of the world, despite the fact that it was not all unified, and dropped any pretense of thankfulness to God. The decree had read: "Being thankful for the security and prosperity provided by a stronger and more centralized government for the good of all, this day will heretofore be designated 'World Unity Gratitude Day.' All citizens of the world will be allowed proper time and compensation to properly give thanks for the common good." This day was now about gratitude to the state.

A history professor had spoken for the better part of an hour about the history of this day. He explained that the day had originally been established for the Pilgrims to give thanks to the Native Americans for saving them from starvation. The white people in turn had shown their gratitude by murdering and raping the native peoples and stealing their lands. Fortunately the North American Union had thrown open the gates allowing the indigenous peoples of Mexico to force the whites to share their wealth and ushering in the glorious International Union. Josh had bitten his lip so hard it nearly bled at one point. History had certainly changed since his school days. He wanted to shout that it was not only the whites and wealthy that had suffered because of the North American Union, but he knew that perception made for an easier sell.

Looking around though Josh had to admit that they had cleaned up downtown rather well for the event. Government buses had spent days hauling the beggars and junkies to camps outside of town. There was little they could do about the gangs. They were here as always, but they knew that today was special. Anyone who disrupted the festival would face harsh repercussions. This didn't seem to concern them; they had the rest of the year to run amok. This government did like most before them and didn't try to fix what was not easily dealt with. Instead, like their predecessors in both Europe and the last days of the American experiment, they used these problems to justify expanding their own power. Howard had tried to explain this. Now Josh finally understood.

Rounding the corner, he spied Earl and Amy Harper sipping beer and chatting. Even though it was late November, the worst of the winter was still ahead of them in North Carolina. Many of the celebrations were inside, but a large number of people crowded the streets, visiting food kiosks and craft booths. A couple of weeks later it would begin to turn much colder he knew.

"Well, hey big man!" Earl Harper called out. Josh waved and walked over to take Earl's extended hand.

"Earl, Amy," he shook Earls hand and nodded to Amy.

"How are you Josh?" Amy Harper hugged Josh and gave him a quick kiss on the cheek.

"Fine, fine," Josh smiled. He watched Earl out of the corner of his eye. Earl seemed unsteady. A few too many beers Josh supposed. "How are things?" Josh asked.

"Humph!" Earl grunted; a sour look invaded his features. "How's it being a government employee you mean? Well, a lot less lucrative than when I owned the agency myself." Earl would never get over this, Josh knew. Earl and Amy had been forced to move from the large home into more meager government assigned housing.

Josh smiled and nodded, looking around to see who was within earshot.

"Hey Josh, did you see the paper? Boy we really got 'em all upset don't we?"

Josh jerked his head back straight and shot Earl a glare. "Excuse us Amy," he took Earl by the arm and pulled him along toward the row of buildings to their side. Seeing that the alleyway between the buildings was empty, Josh dragged Earl several feet down it and pushed him against the wall. Earl's eyes had widened.

"What the hell is wrong with you?" Josh hissed, "You know we don't talk about this in public."

"I'm sorry Josh," Earl stammered, "but did you see it?"

"Yes, I saw it." Josh nodded.

"I mean, it's getting hot. They want us bad... Kind of worries me."

"Are you getting weak on us?" Josh's eyes bore into him, "You knew from the start they would be upset. You knew the risks."

"Yeah, I know, I know, but..." Earl looked down, his face contorted, "I didn't think it would get this hot. You know like it was in the old days, when we could..."

"This isn't the old days Earl. We aren't free to say what we want. That's why this is so important. If you can't take the heat, you should get out now, but I'm telling you this, you had better keep your mouth shut either way." Josh saw the way Earl was cringing before him. He hadn't realized until then that he had him by the lapels and was bumping him against the wall.

"Are you gentlemen alright?" Josh turned to see the uniformed security policeman at the end of the alley. He had been so caught up that the man had walked right up on them.

"We're fine officer," Josh released Earl and smoothed his lapels.

"Perhaps, we should go to the station and discuss this matter."

"That won't be necessary officer. We were just having a little chat."

The policeman eyed them cautiously, "I need to see your identification." He reached with his left hand. His right hand remained lightly on his sub-machinegun.

"Sure, I have mine right here," Josh pulled his wallet out and shot Earl a sharp glare. Earl stood still as Josh handed his ID card over.

The soldier glared at Earl expectantly. "My ID's right there officer." Josh gave a quick nod at his card and cut his eyes over toward Earl in a warning.

"Oh," the policeman had looked down at the ID and spotted the name and the high security clearance. He handed the card back to Josh, "Sorry to trouble you Mr. Lance," he nodded toward Earl, "let me know if you need any assistance with this matter."

"That won't be necessary, thanks." Josh smiled and watched the soldier all the way out of sight. He then pulled Earl toward the entrance to the alley and looked around the corner to check. The policeman was gone.

"I'm sorry Josh," Earl looked near the point of crying. Josh nodded and put a hand on Earl's shoulder.

"Look, they don't know who we are, but if you can't take the pressure tell us now." Josh looked down at Earl and glanced over toward Amy. She was looking their way; concern and confusion etched her face. He smiled and waved at her.

"I'm fine Josh," Earl pleaded, "I just get a bit nervous sometimes. I'll be okay, really." He nodded emphatically. Josh patted his shoulder and they turned and walked back toward Amy.

CHAPTER
37

"YOU know Howard, I don't care too much for lemon in my tea, but I get the feeling that you really hate it." Howard had pulled the lemon from the edge of his glass and thrown it down disdainfully. Josh sat smirking. Four fresh glasses of tea had been set before them by Zee. Josh had taken special notice of the name as he had the blonde waitress it belonged to. It was nearly two o'clock and the lunch crowd had cleared out. Oakland, Josh, Howard and Artemis hunched around a table in the old barbecue restaurant. They occupied a corner in a separate room from the main dining area.

"Properly brewed and sweetened tea doesn't need lemon," Howard wagged a finger, "in fact it is an affront to the tea and an insult to the taste buds."

"I'll remember that old friend," Josh held up his glass in a mock toast, "and I will never serve you tea with lemon in it." He watched Zee out of the corner of his eye and she turned and caught his gaze. She smiled sweetly. His face flushed and he turned away. She was younger than he was, but no kid, probably in her early forties. Pretty, but not beautiful, striking was the best word for her. Josh realized these days that he spent a lot of time staring and admiring. Longing for something really, but knowing that he lacked the courage to complete the transaction. Besides, he hadn't the time for such frivolity. This appeared to be an extra long lunch indulged in by four executives flaunting their privilege. It wasn't.

In Due Time

Josh raised his glass and Howard laughed and returned the toast, touching his glass against Josh's. Josh had been watching Zee, following her out of sight through the door to the small room. When it was safe he resumed the discussion.

"So the land has been purchased as we discussed?"

"Yes," Howard lowered his voice as well, "in Danville, Virginia." They felt it was safer to talk outside of the office, Gen. LaVail and his men were there so often that Josh wondered if the building might be bugged, and this was something that could not be discussed with the other members of the Ox.

"Under what name?" Josh asked.

"James Mack," Howard looked around as he spoke.

"Sounds good," Josh said, "so we need a code that only the four of us know. I've thought about this. There will be three levels," he held up his index finger, "one is low level, meaning leave casually without raising any suspicion. The code for that will be, 'Mr. Mack wants to see you.' Two is more urgent, meaning leave quickly and be prepared for anything. That will be, 'Mr. Mack needs to see you.' Finally," he held up a third finger, "level three will mean drop everything and get out immediately. That will be, 'Mr. Mack demands your presence.' Okay? Whatever, but the keys are, 'wants,' 'needs' and 'demands.' Got it?" He scanned the faces around the table. They all nodded grimly. "Guys I regret that this is necessary, but I don't feel that everyone in the Ox can be trusted. Someone could turn on us, we have to be prepared."

Everyone was silent. Josh slapped his palm on the table and said, "Enough of that, lets talk about something fun. Art, you know anything fun?"

"Well," Artemis grinned, "my time device is coming along."

"What?" Josh bawled, "I had about forgotten about that. It's been so long since you've said anything; I thought for sure you had given up on it."

"As he should have," Howard barked, "I've never seen such a smart man waste so much time on something so bogus."

"Oh, you two laugh if you want," Art fired back, "come by my lab, at home, this evening and you won't laugh then. I'm ready for a live test."

"Are you really?" Oakland piped up.

"Yes, really!"

"Don't waste your time man. It's not possible." Howard said.

"Oh let him dream Howard. Man's got to have something to tinker with," Josh waved Howard off and leaned toward Artemis, "Just don't go and electrocute yourself or anything, you hear."

"I'm telling you, come by and we'll test it. I need witnesses for this anyway."

"Alright, alright we'll see." Josh sat back and watched as Zee walked past the doorway and bent to pick up a pen she had dropped.

"Later today," Artemis banged his fist, "you'll see. I'll shut you all up."

fff

Josh stood at the door of the lab with Howard and Oakland. Art had his head down. Julie had let them in; Art had obviously not even heard the doorbell. He had always been that way, even when they were in college. Sometimes Art would be so lost in his experiments that he would forget to eat lunch. Josh cleared his throat loudly. He looked up.

"Oh," Art mumbled, "come in, I didn't see you there." The three of them walked into the study and each took a seat. Art continued working with his head down for several more moments as if they weren't in the room. Josh smiled, the man was unflappable. Sometimes back at Carolina, he would turn the stereo up to see if he could distract Art. It never worked.

"Art?" Julie stood at the door with her coat on. Art glanced over. "I'm going to the store now."

"Okay," he smiled and nodded as she turned to leave.

"How's Lance liking Emory?" Josh asked.

"Fine, teaching suits him." Artemis smiled. Lance Pike had followed his father's example at Duke and was now teaching Quantum Physics at Emory University.

Josh nodded and Art reached into the bottom drawer of his desk and produced that funny looking belt Josh had seen him tinkering with in the past.

"Looks like you've made some improvements," Josh observed. There were fabric pouches with microchips sewn in and wires emanating from the middle with electrodes on the end.

"Improvements!" Art snorted, "Hell, I've redesigned the whole thing more times than I can count."

"What are those wires for?" Rice Oakland asked.

"Power source," Art grinned, "You see, in order to make this work, you need an electrical charge." He stood and paced behind the desk as he spoke, "I have actually tested this with an inanimate object, but I had to hook it up to a truck battery."

"So those wires hook up to a battery?" Howard offered.

"Sort of," Art said, "the best battery of all right here." He tapped the center of his chest. "You see, I'm using the pulses from your central nervous system by way of your solar plexus to give it an initial charge."

"Won't that like," Josh's mouth twisted as he spoke, "short circuit your heart or something."

"No!" Art pointed to a panel on the right side of the belt, "Here is an improvement I've made. This is a power amplifier. Once charged, it will actually generate electricity from a reaction with the electrons in the air. It only needs a minor electrical pulse to put it into motion. Kind of like an automobile ignition."

"Humph," Josh grunted. Howard stared at the ceiling shaking his head slowly and Oakland leaned forward on his knees.

"As a result, it is now safe for human testing."

"Do you mean to tell me," Howard sat forward and pointed at the belt, "that this thing has actually sent something through time?"

"Yes!"

"How do you know? It's an object, it can't tell you." Howard waved his hands about and smirked.

"Because I did what I am going to do with myself. I sent it ahead ten minutes and waited for it to reappear."

Howard laughed. It was one of those deep belly laughs so strong that Josh knew it wasn't natural. He wasn't sure whether he agreed with the sentiment or was angry with Howard for mocking Art.

Instead he watched Oakland's reaction. Oakland sat back and rubbed his forehead. A thoughtful look danced about his face. Maybe it wasn't so far fetched. It was at least making Oakland mull it over.

"Chuckle away Howard," Art's face reddened slightly, "you won't be laughing in a minute."

"What are you going to do?" Josh asked.

"I'm going to show you," Artemis picked the belt up and wrapped it around his waist. He then unbuttoned three buttons of his shirt in the middle of his chest and pulled the waxy backing from the two electrodes and placed them inside his shirt and pressed them into place.

"Art," Josh felt his stomach turn over, "is this really a good idea?"

"Of course it is," Artemis scowled back.

"No, I mean really." Josh held up a hand, "Some things are just too risky to mess with."

"Oh come on," Howard bellowed, "Do you think that little utility belt is actually going to do anything?"

"Art don't do it, I've got a bad feeling." Josh pleaded.

"Enough," Artemis shouted and pushed a button that lit up a display in the center of the buckle. "See," he smiled, "that power is coming from me and I don't even feel it." He patted Josh's shoulder, "It'll be alright."

"Fine," Josh sat down.

Art punched in some numbers from the display on the buckle. Oakland still watched in silence. Josh looked at his watch; it was 7:05 pm. The display showed the current date and the time of "7:15." There was a big red button beside the smaller black ones. In a grand gesture, Art placed his right index finger on it and pushed. The belt began to vibrate softly and the display glowed brighter. A small hum began to rumble from the belt as if it were angry. Josh swallowed hard; Art's skin was beginning to glow with a pinkish tint.

Josh squirmed in his chair and looked over at Oakland. He was staring ahead with his eyes wide. Howard's mouth hung open. A bright light popped like a flash bulb around Art and he slowly faded from view.

"Oh my God!" Howard leaped from his chair. "It vaporized

Art!"

"Dear Lord," Josh choked out. "Where did he go?"

"It freakin' fried him I tell you!" Howard shouted. "He's gone."

"Oh no," Josh put his face down in his hands. He lifted back up; his eyes wide and moist. "What are we going to tell Julie?"

"Julie my ass!" Howard yelled, "What are we going to tell anybody. What about the law? They're going to think we killed him or something."

"Hey!" Oakland raised his voice.

"I knew that idiot would finally get bitten by one of his hair brained ideas, but my God! Not this," Howard spit out.

"Hey! Cool it!" Oakland roared, waving his arms in the air. The other two fell silent. "That's better, let me think."

"What are we going to do Oakland?" Howard mumbled.

"Oh dear Lord," Josh croaked, "He was my best friend."

"There's one thing that you two haven't considered."

"What's that?" Howard asked.

"Maybe he was right."

"What?"

"Maybe he actually traveled and he'll be back here in ten minutes."

"I always knew that Art was a little cuckoo," Howard sputtered, "but I've always given you more credit that that."

Oakland pointed to the clock on the wall, "7:10, we'll know in five more minutes."

Over the next five minutes Howard paced wildly about the room. Josh sat and stared morosely through the window and Oakland watched the spot Artemis had disappeared from thoughtfully. Occasionally his lips would move in some silent calculation then he would lightly tap his forehead.

"Well," Howard pointed at the clock. "7:15! Where is he?"

Oakland held up one hand and gave Howard a stern look. They were silent for another minute.

"You see," Howard pointed again. "He's gone, zapped!"

Howard continued to rant and wave his arms about. Oakland looked as if he wanted to slap him. Josh stared straight ahead; a tear rolled down his cheek and was replaced by a couple of more in his eyes, blurring his vision. Through the tiny pools, he began to see something strange. A pinprick of light softly pierced the air in front of the desk. He wiped his eyes and sat up. The light expanded slightly to the size of a baseball. It was a warm pinkish orange hue. It grew until it was like a basketball then brightened and began to flood the room with light. Howard and Oakland stood with their mouths open watching. Another lively flash surged through the room and faded out and there stood Art before them just where he had been before.

Josh stood up. Art looked pale and his eyes rolled back in his head. He reached out and caught Art as he pitched forward and eased him to the floor.

CHAPTER

38

SMALL rings spread about the glass of water as Josh bounced his leg nervously. He occupied the chair beside where Art lay on the couch. Howard and Oakland watched from across the living room as his eyes fluttered open. Art cut his eyes over to where they sat.

"Is he okay?" Howard asked.

"I don't know yet," Josh held up a hand toward Howard. Oakland's lips curved slightly upward as he eased forward expectantly in his seat.

"Art?" Josh asked tentatively.

"Yes," Art croaked out and nodded slowly.

"Are you okay?"

"I think so," Art turned his head and looked at Oakland then back at Josh. "What happened?"

"What do you remember?" Oakland asked as he pulled himself from the chair.

"Well," Art eased his legs onto the floor and leaned against the arm of the couch. "After I pushed the button the whole room started to glow. Then there was a bright flash that blotted everything out for a few seconds then when things came back into focus..." he swallowed hard and took the glass Josh offered him. "Well, you were all in different places from where you had been, and then I was here."

"What did you feel?" Oakland asked.

Art took a drink and furrowed his brow. "Tired mainly; did you check my vitals?"

"Yes," Oakland stepped closer, "everything seems fine. Pulse, BP, breathing… All fine. We should probably do an EKG on you though."

"Tomorrow," Art held up a hand. "I'm feeling fine, just like I've done a day at hard labor."

"I guess we should go," Oakland gestured toward Howard.

"Yeah," Howard said, "see you tomorrow." Art nodded. Josh kept his seat. He wasn't going anywhere yet.

"Is Julie back?" Art asked once the front door closed.

"Not yet," Josh shook his head.

"We don't have to tell her about this do we?"

"Nahh, no reason to," Josh smiled.

"Good."

"Art, if you don't mind my saying; you scared the Hell out of me just then."

"I'm fine."

"I mean it man," Josh smiled, "I've lost so much. I don't want to lose you too. Besides, Julie's much too young and pretty to be a widow." They both laughed.

Art took a long drink from the water glass.

"After I lost Alice and the kids," Josh continued, "you and Julie were about all that pulled me through."

"I'm sorry," Artemis stared at the floor. His smile sagged into a frown.

"Huh?"

"I mean about Alice and the kids, I'm sorry."

"That wasn't *your* fault."

"Sometimes it feels like it was," his voice cracked and he looked up toward the ceiling. Josh studied his face, his eyes seemed to moisten.

"What? What makes you think that?"

"Oh," Art's eyes regained their focus. "Uh, you know, um… I just tend to feel guilty about everything." He let out a nervous chuckle, "That's all."

Josh watched him for several seconds. Art looked at him, but didn't make eye contact; instead he seemed to be looking at his chin. He finally nodded, "Of course. Sure."

$$fff$$

The next evening Josh strolled through the mall. He didn't really know why he had stopped there. He had just felt the urge. The stores were about to close. What stores there still were, that is; taxes took most of the pay from people's income and they were given International Union Benevolence stamps to bring them up to a "proper sustenance level." Of course those who could afford it had ways around this. Loyalty and "indispensability to the greater good" were always rewarded, so Josh wasn't affected.

He stood peering into a clothing store. The woman had her back to him, but he recognized her. She turned her head and he smiled as he caught her profile.

"Come here often?" Josh asked as he slipped up behind her. She jumped slightly and turned. "Sorry... didn't mean to scare you."

"That's okay," she said turning, "oh, it's you."

"Yes, my name is..."

"Oh, I know who you are, Mr. Lance."

"It's Josh please, and if I recall your name is Zee?"

"Very good," Zee nodded with a smile.

"I have a good memory," Josh tapped a finger to his temple with a wink.

"So... what are you doing out tonight?"

"Oh, nothing," Josh said. Her eyes had a certain sparkle up close. They were a deep blue. Flecks of gray seemed to shine through. "Just looking around."

"Where are your friends? You guys seemed to be having quite a time."

Josh chuckled, "I guess they're all home."

They walked casually through the mall as they continued talking; finally they were occupying a bench. Josh didn't really remember sitting, but there they were. He could hardly believe that an hour had passed when Zee stretched and glanced at her watch. Josh tried to avert his gaze, but he couldn't help noticing the tightness of the fabric of the front of the blouse as she stretched. Her eyelids fluttered slightly then narrowed as she focused on the timepiece.

"Oh, my... Well, I must be going." She said.

"Please allow me," Josh motioned toward the exit, "It can be dangerous outside these places nowadays."

"True," she walked alongside Josh as they moved out to the sidewalk.

"It's not like it used to be. The criminals run roughshod now... you know, the greater good..."

Zee held up a finger, "I don't think we should be heard talking that way. You never know whose listening." She quickly looked around then leaned in and whispered, "But I know what you're talking about."

At her car, Josh stopped as she opened the door. "Look, Zee, I've enjoyed talking to you. Maybe..." Josh paused, "maybe we could talk again sometime."

Zee looked up at him and smiled, "Okay."

CHAPTER
39

EARL Harper handed the folded bills to the man sitting in the passenger seat. He flipped through them, turned them over and examined each bill; lips moving as he counted. Earl fidgeted about in his seat, shifting his eyes from side to side.

"Calm down," the man snarled at Earl. Finally he looked up and smiled, "All there," then pulled a paper bag out from under his legs and handed it over.

Earl quickly looked into the bag and checked its contents. One nine millimeter handgun and one hundred rounds of ammunition, as promised. Earl smiled sheepishly and nodded.

"Pleasure," the man opened the door and hopped onto the curb. Earl pulled away and soon the man whose name he didn't know and didn't want to know was but a memory.

Earl reached over and put the bag onto the floor. He should hide it better, he knew that. What if he got stopped or went through a check point? Oh Lord, the worrying never stopped. In the old days he never worried that much. His house was nice and in one of the best neighborhoods, but since the insurance industry had been absorbed as a government function they now lived in government employees' housing. It was better than regular government subsidy housing, but not much. His old neighborhood was gated. He was never concerned about gang members conducting drug deals at the end of the street. Now it was common.

The neighborhood watch Earl had headed up had done some good until it had been disbanded by court order six months ago, like most such watch groups had been. The International Court had ruled that these groups had employed an unacceptable level of racial profiling in the pursuance of their goals. Now it was every household for itself and home invasion robberies had become the sport of the season.

One hundred rounds, Earl mused. He doubted he could ever need that many. Target practicing was a crime and if there were a confrontation he was sure it would end long before that. He also knew that it would be a long time before he would be out from under the cloud such an action would place him under, but maybe he could at least save his family. The robberies bothered him, but the one from two days ago scared him to death.

Two streets over, the Malcolm family had been robbed. As would happen a neighbor had noticed something amiss and called the police. When they arrived an hour later, they found them in the living room. The children were duct taped together on the floor, but largely unhurt. Their parents were another matter. Mrs. Malcolm had been abused, her clothes in shreds and they had both been beaten unconscious. She would recover. His recovery was much less certain.

Earl couldn't let this happen to them. His father had a saying, "better to be tried by twelve than carried by six," the old man would remark with a rueful laugh. Those were the days when there still were twelve person peer juries. Now your only option was a panel of three European judges. There were some things even the global government couldn't change though, Earl smiled. It still generally took six men to carry you to your grave.

fff

Julie Pike set her book down on the end table beside the couch and stretched. She let out a deep yawn and arose to head toward the kitchen. A cool glass of water was what she needed. She smacked her lips as the cool liquid flowed from the refrigerator door into the glass she had grabbed. She jumped up on the counter and took quick sips as she kicked her feet back and forth. Even now in her fifties she still possessed the playfulness of a little girl. What time was it, she set the glass down. Where was Art? Better find him.

"Art," she called jumping down from the counter and heading toward his study. Down the hall, past the bathroom to his study beside the back door, "Art!"

"Huh?" He looked up quickly. He was reading that forbidden book again. She had noticed him looking at it more in recent days. He closed it and set it down on his desk abruptly.

"Honey, you're going to be late." The Ox was meeting at Josh's tonight. Julie was always glad to have the house to herself.

"What?" He looked over at the clock and jumped up. "Oh no, you're right."

"Chop-chop young man, march yourself upstairs and go get ready," she grinned pulling him by the arm.

"Ooh, are you going to spank me when I get home?" Art asked as he kissed her.

Julie laughed and swatted him on the rear, "Get going." She was still smiling when he headed out the front door. She took the paperback from the end table and again found the page she had marked, but then decided that she really didn't want to read. Nothing on television grabbed her attention, so she walked out to the back patio. It was growing dark and cooler, she decided against lingering outdoors.

Pausing by the door to Art's study, Julie noticed the scrapbook setting out. Art never left it out. He always kept it locked away in a desk drawer. She wandered in and laid a hand on the cover. Tracing one finger about the edges she looked around, then felt silly because she knew she was alone. No, she thought, leave it alone. This is private and special. Art would be upset. She turned and headed toward the hall. At the door, Julie paused and shook her head. She went back to the desk, grabbed the scrapbook and hurried into the living room.

CHAPTER 40

"SO, are you…" Art hemmed.

"What?" Josh asked. His mind was still in back in the meeting, in his study. Josh had remodeled and was rather proud of his new office. They were the only two remaining. The others had left once they adjourned.

"Um… are you seeing that waitress, still?"

"Zee?" Josh shrugged, "I guess."

"You don't sound too enthused."

"She's nice," Josh said. The meeting had been the usual steady stream of word of mouth accounts. They summed it all up into a document they called, *Pronouncements of the Ox!* They were always careful to edit out anything that might give clues as to their identity. Owing to Josh's working relationship with General LaVail, they knew just how effective they were. LaVail would try to downplay it, but he had grown increasingly candid with Josh. LaVail's arrogance often got the better of him and Josh's stroking of his ego helped him speak more freely. LaVail couldn't speak so freely with those under his command and rival generals might use any such confessions to advance their own goals. So, Josh presented the perfect avenue for LaVail's bragging.

"But?" Art dragged out the word.

"But what?"

"You just seem like you're trying to find something wrong with her, that's all."

"Ah, she's nice, just…" Josh frowned, "well…"

"Well, what?" Art sputtered, "Look you can't spend the rest of your life comparing every woman to…" Josh shot him a sharp look. Art smiled sadly and reached out for his shoulder. "I'm sorry… but… well, you just can't. You've got to start being happy again sometime."

"I know," Josh looked down. "We'll see."

"Stop being a hermit, okay?" Art half grimaced. Josh let out a soft laugh.

"Okay."

$$fff$$

As Julie sat reading the scrapbook her eyes grew wider. Each page produced something strange and foreign and she would let out a little gasp. She was shaking her head and knew that she should put it away before Art got home, but she didn't. Finally she closed the cover and laid it on the coffee table. She leaned back and that's where she was when the key turned in the front door. Art's happy smile quickly faded when he saw her glare.

"What's wrong?"

Julie simply reached out and picked up the scrapbook. She held it up with the cover facing him and slowly waved it about. His frown was replaced by a look of terror.

"What is this?" She asked quietly.

"You didn't read it did you?"

"Yes, I read it," her voice rose slightly through clinched teeth.

"You were never supposed to read that! You…" he shook a finger at her.

"Don't you dare," she shouted, "if this was just some kind of ordinary diary, I would probably apologize, but it's not. Is it?"

Art gritted his teeth and hung his head. He slowly shook it back and forth without speaking.

"These…" Julie paused, "these things. These crazy things… They never happened! What in the world is this Art? You'd better tell me right now."

Art walked over and flopped down beside her on the couch and started to cry. He was an emotional man, full of fears, but this book… There had always been something about this book that both fascinated and terrified him down to his very soul. He was protective of it like a favored child. Julie had spent hours wondering what secrets it held, and now… could these crazy things be true? These things… these insane things. She looked deep into his eyes as the tears poured forth. These things couldn't be true, could they? She watched Art's eyes, those deep sad eyes. The fear, regret… and something else, despair, yes… despair. Julie knew Art too well. He believed this. With every molecule of his being… it must be true.

ƒ ƒ ƒ

Zee was waiting in the doorway looking out as Josh drove up. She wrapped herself around him when he walked through the door. He hadn't planned on coming over but she had insisted. She really wanted to see him.

Josh closed the door and they found their way to the couch. A sweet melody drifted from the radio droning softly in Zee's bedroom. Would he be in there again tonight? He didn't know. The lights were out and a glowing fire bathed the room. She stroked his hair as his head rested on her soft breasts. He lightly ran his hand along her outer thigh and hip. Josh genuinely liked Zee and she was crazy about him. So why was it, he wondered, that he could not turn loose and return those feelings. The warmth and desire in the room restored his feelings, but still there was something he couldn't let go of. Something holding him back.

She began to caress his cheek with her right hand and soon she brought her left hand down to his other cheek. Josh looked up into her deep blue eyes. The fire sparkled in them. Her lids fluttered shut as she leaned down parting her lips and kissed him deeply. He kissed her back. Her lips were strong and smooth. After a while he pulled back and turned to the fire, sitting with his back to her. Zee pulled herself up behind him with her legs around his hips. She rubbed his back with her left hand and reached around to stroke his thigh with her right. This felt so good, Josh thought. Why couldn't he just enjoy it?

She ran her fingers up his chest and to his chin, rising up on her knees and turning his head back to her. Zee kissed him again; her tongue lightly tickled his lips. She broke the kiss off and ran her lips along his cheek and whispered, "Will you stay the night?"

Josh sat back and stared at the fire again. For a moment he didn't answer then he turned back to her, "I can't."

"Why not?" She eased back some.

"I don't know." He barely croaked out.

"You don't know?" Zee studied him carefully.

"No," he looked down.

"Why not?"

"I just don't…"

"I see," Zee looked at the fire, her lips tightly compressed.

Josh looked at her and smiled in a sad way, "I guess I thought I was ready, but maybe I'm not."

"Why not?" That irritating question again. She stared intently, her hands now folded across her chest.

"I guess I'm still not ready to move on after my wife's death."

"How long has it been?" Her eyes opened pleadingly wide.

Josh furrowed his brow and grimaced slightly, "Twenty years."

"Will you ever be ready?"

"I doubt it," he said quietly. Josh patted her on the knee and got up.

Zee looked up at him, a tear eased down her cheek and she said, "You're not coming back are you?"

"Probably not," Josh answered as he looked down. He took one last look at her and smiled then he left.

$$fff$$

Julie stared at Art in disbelief. Art shrunk from her glare. He wouldn't have believed it himself if he didn't know it to be true.

"What are we going to do about this Art?"

"Why do we have to do anything?" He waved a hand like he was brushing off a gnat.

"Why…" her mouth hung open. "I can not believe you think that. Why?" Julie's voice rose, "We have to that's why!"

"Well, I don't know what to do," Art's voice pitched into a high whine.

"I'm not kidding. I can't just forget this." The intent look was one that Art had never seen in Julie's face. "I'm gonna do something."

"Like what?"

"Something," she stood and stomped a foot, "that's what."

"Whatever…" he looked up at her then back down. "You do whatever you feel you have to. I won't stop you."

Julie sighed, picked up the scrapbook and headed toward the front door. Art looked up and watched her turn the knob. She paused and looked back at him. Tears filled his eyes; she tried to smile, but a look of profound sadness was all she could manage. Then she closed the door behind her.

CHAPTER
41

"JOSH, I need to talk to you," Julie spoke quickly. She sounded slightly breathless. The phone was ringing when Josh walked into his house. He had looked at the number on the display expecting it to be Zee's.

"Are you okay?"

"Yes, I'm fine."

"Art..."

"He's fine," Julie cut him off. "Listen, I'll be there in a few minutes. I have to show you something."

The line went dead. Josh stood there with the phone in his hand and shrugged. It was 11:00 o'clock. What could be so important? He didn't have to wait long; Julie had obviously been close when she called. He didn't notice what she was carrying and paid it no attention. She sat smoothing her hair and shifting in her chair when Josh returned from the kitchen with two glasses of water. Julie took a long, nervous sip and set it down.

"What's this all about?" Josh asked.

"This," Julie held up the scrapbook. Josh squinted hard then his eyes opened wide.

"The famous *forbidden* scrapbook?"

"Yes," she nodded. "Here," she held it out.

"Won't Art be..."

"He knows I have it."

"Does he know you're here?"

"Probably," Julie said, "I didn't say, but I'm sure he knows. Read it!" She made two short sweeping motions with the back of her hand toward the scrapbook.

"Okay," Josh opened the book and looked down.

The first story was a profile of the football team at the beginning of Josh's senior year. There was a profile on Josh. The next item was a story about the Durham game. Josh turned the page and recognized the story about his wreck with a picture of the car being pulled out of the lake. He remembered the headline: 'Football Victory Marred by Tragedy.' That was as far as he had gotten before when Artemis had snatched the scrapbook from him and locked it away. He felt a chill run through his veins at what he read next and looked up at Julie with his mouth agape. The opening paragraph read:

"On the heels of its victory over Durham, Burlington Central finds itself grieving today after news of the death of its star quarterback, Joshua Lance."

Julie met his eyes and nodded toward the scrapbook. He looked down and continued reading. It said: "Lance, 17, was killed late last night after crashing his Ford Mustang into Lake Macintosh. Initial reports indicate that the all-state quarterback drowned after the car sank to the bottom in water just deep enough to cover the vehicle."

"What is this?" Josh stammered, "Julie is this some kind of joke?"

"I'm afraid not," she smiled unenthusiastically. "Keep reading."

On the next page was an obituary then a story about how 1,500 people attended his funeral. Then a story headlined: "Burlington Central Falls to Wilmington," with a subhead: "Finch Interception Ends Burlington Central's Hopes."

"Julie," he looked up. "Please tell me what's going on?"

She took a deep breath and looked up at the corner of the ceiling, then back down for several seconds. Finally blowing her breath out between her lips, she looked back up at Josh shaking her head.

"I'll try," she said. "This book was given to Art in 1997 by an older gentleman who just showed up out of nowhere. The man said he was from the future and that these were some of the things that were going to happen. He showed up about a couple of weeks before your wreck. Art was told of several predictions for the next few days and then the man left. They all came true and the man came back. He then told Art about the car crash you would be in and said that his whole life would change for the better if he were there to rescue you. He said to Art that a man with your popularity and family status could give him the inroads he needed to achieve great things."

"Who was this man," Josh sat forward, "and why would he care?"

Julie laughed softly then covered her lips with her fingers, "Um, it was Art himself. His future self."

Josh arched his eyebrows and whistled softly between his fingers that were tented in front of his mouth.

"You see," she went on, "apparently, Art, the future Art," she corrected, "didn't have a very happy life."

"I see," Josh looked confused, "so he came back and saved my life."

"Not only that, but that blue paper, it's stuck in the back of the book," she pointed, "is what he called his 'roadmap' for Art." Julie made mock quotes around the roadmap, "It's a list of instructions to give him insights on his future life and how to be more successful."

"I see," these seemed to be the only words Josh could come up with even though he really couldn't see.

"There's more," Julie tapped the book with her index finger, "You need to keep reading."

Josh opened back to where he had left off. He remembered that Art had moved his mother into her own house to protect her from his father. With his success, Art had paid for the house himself. She had not been so lucky in this other time. A headline read: "Man Kills Wife Then Self."

He found other stories about Art and various memorabilia from his life. He had apparently not gone to college and had ended up working as a janitor. There was evidence of several arrests for drunkenness and court ordered stays in rehab centers. There were also notes of experiments and pictures of a laboratory and machine shop. Apparently he had still pursued a love of science.

This was too strange for Josh to fully grasp, but thus far things seemed to have turned out for the better. He frowned at the stories about the International Union; some things didn't change. Then he turned the page, focused on the next story and froze in his seat. Josh looked up and Julie nodded sadly.

CHAPTER

42

"THIS is unbelievable." Josh put the book down and headed to the kitchen. Julie followed him and watched as he put on a pot of coffee. He leaned against the counter with his head down listening to the hissing from the coffeemaker. Julie stood watching him carefully.

"When are you up to?"

"2032," Josh answered.

"There's more to come," she patted him on the arm and reached into the cabinet for two cups. The coffee finished and they returned to the living room with it.

Josh resumed his reading. The stories reported about a great uprising against the International Union. It was the revolution that Howard always hoped for, the one that would happen if there were only someone worthy to lead it. Apparently in this alternate time dimension there was. In the reports from 2031 stories about a young man from the Carolinas, first identified as a colonel then later as a general, began appearing. A man named Alexander Birch.

The figure in the pictures was older and bore some scars, but there was no doubt. It was Alex. Josh read on impressed with the progress. The news reports from the early years were critical and dismissed him as a criminal. Then later there was a major shift. The army which Alex now commanded managed to capture large portions of the South East. The papers were now in friendly hands and the reporting took on a new tone.

Starting as a captain over a small band Alex had annoyed the globalists and inspired the locals. Then one by one Alex had recruited other independent guerilla bands to join his until he commanded a regiment then eventually he was the commanding general over a small army. Finally in 2035—that was last year Josh reminded himself—Alex had marched his army north. Splitting it into two corps, he enveloped and laid siege to Washington, D.C. After the capture of key figures the International Union negotiated a withdrawal. The war had been won. The globalists withdrew to Canada and Mexico.

The move to reconstitute the civil government was swift. In speeches Alex had insisted they must be careful not to descend into a military dictatorship. He expressed disdain at thoughts of being a ruler. So the next headline made Josh smile for the first time. It read: "General Birch Elected President." The picture made his heart leap. It had three figures with a caption reading: "General Birch is accompanied to his inauguration by his mother and sister."

They were all older, but Josh could tell; it was them. The sight of Alice at the age she should be now grabbed him. A separate article profiled her and bore a close-up of Alice. There were those eyes he had stared into so many nights looking up from the page directly at him. He traced his fingers along the face. A tear fell from his eye and onto the book. Setting it down, Josh wiped his eyes, but it did no good. New tears replaced the old. The ache and longing was back and he laid his face into his hands and sobbed.

Josh excused himself and walked to the door. He stepped outside and breathed in deeply. He exhaled and leaned against the wall on his stoop. A car sat at the curb on the street. A solitary figure rested in the driver's seat and Josh stared for a moment then headed toward it. As he drew near, Art opened the door and climbed out. Art walked around to the front of the car and the two men watched each other silently. Where would he begin? Finally Josh reached out and put one hand on Art's shoulder. The smaller man ducked his head.

"Are you going to stay out here all night?" Josh tugged at him. "Come on."

"Listen Josh," Artemis held up a hand.

Josh shushed him.

"But I…"

"No," Josh pulled at him again heading toward the house. "We have to sort this out and decide what to do about it."

$$fff$$

"So this man you saw," Josh asked. After he had finished reading, they sat talking the rest of the night. "Why did you trust him?"

"I didn't," Art took a breath, "not at first, but he told me things. Things that happened within the next few days," he shrugged.

Josh poked out his lips, "Okay."

"He seemed kind of haggard and a little deranged, but…" Art paused, "I look in the mirror now and I realize that this was the face I saw then." Art tapped his finger to his cheek. "He was just a little more drawn; seemed really sad."

"And he gave you this," Josh put one hand on the scrapbook, "and this?" He pulled a folded piece of blue paper from the book.

Art nodded. "He called it my roadmap for life."

"Roadmap?"

"Yes," Art laid his head back and rubbed his eyes. The sun would be rising soon, "He explained that it included tips and tricks for me to remember, things to avoid, things to be sure to do. The advice was pretty astounding really."

"Yeah," Josh nodded somberly, "I guess there were some things he didn't think about, though."

"No," Art ducked his head. "I guess not… Josh?"

"Yeah?"

"What are you going to do?"

"Well," Josh looked at the clock, "it's six o'clock in the morning. I'm going to take a shower and go to work."

Art looked up with his eyes wide. How could he think of work now? Julie laughed softly; a nervous exhausted kind of giggle.

"I suggest you do the same," Josh stood and clapped Art on the shoulder. "We'll talk to Howard and see what he thinks."

"Howard?" Art arched his eyebrows, "He'll just make fun of us."

"Nahh," Josh shook his head, "Besides, so what if he does? Who else can we trust with this?"

CHAPTER

43

ART lounged on the couch in the corner of Josh's office. His head lolled to one side, drifting in and out of sleep. Josh fiddled nervously with the papers on his desk. He would look at one then another for a while, then reshuffle them and start back at the beginning. Half way down he would conclude that he hadn't comprehended a word on the page. It had come home to him once again; there were some things much larger than work and business.

Art jerked upright at the sudden knock at the door. Josh called out that it was open. He noticed that he had lurched about half way out of his own chair and that his knuckles were turning white from his grip on the arms. He relaxed and sat back as Howard closed the door behind him and walked up to the desk.

"What is this? Return of the Zombies?" Howard smirked.

"What?"

"You two look like hell."

"Yeah," Josh pointed at a chair, "sit." Artemis walked over and took the chair beside Howard.

After twenty minutes of explanation all Howard could muster was, "My God."

"Yeah," Josh nodded and threw a hand up, "whether God has a role in this or not beside, the real question is: what are *we* going to do?"

Howard looked between Josh and Artemis, made a few

unintelligible sounds then shrugged his shoulders.

"Well," Josh continued, "we have to do something."

"Like what?"

"Like take Art's time belt and go back and fix this."

"Sheesh," Howard blew out a slow whistle, "Do you think that's wise?"

"How the hell do I know?" Josh growled, "But I have the chance to save my family and fix all this other mess. What do you think?"

Howard looked over at Art who still sat with his head down. He had barely made eye contact with either of them during this time.

"I'm just saying," Howard protested, "you saw what that thing did to Art. Besides, how do we know that it's reliable enough to do this?"

Josh arched his eyebrows and looked over at Artemis.

"It is," Art said.

"Yeah, whatever," Howard shook his head. "Let's just don't rush into anything."

"Agreed," Josh said, "We'll need to come up with something before I do this."

"Hold on a minute there John Wayne," Howard objected, "Even if we decide that this is doable, why should it automatically be you that goes?"

"I have the biggest stake in this."

"Have you considered that maybe you're also too close to the situation; too emotional; too likely to do something rash?"

Josh slammed his fist down on the desk. "I also have the least to lose if something goes wrong."

"Fine," Howard waved a hand, "whatever. Let's just be sure we have our ducks in a row and that this damned time thing is gonna work before we launch you or whoever off half-cocked."

$$fff$$

"The key to this whole thing is the blue *roadmap*," Howard said. He sat on one side of the kitchen table in the breakfast nook of Josh's condo. It had been two days since he had learned of this mess and he had studied the scrapbook and blue map exhaustively. While standing in his shower it had all come to him. The warm water beat down on his sore muscles. He had always enjoyed hot showers and it was where he did his best thinking. Most of his novels had been plotted there. He was fortunate; his shower didn't have a timer on it like most did. Such were the perks of being a valuable government asset, so he was not limited to one three minute shower a day like most others.

"Okay?" Josh waited.

"I was thinking," Howard thumped the paper, "what we can do is create a copy of it with new information."

"And?"

"And, all you will have to do then is replace the old one with our version. Except our version will contain warnings of things to come. You see it can tell him to stay away from Connor Finch for one thing. Also about the International Union and aiding the revolution."

"How will he aid the revolution?"

"Hell, he's a genius. Art designs weapons and stuff. I think with the proper warning he can do wonders for the cause."

"How will he get it?"

"You're going to give it to him." Howard pointed a finger at Josh.

"Oh, of course," Josh sniffed, "I just waltz in and announce that I am his new friend from the future and, oh by the way, here is a new set of instructions; don't trust the ones from that other time traveler."

"Of course not," Howard shook his head irritated, "you'll have to somehow replace the old one with ours."

"Oh, is that all? I thought you might ask me to do something difficult."

"Okay, okay! I know it's not as easy as it sounds, but you're a resourceful man. You'll find a way."

"I guess I'll have to," Josh looked down, "It's really the best plan we have I reckon."

"Best I can come up with."

"How're Art and Oakland doing with the Time Belt?" Josh looked up.

"They're working on it."

"You know, Art's not too happy with you right now." Josh

grinned, "He thinks that it's already as good as it's going to get."

"He may be right, but I'm not about to let you fly off to the past with that thing until we know for sure."

"Yeah," Josh sighed, "I just want to go ahead and get this done."

"Look," Howard said. "The past isn't going anywhere. We can take our time and make sure we do this right. You understand?"

"Yeah," Josh nodded.

"Another thing…"

Josh looked up, cocking an eyebrow.

"We have to have a plan and you have to stick to it." Howard warned.

Josh snorted, "Well, I guess if all else fails and I can't swap the maps, I could always just kill Connor Finch."

"No!" Howard slapped the table, "You read all of the scrapbook. You know that you can't do that."

"Sure, whatever."

"I'm telling you Josh, you can't go off seeking revenge."

"Actually it would be preemption…"

"Whatever! You have stick to whatever plan or it will be just like when that bunch of greedy bastards in Congress began ignoring the Constitution." Howard stared unblinking. The passion blazed in his eyes. Then he continued more calmly, "You see what happened with that. Our Founding Fathers had a plan and they just flushed that away."

"Yeah, I see, but…"

"No buts!" Howard said, "I know what you're thinking, but you're not going to be able to plot a way around it. If Finch dies too early it will screw everything up as badly as it is now."

Josh looked up. His tired eyes tinged with sadness and nodded slowly.

"We've just got to warn them to stay out of his way."

CHAPTER

44

EARL Harper turned off the car. He stared up at the little rundown house. Damn this new government, they had taken everything he had. To cap things off, something was going on with the Ox. Damn them! They had pulled him into their little web, made him an enemy of the state and now they were excluding him. Lately they had taken to having private conversations in corners that would cease once he came near. Veiled references made him suspect that they were having secret meetings without him too. Well, if they thought they could try to pull something and expect him to go down for it, they could think again.

The Ox and the whole council had a huge target drawn on it. Earl knew this. Papers wrote about them. People had been questioned, fortunately no one who actually knew anything... so far. The rewards mounted higher by the week. The others would laugh about the impact they were having, but Earl wasn't laughing. His freedom was the only thing the world government had not taken from him so far. Freedom, hah! If you could call this freedom, Earl didn't feel very free. Still the thought of taking the fall and actually disappearing into a gulag blanched Earl. No sir... that was not going to happen.

Amy peeked out between the curtains. Earl wondered if the boy was home yet. Hard to believe Earl, Jr. was in high school now. Hell, he was at school more than he was home. Government schools had expanded their hours so much that the teachers now worked two shifts. Earl could still remember when they got out at three o'clock and didn't go year round. Afternoons were now devoted to *Citizenship Skills Development*. Diversity training and World Political Theory Appreciation were but a couple of the topics they were drilled on. First thing every morning the students had *Community Safety* class. Each student was individually quizzed on *community safety* issues. Had they seen their parents or neighbors behave in a manner that would compromise the greater good; or anyone else, for that matter? Had they seen anyone handling any guns, in their own home or elsewhere? Perhaps their parents of friends had expressed views detrimental to the greater good of the community? If so, they should receive proper counseling.

Earl Jr. understood the dangers pretty well, but Earl lived in constant fear something would slip out. Those arrogant pigs on the Council of the Ox made it that much harder. Who did they think they were fooling? Their Quixotic little anti-world government crusade would accomplish nothing beyond getting them all killed. Now he wished he had not followed Wesley and Josh to that first meeting.

Amy had a worried look on her face as he entered. He stood just inside the front entrance and closed the door. The look further unsettled him.

"What is it?" Earl asked.

"Well…" Amy looked down, "The usual, people hanging out and cruising up and down the street looking around."

"And?"

Amy sighed and brushed back her hair. "And someone rattled the back door a little while ago."

"Did you see anybody?" Earl's eyes darted to the back door.

"Yes," she sniffed slightly. Her emotions welled up along with Earl's alarm, "just briefly. He was running away."

"What did he look like?"

"I didn't get a good look. He had a jacket with a hood and he had his back to me."

Earl blew a long breath out walking to the back door. He looked out and saw nothing. He began pacing in a tight circle and lightly rapping his fist into the palm of his hand.

"It was probably just kids, you know…" Amy rationalized, "just messing around."

"Could be, you're probably right." Earl forced a smile and ambled into the bedroom. Opening the closet, he reached up into the back corner of the top shelf. He pulled the pistol out and sat down on the bed with it. He ejected the magazine and turned it over in his hands. Running a finger along the round at the top of the stack his mind wandered. Yes, he might need this after all. Earl pressed the magazine back and put the pistol up into its hiding place.

fff

The next evening Howard Spence found himself on the north side of Durham. He looked around before entering the building. He had been here before. The Asian man in his late thirties barely acknowledged his presence. Chin was not known for his social graces, but he was the best at what he did.

"Good to see you again," Chin said without looking up. "So you need more work done."

"Yes."

"Okay," Chin walked from behind the counter and locked the front door. The exterior was plain with a solid door and no markings. If you were here it meant that you knew someone. Chin returned to his place behind the counter and reached an open hand out toward Howard. Howard pulled an envelope from his coat pocket and placed it in Chin's hand. He opened the envelope and pulled a sheet of paper wrapped around some cash and three pictures. Chin placed the money beneath the counter, set the pictures to the side and began to read from the paper.

"I hope that will be enough down payment." Howard said. Chin kept reading and nodded slightly.

"I trust you," Chin cut his eyes up with a slight grin then moved his eyes back to the paper.

Howard glanced around the room. He knew that Chin trusted no one, but nobody dared to short Chin, not if they wanted more work done. He also knew that Chin would keep his mouth shut; a valuable skill.

"So you want the documents all to be dated in 1996?" Chin looked up.

"Yes," Howard nodded.

"Three different portraits of the same man it appears," Chin studied the pictures side by side. Howard made no reply. "And you want ten thousand American dollars with dates and serial numbers for the early 1990s?"

"That's right."

"Why?"

"Huh?" Howard stammered.

"I mean I can manufacture the cash and identities you want, with some research, but why date them from forty years ago?"

"Chin, you know better…" Howard shook a finger.

"Okay, okay," Chin waved a hand. "I know no questions."

"You can do it, right?"

"Sure, this will be a little more expensive than before."

"How much," Howard asked.

Chin shrugged, "Twenty-five percent premium for the documents and the counterfeit cash, for the research."

"No problem," Howard said and turned to the door. He slid the deadbolt back and took one last look behind him. Chin was watching him closely. Howard smiled nervously and left.

CHAPTER

45

"COME in," Josh waved to Art and Oakland and pointed to the back corner of his office with the four chairs surrounding the small table. Howard already occupied one of the chairs. He lifted his head from the blue paper he studied and threw them a sideways glance.

"Well?" Howard sat back with his head cocked to one side. The other men pulled their chairs up to the table.

"I think it's in good shape," Oakland nodded and glanced over at Art. Art was nodding also.

"You sure?"

"As sure as we can be," Oakland put a hand on Art's arm. Artemis glanced at Howard.

"Improvements? Testing?"

"Yes," Oakland said looking over at Art who still stared out the window. "At least we tested the changes the best that we can."

"What about objects? Identity documents, cash?"

"As long as he's touching it," Oakland nodded. "It should work."

Howard sat back interlacing his fingers behind his head. He studied Art for a moment before proceeding. "Art? What do you think?"

Artemis turned his head and stared at Howard for a moment. "It'll work."

"I'm not your enemy Art," Howard's eyes bore back into Art's. "I'm just that objective third party asking the hard questions."

Art ducked his head and slowly nodded. "Yeah, okay."

Art and Oakland left and Howard kept his seat across from Josh. Howard pulled the paper out and placed it between them. Josh let out a sigh.

"We want to make sure that we have everything in place. We're just about there," Howard patted the table. "I want you to review this blue map and make sure that everything looks right to you. Make sure I haven't left anything important out."

"What about the identity papers and money?" Josh asked.

"Tonight," Howard said, "God willing."

"Are you expecting trouble with that?"

"Nahh," Howard shooed the idea away with his hand, "but it is Durham, anything can happen over there. Besides that, no, my guy there is pretty dependable."

"Yeah," Josh nodded slowly.

"Of course the good part is that it is lightly patrolled there. The army doesn't like to go there either." Howard smiled, probably for the first time of the day.

𝆑 𝆑 𝆑

"Come in Colonel," General LaVail waved from his desk.

"Sir," the colonel took a seat in the front of LaVail's desk. "We have some information on a forgery operation in Durham."

"Okay," LaVail sat back motioning the colonel to continue.

"An informant came to us last week. My officers have been checking into it."

"Anything special about this one; any value in surveilling it or should we just take it down like the rest?" LaVail rocked slowly in his desk chair.

"Not that I can tell," the colonel shook his head. "I suggest that we close his operation, and then bring him and his equipment in for examination."

"When?"

"This evening?" The colonel stood. LaVail nodded and the colonel saluted.

"I'll prepare the orders," LaVail returned the salute.

f f f

Howard looked around slowly as he closed the door to his car. He ran a hand along the back of his neck, gently massaging a knotted muscle. Relax, he told himself. All the tension of recent days was getting to him. That had to be it, but there was something else. He couldn't put his finger on it, but he suddenly felt it worse. Looking around again, he tried to regain control of his pulse as he reached for the knob. He opened the door and stepped into Chin's shop.

He looked around. They were alone. Chin looked up from the old wooden counter separating his workspace from the rest of the room. Howard eased up to the counter.

"Is it ready?"

Chin nodded. Howard reached into his coat pocket and pulled an envelope out and slid it across the counter to Chin. Chin stuck it away under the counter without checking it. Howard had always paid faithfully and Chin knew it. Chin pulled a small leather packet and set it before Howard. The packet strained against its seams. Howard opened it and quickly surveyed the contents. Cash, passports, driver licenses and other documents all seemed to be in order. Howard closed it and smiled.

"Did you destroy all the files?"

"Of course," Chin's lips curled slightly on the edges.

"Thank you," Howard nodded and turned to leave.

"A pleasure as always," Chin said. Howard looked back and smiled then closed the door behind him.

Howard still had a queasy feeling in the pit of his stomach. He scanned the parking area carefully before proceeding then looked around and under his car before he climbed in. He had driven several blocks when he met the line of security police cars. Four in a row, something was up, but he wasn't about to turn around to see what. Instead, Howard drove on into the night. It would be days before he would hear of what happened.

CHAPTER
46

"**W**HAT is it?" Josh asked. Anxiety lined Howard's face as he stood on Josh's front stoop. Howard frowned in response.

"Inside," Josh hooked the air with his thumb and Howard pushed past him. Josh closed the door. What could be wrong? The documents were in order, the antique cash, heck; they even had the blue instruction "map" in final form. Last minute reviews of their plans and they should be ready.

"So?" Josh asked sitting down. Howard laid his head back on the couch and sighed.

"Chin... the forger," Howard rubbed his eyes, "well, he's been arrested."

"Oh crap," Josh spat. "Do you think he'll talk?"

"I dunno," Howard's voice sounded tired. For days they had all been running on adrenalin and little else. "With enough torture..." he shrugged, "anybody's guess. The good news is, I'm not sure how much he really knows about who I am."

"Then we're alright?" Josh asked hopefully.

"Maybe," Howard twisted his mouth slightly. "What I'm more worried about is his equipment. Our documents are on there, including pictures."

"I thought he deleted all that."

"He did... I think... but..." Howard grimaced, "They have people who can recover just about anything."

"Oh," Josh murmured.

"It will probably take them a while, but…" He blew out a loud sigh, "We'd better not waste a whole lotta time."

$$fff$$

Earl's eyes fluttered open. He looked over at the clock; 2:35 a.m. Why was he awake? His heart palpitated at the sound. That's why he woke up; a loud squeak then a lower scrubbing sound from the back bedroom; Earl Junior's room. What was that boy doing? A resounding crash brought him upright in the bed.

"Hey!" The sound of Junior's voice was followed by running feet. "Dad!" Earl jumped from the bed and ran to his closet. He grabbed his gun from the top shelf and ran to the bedroom door. He flipped the switch outside his door, illuminating the living room. Junior ran toward him, his eyes wide, with a small, dark man dressed in black behind him. A flash, a deafening bang and Junior tumbled to the floor.

"No!" Earl cried. The small man twisted toward him and fired again. Splinters flew from the door jamb onto Earl's head. Earl raised his gun and fired twice, the man doubled over, a pistol falling from his hand. A second figure appeared from Junior's room with a crowbar in his hand. Earl fired again and again at the man until his pistol clicked twice. On the third shot he dropped the crowbar and slammed into the wall, then scrambled back into Junior's room. A dark splotch stained the wall he had fallen against. Earl ran to the door and saw the man slide out the window. He could hear him tumble to the ground and scramble back up. The last Earl saw of him was his back as he ran away.

Earl turned around as he heard Amy scream. She threw herself onto the floor beside Junior and pulled his head into her lap. Incoherent words rolled out between guttural sobs. Earl fell to his knees beside them. The boy was white and still. Earl reached over and touched him and knew he was gone.

$$fff$$

Hector stumbled through the back yard incredulous that he had been shot. That bastard! Why did he have to shoot me? Blood kept pouring from his side as he trudged along. He knew he had to get away from there. The throbbing began to work its way through the haze that the drugs had cast over his brain. When Hector had climbed into the window he felt no pain; that was no longer true. He passed between two houses and walked into the street in front.

They had expected this house to be like the rest. The people of this neighborhood depended on the government for their every need. They closed their blinds and huddled inside, trusting the police to rescue them. Their gang always made sure the police were busy elsewhere before they went in. After looting the place, they usually had plenty of time to have all the fun they wished, then leave and go about their business. This was not supposed to happen.

The compact .38 special he had bought from the same dealer who supplied his drugs dangled from his right hand. He ambled over and tossed the gun down a storm drain he saw in front of him at the curb. The blood oozed between the fingers of his left hand. He put his right hand on top to stanch the flow. Fifty yards later he collapsed where the police would later find him.

$$fff$$

Captain Alberto Alvarez walked through the front door of the Harper home. Two young men lay dead on the living room floor. A man and a woman sat across the room at a table beside the kitchen. The woman was crying and started to rise. A soldier pointed his pistol at her and warned her to stay where she was.

"Mr. Harper?" Alvarez walked over to Earl.

"Yes," Earl looked up through red eyes.

"Do you know these men?"

"The blonde boy is my son."

"I see," Alvarez pulled out a note pad. "And why did you shoot these two?"

"I didn't!" Earl stood up and a soldier shoved him back into the chair. "I only shot the other guy… HE shot my son!"

"Okay," Alvarez made a note, "so this man," he twisted and pointed toward the dead intruder, "shot your son."

"Yes."

"So, he shot your son because you were trying to shoot him."

"NO!" Earl's eyes blazed.

"Was your son," Alvarez ignored Earl's outburst, "also trying to shoot him?"

"No one was trying to shoot him."

"Is he not shot?" Alvarez raised an eyebrow.

"Yes, but…"

"What is that blood on the wall over there Mr. Harper?" Alvarez pointed to where the other intruder had fallen back against the wall. "And all those holes?"

"I told your men already…"

A soldier called to Alvarez from the doorway and the Captain turned his back on Earl and walked away. The two stood whispering and casting glances back toward Earl and Amy. Her tears had slowed to an occasional involuntary heave from deep in her chest.

"Well, Mr. Harper," Alvarez strolled back over, taking a circular route so he could step over Earl Junior's body. He stood looking down at the boy for a moment then walked back to the table. "It appears that we have found a third victim of your shooting spree." Earl sat glaring. Alvarez grinned, "Three dead men and an illegal gun… it is not looking good for you."

"So…" Alvarez nodded toward one of his soldiers. "You are under arrest for homicide with a prohibited weapon." The soldier pulled Earl from the chair and put a handcuff on one wrist. Earl looked at the man with alarm. "Give him your other arm, Mr. Harper, don't try to resist." Alvarez warned. Earl relaxed and the other wrist was cuffed behind him as well.

Amy sat with her mouth open. Tears streamed down her face as Earl was led from the house. She looked over at Alvarez who had stood and peered down at her.

"Now Mrs. Harper," he motioned for her to stand. "You are also under arrest…"

"What for?" Amy's voice was near a shout.

"… for occupying a dwelling containing a prohibited weapon."

"No," she yelled and slapped the table as she stood.

A soldier grabbed her arm and twisted it behind her and shoved her forward against the table. It struck her low in the belly. The air rushed from her body as the soldier drove her face first onto the table with his elbow in her back. She wanted to scream, but couldn't. She felt as if her wrists were being twisted off as the handcuffs were tightened about them. The soldier pulled her upright and Alvarez waved him toward the door.

Alvarez walked over to a sergeant in the living room. He nodded at the sergeant and looked about the house.

"Hate crime?" The Sergeant asked.

"Perhaps," Alvarez shrugged. "We'll leave that to the prosecutors."

"What of the boy? It does appear the other dead man shot him."

"So?" Alvarez asked, "We can do nothing about him, but Harper… we can keep him from shooting anyone else. Besides, I was reading Harper's profile. He's has been overheard often complaining about the government closing his business." He chuckled, "One less rabble rouser."

CHAPTER
47

HOWARD sat at the table in the corner of Josh's office staring blankly ahead; his head slowly shaking ruefully. Josh paced between the corner and his desk in the middle of the office.

"It's hit the fan now man," Howard said. "It's just gonna get worse."

"Yeah, well…" Josh shook a finger toward Howard, "we've got to figure out how to get Earl out of this."

"What makes you think we can?"

Josh raised his hands straight out to his sides, palms up and let them fall, slapping his legs. "Well, we've got to do something."

"Like what?"

"I don't know, but this complicates the hell out of everything."

"Sure does," Howard nodded.

"We've got to put our plans on hold now…"

"The Hell we do!"

"Look," Josh stopped, facing Howard. "I can't leave with this going on. I've got to stay here and help him. I mean, his son is dead and he and Amy are both in jail…"

"You got them lawyers, Josh. What more do you think you can do?"

"I don't know, but I'll think of something. I always do."

"Not this time," Howard said. "The best thing you can do for them and all of us is take your little trip through time and fix this crap before it ever happens. See the big picture man."

"But…"

"First Chin, now Earl… Look Josh, there are too many people who know about us in jail now. For all we know a squad may be on the way for us now. No," Howard shook his head, "we have to stay the course and hope it's not too late."

"But how are we going to concentrate on that now…" Josh pleaded, "with all this…"

"We will because we have to, that's all there is to it!" Howard eased back his chair and half stood leaning on the table. "Look Josh, at the beginning I didn't buy into any of this, but you were so gung-ho. You asked me to suspend my disbelief and I did. Now I honestly believe this is possible. It pains me but, I think Art really has it figured out, so…" Howard sat back down and sighed.

"So…" Josh sat down across from Howard.

"So, we have to do this, we no longer have a choice."

Josh looked down for a few seconds before answering, "You're right… we have to."

𝆑 𝆑 𝆑

The light was a rude shock to Chin's eyes. How long he had been in the dark he didn't know. His arms ached severely from the hours of having them chained above his head. Now Col. Romochek stood with his hand on the light switch. Chin was near senseless. His legs ached from standing; his head throbbed from sleep deprivation. When he tried to sleep, the shackles dug into his wrists, so sleep evaded him, but eventually fatigue would overtake him and he slept despite the pain.

"Having fun?" Romochek asked.

"Barrel of monkeys," Chin half groaned.

"Bring him into the interrogation room," Romochek motioned to a pair of soldiers behind him.

Chin was half walked, half dragged into the room. Romochek sat behind a table. The soldiers deposited Chin into the chair opposite him.

"I trust now that you've had some time to consider your

predicament, you will choose to be more cooperative." Romochek tilted his head back looking down his pointed nose at Chin with a cold smile.

Chin glared at him but said nothing. He looked down and spit on the floor. A foolish smile came across his face and he began to hum softly. Romochek tried to decipher the tune—Jesus Loves Me, yes that was it. Chin was delaying; Romochek would have none of that.

"You're techniques for deleting the data from your computers is quite good," Romochek complemented. "It would go well for you to tell us how you did that and how to recover it."

Chin looked up and grinned. He gave a dismissive wave and said, "What can I say man, I'm just that damned good." He laughed, "There is no recovering the data."

Romochek kept his face even. He did not want Chin to know how deeply this irritated him. They had been at this for days. Nothing seemed to be working.

"Your skills are quite good," Romochek commented, "where did you learn all of this?" Chin locked onto Romochek's eyes and smiled between his swollen lips, the bruises glistened on his checks.

"From your momma." Chin had managed to slip this answer into most of the queries since his arrest. The impassive look faded from Romochek's face as he swiped across the table with the back of one of his mighty hands. Chin toppled sideways out of the chair. Romochek moved around the table and drove the toe of his boot into Chin's lower abdomen. Chin landed a couple of feet away and lay doubled over moaning.

"Take him to his cell," Romochek barked.

"Chain him to the ceiling?"

"No," Romochek murmured. It hadn't worked before; he could sleep on the floor while Romochek decided what to do next. Perhaps easing up would take him off his guard, perhaps it was pointless to continue this; throw him in the gulag and get it over with. He walked into the observation area on the other side of the two way mirror.

"What do you think Major?" He asked his adjutant who had been watching.

"With due respect Colonel; I don't understand why you are spending so much time with this man." The major shrugged, "We see small time forgers like him often."

Romochek didn't answer immediately. He paced the room with his hands behind him. Something about this one had bothered him. There was something he couldn't put his finger on. So highly skilled; just the type people with the most to hide would go to. The Colonel rubbed his eyes and groaned. Even so, it was unlikely he would give them anything of worth. Finally he turned and swatted at the air in a dismissive manner.

"You're right," Romochek said, "he probably just deals with small time hoods. The man knows nothing. Arrange a transport."

The major nodded and smiled. "Yes sir." Then he turned to leave.

"And Major," Romochek said when the major reached the doorway. "I want to personally escort him." The major hesitated and shot a quizzical look. "That is all, Major."

CHAPTER 48

EARL leaned against the table in the interview room. He rested his face in his hands with his eyes peeking out watching his reflection in the giant mirror. The hearing was not going well. So far it had been more about his personal views and history than it had about the shooting. Initially his attorney, Alan Spanger, tried to make it a matter of self defense, but the judges had told him this was not an option. The day, so far had been a parade of anyone who had ever witnessed Earl making an anti-world-government or pro-American statement. The woman who had handled the transfer of his house to the government had spent two hours on the stand. The prosecutor expended copious amounts of air validating her progressive credentials going all the way back to birth. She had literally been born during a Viet Nam war protest on the streets of Berkeley to a mother who was so devoted that she refused to leave even though she was likely to deliver at any time, which she did. He smiled as he described how she had cursed and wished death upon the police officers as they delivered the baby.

"And he said what!" The prosecutor had asked with a dramatic look of horror on his face.

"He said that part of him would like to 'strike a match to the house' rather than let the people have it." She responded with a frightened look. "I asked him why that was, I mean he was being fairly compensated for it. He laughed and berated me saying that it was less than half what it had been appraised at a few years earlier. I tried to explain that in the interest of social justice we all had to make sacrifices."

"So, Ms. Patella, what did he say to that?"

"Well…" Patella hesitated and looked down reddening before swallowing hard and looking back up. "I'm afraid he was rather rude… Um, well, I don't know if I can repeat those words in court."

"Perhaps you can just paraphrase them for us," the prosecutor nodded sympathetically.

"Okay," she said, "uh… well, he said that I could take my social justice and… um… stick it somewhere…" She ducked her head suddenly.

"I think we get the picture Ms. Patella." The prosecutor sneered and pointed at Earl. "Your honors, is there no end to this man's disdain for the greater good?"

With the self-defense angle being disallowed, Spanger headed into his plan B. He called upon psychologists and pharmaceutical experts and began making a case for a treatment program. He had argued that Earl's upbringing had programmed this kind of thinking in him and that with appropriate outpatient treatment, this was correctable. Proper levels of medication and psychological feedback could retrain his thought patterns so that he could understand the necessity of giving back for the greater good.

"This man," the prosecutor had replied pointing at Earl, "Is beyond redemption. There is no medication, no psychological reinforcement that can cure the damage that has been done to him in his life. The evil is so entrenched in his thought process that it descends into his very heart. That is what leads to such tragedy…" he paced looking down thoughtfully, "He so lacks understanding that he could not see how these two young men had lost patience with getting their fair share that they felt they must go out and get it for themselves. Rather than cheerfully sharing his bounty, he chose instead to murder them and in so doing brought about the death of his own son." He swept back his hair with a look of desperation and sighed dramatically, "No your honors, society must be protected from Earl Harper and his kind. We won't be safe until all of his ilk are locked away where they can no longer oppress others. We know who they are, an examination of their old government questionnaires from school records to community surveys -- MILLIONS of pages of them – tell us! When will the government get wise and remove this cancer from society?"

$$fff$$

"We are going to transport you to another facility," Col. Romochek flipped on the light in Chin's cell. Chin lay on the floor and shielded his eyes from the bare bulb. After hours in total darkness, the light was hard to adjust to.

"I was just starting to have fun," Chin sat up and hugged his knees to his chest.

"Tell me Chin," Romochek knelt a few feet away, bringing himself down to Chin's eye level. "Have you always been such a joker?"

"No I learned it in here," Chin did his best to smirk. His eyes were puffy and his mouth was swollen. "I guess you just inspire me Colonel."

Romochek chuckled slightly. "You know, this could have been a much more pleasant experience had you cooperated."

"What? And spoil your fun?"

Romochek grunted and stood upright. He glared down at Chin and motioned to the soldiers behind him. "You are a tough nut, I'll concede that."

"Where to now?" Chin asked as the soldiers lifted him to his feet and began shackling his arms behind him.

"A processing facility where you will stand trial, then on to an education camp," Romochek's smile chilled Chin's blood. "You should enjoy it there. The work you will do will free you from your old patterns." He nodded to the two guards and they stepped back. Romochek took hold of Chin's arm and pulled him through the door of the cell. They walked along the hallway leading to the exit. Chin looked around, the two guards followed many yards behind.

"Why the personal escort," Chin asked.

"I enjoy your company Chin," Romochek looked straight ahead. "I have enjoyed the cat and mouse game and I admire your spirit. It is a shame that it will be broken so completely."

"Oh, you like me," Chin smirked between grimaces. One of his ankles was swollen and his limp pronounced. Romochek laughed softly.

The outside door opened and they walked into the daylight. The sun beat down and Chin's eyelids drooped at the sudden glare. The transport car was more than fifty feet away. About ten feet outside the door of the building Romochek let go of Chin's arm. Chin looked back at him and he nodded for Chin to continue walking in front of him. Chin turned his head back to the front and looked toward the waiting car. Then he heard the metallic slid of a pistol action.

"Halt!" Romochek shouted. This was followed by a loud boom. The bullet struck Chin in the lower part of his hamstring just above his knee. Chin tumbled onto his right side. Romochek yelled for Chin to stop and fired his pistol again, this time striking him behind the left knee and blowing out his kneecap. Romochek strolled around to Chin's front. Chin's teeth were clenched tightly. His face contorted. Romochek twice more cried halt and placed bullets in each of Chin's shoulders. Tears were streaming from Chin's eyes now and a low moan escaped his lips as Romochek squatted before him.

"Are your jokes funny now," Romochek asked and placed the muzzle in Chin's ear. Chin's eyes still flooded, his teeth clenched tighter and he slowly nodded. Romochek's pistol roared once more.

"Such a pity," Romochek spoke loudly as he stood. "This man should have known that he couldn't escape." Romochek wiped the blood from the barrel of his pistol onto Chin's shirt and slid it back into his holster.

CHAPTER
49

"W E'RE going to have to step up the time table on our plans," Howard said in a low voice. Josh didn't know why Howard was using the hushed tone. The door was closed and no one could hear from outside. If the office was bugged, the listening devices would be sure to pick their voices up anyway, but he understood Howard's paranoia. The news about Chin had spooked them both.

"When?" Josh asked.

Howard stared at Josh soberly, "Tomorrow." Josh sat back in shock.

"So soon?"

"Yes," Howard said, "we have no time to waste. All the stuff is in place up in Virginia. We'll do it there."

"Okay," Josh said hesitantly. Howard eyed Josh carefully. There was no turning back now, but... Josh's butterflies were quickly evolving into bats. He couldn't screw this up. He just couldn't, or they were all doomed.

"We have no choice," Howard kept studying Josh. "Now we have to go over the plans for the operation. You will have to know what you must do when you get there."

"Fine, but... why Virginia?"

"I'm getting to that," Howard answered. "You will have to have transportation and lodging. You won't be going directly to the time. We'll drop you in a little earlier so you will have time to work, hence the lodging."

"I'll have cash," Josh said.

"True, but…" Howard tapped a finger on the table. "Large cash purchases draw too much attention. I would have had Chin create a credit card for you, but there's a problem with that. We would have no way to create an account to support it and substantial credit card purchases are always verified. I pondered how to get around this and I think I found a solution." Howard talked on for several minutes and Josh slowly nodded and smiled. This just might work.

"Now we have a list of places where you can find young Art," Howard said, "but it's going to be up to you to find a way to switch the maps on him. You're a smart cookie. I know you can do it."

"Yeah," Josh ran his fingers through his hair and sighed. "I'll have to. Oh!"

"What?" Howard raised his eyebrows.

"Earl's trial," Josh looked at his watch, "It will be wrapping up today. Don't you think we should go there?"

Howard was shaking his head. "Too risky."

"Well," Josh said, "I think I should at least be there."

"Bad idea Josh, what if they are onto us?"

"I think it will be a bad idea if I don't go. That will look suspicious."

"I don't know," Howard said after a couple of moments. "Maybe…"

"At the very least, I think Earl should see that we're there for him… you know, it might give him strength."

Howard stared at Josh for a minute. "OK, you go, but if you smell a rat get out. Otherwise I'll have to go back in your place."

𝆑𝆑𝆑

Three black robed judges were perched on high peering down on Earl like so many hungry buzzards. Earl squirmed silently, his eyes cast downward. Amy had been on the stand. She had broken down in tears prompting the chief judge to call a recess. At that point he gave her a stern lecture. She was informed that she should save her tears for the two men her husband had murdered. He further informed her that if she showed such emotion again she would be held in contempt.

"Your honor," Alan Spanger stood, "I renew my request that the weapons used against my client be admitted into evidence. There is a crowbar in evidence that was raised to strike him and there is the bullet that was fired into the door frame beside his head, not to mention the one taken out of Earl Harper, Junior."

"Mr. Spanger," the judge looked downward through his half moon reading glasses. "Your request is so noted and denied. The victims' attempts at self defense have no bearing on your client's aggressive actions."

"Your honor, that is a prejudicial statement, I call for a mistrial."

"Mr. Spanger," the justice's face reddened and he slammed a fist on the bench, "there is nothing prejudicial about my words or elsewhere in this preceding. Any further such statements and you will be charged with contempt of court."

"But..."

"Do you understand?" The justice roared.

"Yes your honor," Spanger's face bore a sour look as he looked over at Earl who was peering up helplessly. He looked back at the judges, "Your honors, I have no further evidence or witnesses. Defense rests."

"Very good Mr. Spanger, my colleagues and I are ready to render a verdict."

Spanger stood up, "Don't you need to deliberate your decision?"

"We have no need," the head judge smiled. "The evidence is clear cut." Earl looked down, his face sagged. "Defendant will rise." Earl stood and held onto the table. "The defendant is pronounced guilty of two counts of first degree murder, of the two strangers, and one of second degree murder, in the matter of his son. He is hereby sentenced to life in prison." Earl sagged back against his chair. Two bailiffs came to handcuff him. Josh tried to get Earl's attention as he was led out. Earl would not look his way.

The door to the courtroom swung shut behind Earl. Josh sat back and glared up at the judges. They gaveled the court back into order and announced that Amy Harper's trial was set to commence the following day.

CHAPTER
50

EARL lay on his right side facing the far side of the cell. In the next cell a man resembling a large black Buddha grinned at him through teeth almost as yellow as the gold one in front. Urine odors assaulted his nose from the mattress beneath his head. Earl sat up and tried to ignore black Buddha's stare. Alan Spanger had patted him on the shoulder and told him how sorry he was and wished him luck. What luck? There was no luck where Earl was headed. A life of *this*, that's what luck Earl had waiting for him. Josh had been sitting at the back of the courtroom. He was the only one of Earl's 'friends' who had bothered to show up. Josh had looked like he wanted to say something, but Earl pretended to not see him. More than anyone, Josh was to blame for this. Them and their stupid Ox thing, who did they think they were?

Earl jumped at the touch. Fingers had reached through the bars and caressed his hair and rubbed his ear. The skinny white man leered down at Earl, cackling, his boney fingers sticking through the bars. Black Buddha shared the laugh. The body odor drifting into Earl's cell from the two nearly gagged him. At least he was in this cell alone... for now.

Earl walked over to the door of the cell and began calling for the guard. He banged on the bars and continued yelling. A guard appeared around the corner glaring at Earl and screamed for him to shut up. Earl urged him to come over.

"What do you want?" The guard barked. Earl looked around, the boney white guy winked at him and Black Buddha's shoulders shook as he chuckled.

"I need to see the Captain."

"Why would the Captain want to see you?"

"I need to tell him something."

"What?"

"It's important, please!"

"Oh alright," the guard turned and walked out of the jail area, closing the door behind him.

"What do you want Harper?" The Captain growled as he came through the door.

"Captain, I've got something important," Earl motioned for him to come closer. The Captain eased to where he was just out of Earl's reach and stopped.

"I'm listening."

"I need to speak to Colonel Romochek," Earl said in a loud whisper.

"What for?"

"It's important," Earl said. The Captain rolled his eyes.

"What is?"

"I have information," Earl looked over both shoulders and back. "I want to make a deal."

"Time for deals is over Harper, you've been sentenced already. Your ass is ours."

"This will be worth something," Earl pleaded. "It'll be worth reducing my sentence and freeing my wife."

"What could you possibly have that would be worth that?"

"I can't tell you," Earl pressed his face between the bars. "I'll tell the Colonel."

"Quit wasting my time," the Captain turned and walked toward the exit.

"No, please, come back!" Earl yelled, watching the Captain open the door leading out to the guard's area. "It's about the Ox!" The Captain stopped and slowly turned around.

$$fff$$

In Due Time

It was dark outside the window to Art's office. Josh lounged in a high backed leather chair across from his old friend. Art poured two glasses of wine and corked the bottle. Josh sloshed the red liquid around, staring into it. The rich texture and hearty aroma soothed him.

"To you," Art held up his glass. Josh touched the rim of his glass to Art's.

Josh took a sip and propped the glass against his leg. "This could be the last time we do this." He frowned, "If things don't go well."

"Are you sure you want to do this?"

Josh shook his head slowly. "No, but I've got to."

Art nodded slowly, his cheeks sagged sadly. "You be careful and come back here."

"Here's to my returning to a better world," Josh held up his glass.

"I'll drink to that," Art said.

"What's that," Josh pointed at a small dagger sitting beside a stack of books on Art's desk. The blade was only about twelve inches long, but the handle had a full guard surrounding it like most military swords do.

"Oh, you've never seen this?" Art asked, picking the dagger up and handing it to Josh. "I usually keep it in a drawer, but I had it out looking at it earlier."

"Where did it come from?"

"I got it from my father," Art explained, "one of the few things I got from him. It belonged to an ancestor, David Artemis; I was named for him. He was from my grandmother's side. He was a first lieutenant in a North Carolina unit during the Civil War. That was his sword."

"It's too short to be a sword." Josh turned it over in his hand, running his finger along the edge of the blade.

"It got broken near the end of the war, so he ground it down to a dagger. It was very useful for close combat," Art smiled slightly. "I hear a good many Yankees knew its bite."

"I'll bet they did," Josh grinned.

$$fff$$

Howard strolled down the trail leading from his condo, massaging the tightness in his neck as he went. He wondered how the world could be in such turmoil on such a beautiful night. The tension in his shoulders told him otherwise. The wide walk meandered past the common garden behind his condo from the street then on down the hill where he walked now. It led beside the common overflow parking area at the bottom of the hill then up the next, behind the other buildings then out to the next street. Howard stopped at the white Ford SUV parked in the overflow parking. It sat there adorned with its Virginia tags unbothered. He continued on by and headed out for a loop around the far buildings.

Dark circles lined under Howard's eyes. Three to four hours of sleep per night just weren't enough. The adrenalin of the previous days was telling on him, but, if things went well tomorrow, Howard mused, it would all be worth it. He wondered how it would be if Josh were successful. Would things suddenly change, would he know they had changed? Perhaps he wouldn't remember the recent years they had endured at all. Maybe he would have new memories and not even be aware of what they had done. He soon found himself back at the bottom of the hill in front of the SUV. He took a deep breath and headed up the hill toward home.

Something was out of place, what was wrong? He quickly looked back at the SUV. It was still where it belonged. The intrigue was beginning to spook him, he wiped his brow. Howard studied the vehicle for a moment, remembering when he bought it. It had been purchased and registered under the name of James Mack, an alias Howard had set up. That was how he first came to know Chin. He had discovered James Mack's headstone in a local cemetery. It was a small one with a carving of a lamb adorning the top. James had been born the same year he was and had died two years later. Howard hoped that James didn't mind him borrowing the identity.

An underground source had shown Howard how to disable all of the tracking chips and the black box in the SUV. Once a year he would drive the vehicle to a remote area and laboriously reconnect the surveillance equipment and drive to Virginia to reregister and inspect it. The inspector, upon plugging into the black box, would comment on how little he drove the SUV. Howard would shrug and mumble something about protecting the environment. The diagnostic equipment would then go on to determine what speed laws had been broken over the previous year. It would double check to see if there was a record of a ticket being already issued by the tracking satellites communicating with the black box. If one was not found, a fine would be assessed on the spot. If a security police officer had issued a fine manually, it would almost always have to be paid a second time during the inspection, or even a third.

The SUV was just fine; he decided and continued up the hill. He was over half way there before he saw it... Several police vehicles occupied the parking area in the front of his building. Howard's car was blocked in by a HumVee and several soldiers in black riot suits had sub-machineguns trained on his condo as another pair swung a battering ram against the front door. A soldier stood at the back corner with his weapon covering the common garden area of his building. After the second whack the door gave way with a groan. Howard eased back down the trail, realizing that he had better leave before they discovered that he was not in there.

Further down the trail he passed over a dip that hid him from their view. He heard shouting from the top of the hill and picked up his pace. Howard's heart wanted to explode by the time he reached the SUV. He reached into his pocket and quietly thanked God that he had the keys with him. The engine roared to life and Howard wasted no time driving the opposite direction out of the parking lot. From the pocket inside the door, he pulled a cell phone he kept there that was also in the name of James Mack. He always left the battery out of the phone to avoid being tracked with the Global Positioning Satellite chip inside. He had learned that cell phones could be tracked even when they were off. The only way to prevent that was to remove the battery; no power source, no tracking. He made sure that he recharged and replaced two batteries in the SUV weekly in case this day ever came.

As he rolled up to the stop sign, Howard slid a battery into the phone and turned it on. He punched in a number from memory. It rang four times before he got an answer.

CHAPTER
51

RICE Oakland reclined in his easy chair reading the newspaper. The front page story detailed a new program for government testing of children to improve their chances of successfully contributing to society through any necessary behavior modification. A recent government sponsored study had reported that 82% of all children needed medication to help them channel their energies and attention properly. This new ground breaking initiative would determine the best medication and appropriate levels for each child. A battery of tests would also be administered upon entering school to design any manual psychological feedback program that would be helpful in preventing any sort of "anti-social" behavior. The article concluded by saying that many experts believed that the 82% figure would prove to be extremely conservative once all data was in under the new program.

Oakland set the paper down and turned up the television volume. There was a picture of Earl Harper in the background beside the news anchor.

"A local man will spend his life behind bars for crimes against the state. Earl Harper was sentenced to life in prison for a triple homicide. We go live to Veronica Crum for the full story." The scene switched to a young blonde reporter staring straight at the camera. She wore a blue suit coat with the collar of the white shirt beneath it stylishly resting on top of the suit collar. As she opened her mouth to speak a sudden gust of wind fluttered the leaves on the tree behind her and flipped up the collar on her white shirt, which she quickly smoothed down. The only thing that didn't move in the picture was her hair.

"Earl Harper learned today that there is a price to be paid when you choose to terrorize others with a gun." Veronica spoke the last word louder and let it hang in the air for a second. "The mother of one of his victims had this to say." A prerecorded tape showed a squat woman speaking rapid Spanish with the voice of an interpreter following.

"My son was a kind and loving boy." The interpreter said, "He needed food and medicine for his children. I don't understand why this man had to kill him."

"Also," Veronica said in a pre-recorded voice over, "his girlfriend and mother of one of his five children had this to say." The clip switched to a girl of about seventeen wearing a t-shirt and worn jeans with a hole in one knee.

"Our baby has been so sick lately. He really needs the medicine and he had other kids he had to care for too. Now I don't know what we will do." The scene switched back to Veronica standing on the back lawn of the television station.

"The court also ruled that the death of Earl Harper, Junior resulted from a forced reaction to Harper's assault on the other victims. Kent." Veronica nodded.

"Veronica," Kent said from the anchor chair on the left side of a split screen with Veronica on the right; "is there a lesson in this for others?"

"Yes there is Kent," Veronica said. "Everyone has to shoulder their share of the burden in society and such acts of violence against the less fortunate will be punished."

"Thank you Veronica," Kent nodded grimly.

Oakland turned the volume down and growled. He fought the urge to throw the remote at the TV. He tossed it over onto the couch and pushed back in his chair. He was nearly asleep when the phone rang.

"Hello," he mumbled. A second later his eyes widened and he

bolted out of his chair. He looked across the room where Alisa quietly worked on a crossword puzzle. "Get the kids and go to your mother's."

"What?" She looked up.

"Just do it!" He nearly screamed, "And stay there until I call and say otherwise."

fff

Howard was rolling up to the curb as Oakland emerged from the woods that separated his house from the street behind it. Oakland jumped into the passenger seat and Howard accelerated away before the door was closed.

"What happened?" Oakland asked between gasps, he could remember when running all day was a given, but that was a long time ago. He struggled to slow his breathing, his senses had gone hypersensitive.

"I don't know, but they're all over my place," Howard watched his rear view mirror.

"Why?"

"Somebody must have talked," Howard shot a glance over at Oakland. "Chin's been dead for days, so if he told them anything they would have grabbed me before now. It had to be Earl. That means the whole gig is up."

"Crap," Oakland groaned.

fff

Josh turned the dagger over in his hands. He traced all the details as he wandered about Art's office idly chatting. He tried to imagine what it would have felt like to go into battle with nothing but a single shot musket and this dagger. Just the adrenaline and sweat of brave men mixed with the smell of burning gun powder and the raw earth.

"Well tomorrow, I guess we'll know if that little thing over there," Josh pointed the dagger at the time belt resting on Art's desk, "will do the job we have set before it."

"Yes, I guess so," Artemis nodded.

"I just hope it's good for a round trip."

"Me too."

"But for now," Josh walked over to the door and set the dagger on the second self of a bookcase beside the door, "I must answer the call of nature."

"I'd better go check on Julie." He rose and followed Josh out the door. They passed the door to the back patio and Josh turned left into the hall bathroom.

Art continued on to the living room. He plopped down beside Julie on the couch. She laid her head on his shoulder and he caressed her cheek. The phone rang, Julie rolled her eyes and jumped up.

"Hello," her face took on a peculiar look. "Okay, I'll tell him." She covered the phone with her hand. "Art, it's Howard, he says that you have an urgent message from a Mr. Mack."

$$fff$$

Josh was drying his hands on the towel hanging on the rack beside the sink when he heard the crash. What the hell was that? Loud yelling came from the front of the house. Josh reached for the door handle, but the sound of running boots from the hallway backed him off. Someone yelled to others to clear the house, to make sure no one else was here. The door knob started to turn. Josh faded back against the wall behind the door. A small stool sat behind the door and he stepped up on it. The door swung back suddenly driving the knob into the wall. An eighteen inch space from the door hinges to the corner gave him just enough room. Josh pressed himself flat against the wall and held his breath.

"Anybody in there?" A voice called. There was a moment of silence. He could see the black assault uniform through the crack of the door. The boots took two shuffle steps into the bathroom. Josh tensed, ready to spring. He decided then and there that he would not go quietly. Finally the boots turned around and took a step. "No, nobody," the owner of the boots answered.

Josh relaxed and nearly toppled off the stool. Art and Julie! He wanted to charge out and rescue them. No, that would be foolhardy. He would have to get outside and see what he could do then. Maybe he could head around front and ambush the soldiers. Josh eased off the stool and peered out around the door. He checked the hall. It was empty.

Josh tiptoed down the hall. As he passed the door to Art's office, there was a soldier with his back to Josh rifling through Art's things. Josh slipped out the back door, pulling it shut as silently as he could manage. Occasional wind gusts pressed against the house making it creak. Maybe he could use that to mask his movements. Crouching down, he duck walked under the window of Art's office. He could see activity around the front of the house. It would expose him too much to go up the side of the house. The woods, he would come around the edge of the woods. He flopped down on his belly and crawled the rest of the distance to the woods behind the house.

The damp earth soaked through the fabric covering Josh's knees as he knelt beside a bush. He had to catch his breath and figure out what to do next. A hand on his shoulder nearly sent him into a spasm. Another hand clasped over his mouth and a voice shushed him. He turned his head slowly. Oh thank God! Howard's face loomed out o the darkness. Oakland sat close behind.

"Howard, you nearly scared the bejesus out of me!" Josh whispered. "What is going on?" Howard briefly filled him in. Josh nodded back toward the house. "We've got to move around to the front and get Art and Julie."

Howard shook his head. "No. We've already been around there. There's nothing we can do for them."

"We'd just be getting ourselves killed or captured too." Oakland added.

"You don't mean…" Josh's eyes grew wider. "They're not…"

"You don't want to see what's around there Josh," Howard's eyes cast downward.

"Okay," Josh nodded reluctantly.

"We're going to have to go ahead and do it tonight," Howard said. "Almost everything we need is up at the cabin in Virginia."

"I guess we'd better get going then," Josh said sadly.

"Almost everything," Howard repeated with extra emphasis.

Josh looked up at Howard, the whites of his eyes reflected the moonlight, then he slowly looked toward the house. "Oh no."

"Oh yes," Howard nodded. "Tell me where the time belt is and I'll go down there and get it."

"Oh no you don't," Oakland said, "this mess is going to your head. You think you're some kind of commando all of a sudden. You wouldn't stand a chance if you ran into a soldier in there. I'll go."

"No," Josh looked at Oakland, "I know where it is, if they haven't moved it. Besides you have all the stealth and grace of a herd of buffalo. I'll do it."

"Okay," Howard reached into his pocket and pulled a semi-automatic pistol out and handed it to Josh butt first. "Take this just in case."

Josh slipped it in the rear waistband of his pants. He returned the way he had left. First he crawled through the grass on his belly. Then duck walked under the window of Art's office. A shadow moved across the window. Damn, the soldier was still in there. He carefully opened the back door. It was still unlocked as he had left it. The wind helped mask the sound. Looking around, Josh eased up to the corner where the hall hooked left on one side and opened into the doorway to Art's office on the right side. He pulled the pistol out, being careful to keep his finger off the trigger. He couldn't afford an accidental discharge. The game would be over then and there. He peeked around the left corner. The hall was clear, so he moved slowly to the edge of the doorway. He fought to control his breathing as he moved up to the edge of the doorway. If the soldier saw him, he knew he would have to execute a flawless headshot and grab the time belt and dash for the door. That was his only chance.

Josh inched around the doorframe. His heart leapt then he relaxed slightly. The soldier was standing with his back to him as before. The man was rifling through a file drawer. The time belt still sat on the desk where they had left it. He guessed that it probably looked like a toy to the soldier, so why bother it. The best option, Josh figured, was to ease up behind him and take him out with a quick shot to the back of the head; execution style. Then he would be in arm's reach of the time belt, grab it and make haste, but all that noise. Should he first reconnoiter the rest of the house and see who was still there? No there was not enough time. He was about to move on in. Then he thought of another option. Josh slid the pistol back in his waistband and reached over into the bookcase beside the door. The dagger was still where he had laid it.

The dagger fit nicely in his hand. He gripped it as he took light steps. If this guy heard him, Josh was sunk. When he was one step behind the soldier, Josh leapt forward and reached his left hand around to cover the soldier's mouth. He gripped the man's jaw tightly and rammed the dagger in low on the right side of his back. The dagger slipped in under the edge of the Lance & Pike bullet proof vest and sunk into the soft tissue. The soldier kicked back at Josh, his boot grazing Josh's calf. Muffled cries escaped around his fingers. He hoped no one was near enough to hear. He adjusted the dagger and jabbed at an upward angle several times. The soldier finally went limp in Josh's arms and he eased him to the floor. The open eyes taunted him. His stomach cramped and a wave of nausea briefly seized him. No, he had to get a hold of himself. He couldn't afford to be sick now. This was war and Josh had to see this through. He grabbed the time belt and retraced his path back out to the woods.

CHAPTER 52

"THERE was nothing we could do for them you know," Howard said as they drove along. "I know," Josh growled from the back seat. Oakland stared straight ahead from the passenger seat.

"I'm just saying…" Howard started.

"Okay!" Josh cut him off. They navigated the back roads leading them up to Virginia. The secondary roads were less likely to have checkpoints than the main roads. The air was tight, though as they watched for any stray patrols. Their target was the cabin in the woods above Danville. There it would all come together or fall apart.

"Uh oh," Oakland muttered.

"I see it," Howard answered. Josh leaned up and looked between them. A police unit partially blocked the road with its lights flashing.

"Oh crap," Josh groaned. "So close."

"Just be cool," Howard said without turning around. "This is probably nothing." Oakland kept his eyes to the front. Howard lowered his window and rolled to a stop.

"Evening officer," Howard kept the vehicle in gear with his foot on the brake.

"Identity card please," the young soldier asked. Josh glanced around. He was alone there.

"Certainly," Howard reached into his coat pocket and pulled out the fake global identification card and handed it over. The security police soldier studied it and looked into the vehicle.

"What was the nature of your travel into North Carolina tonight

Mr. Mack?"

"A visit to my mother," Howard smiled. Josh had never seen Howard so cool. The man suddenly had ice water in his veins.

"And these other gentlemen?" The soldier nodded toward Oakland.

"Oh," Howard threw a quick glance about. "We were repairing a deck on her house."

The soldier's portable radio squawked and a message began coming through. He turned to face toward the front of the vehicle as he listened. Josh thought his heart would explode. He began feeling feint when he heard a description of their vehicle come through. The soldier's right hand moved toward his sidearm. Before he could reach his pistol, Howard grabbed his wrist and jerked the arm inside and floored the accelerator. He gripped the arm tight. They careened down the highway as the soldier twisted around, struggling to hit Howard with his free hand. Howard darted his head avoiding the blows causing them to fishtail about the road. When the speedometer hit seventy miles per hour, Howard suddenly let go. By then they were at a slight dip and curve in the road and they began to slide sideways. Howard jammed the brake pedal to the floor causing them to spin around twice. A speed limit sign loomed at Josh out the window. They were nearly stopped as the sign scrapped down the side of the door. Josh breathed a huge sigh of relief. They were upright and seemingly okay, albeit facing the opposite direction of where they had started.

"What was that old joke…" Howard struggled to catch his breath. "Do you smell that?"

"I ought to," Oakland nodded and looked over at Howard. "I'm sitting in it." All three let out a nervous chuckle.

"Dear Lord," Josh said, "Did I scream like a little girl?"

"I think we all did," Oakland said.

Josh sucked in a breath, looking straight at where the headlights shined on the still form in the road. The torso lay with one shoulder on the pavement, the hips at a ninety-degree angle and the head back in an unnatural position.

"I guess we're committed now," Josh said quietly.

"It would appear so," Howard answered.

$$fff$$

"What the hell happened here," General LaVail shouted as he climbed from his car. Colonel Romochek walked over from where the body lay on the ground.

"A very interesting event," Romochek said, "it would appear."

"Someone murders a soldier at a checkpoint," LaVail blustered, "and it appears *interesting*?"

"I think you will believe so," Romochek handed LaVail a card. "This was found near the body."

"What is it?" LaVail grumbled, not looking down.

"ID card with a Danville address but," Romochek nodded toward the card in LaVail's hand. "I think you will find the picture most interesting."

LaVail looked down at the face smiling from the picture for a few seconds then back up. "Spence," he spat between gritted teeth.

Romochek nodded, "It would appear that they are headed in the direction of that address."

"Lance and Oakland are still unaccounted for," LaVail paced about, "I'd bet anything they're with him."

"More than likely," Romochek smiled.

"Damn it!" LaVail yelled, "That bastard Lance." Romochek stood by silently. "Damn him to hell! He fooled me so completely. I violated my cardinal rule because he had me so snowed." The General smacked his palm with his fist. "Christians! Stupid Christians! They put their damned legends ahead of everything else," he slapped the hood of his car drawing everyone's attention. His glare sent their eyes elsewhere. "They can't be trusted, they think their god is more important than the greater good." LaVail paced for a moment in silence, his steam reduced little. "Colonel, let this be a lesson. Don't ever trust a Jesus freak." He spat on the road disdainfully, "Maybe now the government will let me eliminate the rest of them. Smoke them out and hunt them down like the vermin they are. We can never have effective control otherwise."

CHAPTER
53

THEY had been silent the rest of the drive. Other than a scrape down the side and a crack on one of the door windows, the SUV was largely unscathed. The tension mounted as the cabin drew nearer. The three climbed from the vehicle with their guns drawn. They were ready for whatever might lurk nearby. Other than crickets and tree frogs, the night was still. Howard opened the door to the cabin and they went inside. They entered into a small den with a sleeping loft above. At the back of the cabin was a kitchen which passed through into a larger bedroom. Josh and Oakland sat around a small table which occupied a breakfast nook between the kitchen and den. Howard retrieved a backpack with some items including the packet he had put together for the journey from a closet in the back bedroom and laid it at the center of the table. He pulled a set of instructions from the packet and unfolded it on the table. Soon he and Josh were reviewing their plans.

"I'd better keep an eye on things," Oakland stood up and headed for the ladder to the loft.

"Good idea," Howard nodded.

Oakland climbed the ladder and left the light off in the loft. He sat down beside the front window. The yard stretched out about twenty yards to the woods. It was quite dark outside and Oakland's eyes slowly adjusted to the low light. Much more slowly than they used to, he noted. He looked around the room. There were two other windows, one on the end and one in the back. Good, he would be able to watch three sides of the cabin from here.

Oakland rubbed his head, remembering when he first met Josh. He remembered him from their high school football days—both were all-state—but, he never really knew him until he landed at Rhynelow all those years ago. Now they were here in a cabin in the woods, waiting to die. Josh had been so success oriented back then, everything was business; all about making a buck. Any time someone brought up a political matter he would say, "We're making money, that's all that matters." It was hard to believe this was the same man.

Things had started to change in Josh as his kids grew. Fatherhood changes a man, Oakland reminded himself. It sure had made a difference in him. Josh became more concerned about what kind of world they would live in and what kind of government had been foisted upon them. Then suddenly they were all gone and then everything changed about Josh. He was still a great leader and a savvy businessman, but suddenly everything was different… he was different.

The earthy smell of the cabin soothed Oakland in contrast to the dire situation that brought him here. Any other time he would find this night quite pleasant. He drew in a deep breath and blew it out. How the hell did he get into this? Alisa had griped that this Ox thing would end up getting him killed. It would appear that before the night ended she might be right.

$$fff$$

"The vehicle is in front of the cabin and there are lights on inside," Romochek said.

"Very good," LaVail nodded.

"Shall we move in sir?"

"No, let's take our time Colonel," LaVail responded. "They aren't going anywhere. We have them trapped." LaVail paced slowly by his car which sat on the main road leading up to the cabin.

"Shall we burn them out?" Romochek raised an eyebrow and smiled, "Beautiful night for a bonfire."

LaVail laughed, "Indeed it is, maybe even a barbeque. The yokels here like barbeque I hear." He narrowed his eyes thoughtfully peering into the woods. He couldn't actually see the cabin from where he stood, but he knew the direction. "Maybe," he paced and tapped his temple. "Hmmm... No, I want to see their bodies, intact... not as charred heaps. I want to see their suffering. In fact, if possible bring Lance to me alive. I want to watch him squirm and beg for his life," he grunted out a quick guttural laugh, "or death... Oh yes, I want to see him plead for it to end."

"Yes sir," Romochek said, "when?"

"As soon as you have your men in place, but take your time and make sure it's set up right." LaVail smiled and looked over at Romochek, "It's been a while since I've taken part in a field op Colonel. I'm looking forward to this."

$$fff$$

The cicadas sang and the droning voices below hypnotized him. Oakland jerked suddenly, realizing that he had nearly fallen asleep. The adrenaline had subsided, his heart beat at a more normal pace and he finally became aware of how tired he really was. His eyelids pulled downward, but Oakland knew he must stay awake. Peeking over the window sill, he could hardly believe that this peaceful stretch of forest could hold any threat.

He crawled over and looked out the back and then side windows. Everything was still. At the front, a tree frog was making his way up the middle of the window. Oakland smiled and watched for a moment. Chuckling, he reached up and tapped lightly on the glass under the frog. The light green creature climbed several steps away from the large black finger. He rubbed his forehead and slumped down under the window, trying to control his laughter. Why this was so funny, he wasn't sure. It must be the fatigue, Oakland thought. Turning over back onto his knees, he looked at the frog again. He had never paid them much attention, but now it struck him just how funny looking tree frogs really were. Just as he was about to reach up to tap again, something moved at the edge of the trees.

He crouched down lower, with just his eyes peering out over

the bottom of the window. Probably just a deer, these woods were full of them. After a moment, he began to relax when he saw more movement at the other side of the tree line. That was no deer!

$$fff$$

The same fatigue weighed on Howard's eyes that dwelt deep in Josh's bones. Aching knees and a stiff lower back cried out for attention while he tried to absorb all that Howard was saying. His life would depend on it; all their lives would. Howard tapped the paper, emphasizing a point. Everything except the set of instructions had been inventoried, reassembled and put back in the leather pouch. Josh nodded; this was really going to happen.

"Hey!" Oakland called out in a loud whisper. "I think we have company."

Howard stood up and put the instructions back into the packet, snapped it shut and zipped it into the backpack. Josh headed toward the front window to look out. Howard grabbed him by the shirt and snatched him back.

"No," Howard hissed, "they'll see you."

"Oh bubba, we've definitely got company," Oakland whispered over the railing of the loft. "You two better get moving."

Howard grabbed the backpack and time belt from the table and pulled Josh along by the arm into the back room. They had punched in the proper date coordinates into the time belt earlier. Howard had feared that this might come about suddenly so he was taking no chances. The front door exploded and flew from its hinges. Two soldiers leapt into the room. Three bangs pealed around the cabin from the loft and the two soldiers went down, one holding his neck and the other bleeding from the cheek. A third soldier popped through the doorway and raked the loft with submachine gun fire. Oakland screamed out and flipped over the railing, collapsing a coffee table under his weight.

"No!" Josh screamed as Howard dragged him by the arm. Howard slammed the door to the bedroom and locked it. Josh fumbled with the time belt and Howard nimbly fastened it about him and shoved him against the wall. Josh began to protest that Oakland needed their help. Howard shook his head and mouthed one word, "Go."

There was a loud whack on the bedroom door. A second and the door cracked and flew from its hinges. Howard glanced back over his shoulder. A trooper screamed for them to put their hands up and Howard looked back at Josh and pushed the red button on the belt. The room about them began to glow blue. A low hum quickly increased to drown out all other sounds. The last thing Josh heard was two loud pops. Howard fell away from him as everything faded into blue.

CHAPTER
54

A SQUIRREL was staring Josh in the face from just inches away. He jerked upright, his back spasmed and the squirrel dashed up a nearby tree. The creature stopped halfway and watched Josh carefully, letting out a hoarse warning chirp every few seconds. Josh laughed.

"I'm not afraid of you little buddy," he called. It was early evening, the sun a little over halfway toward the horizon. Howard, Oakland, the soldiers! Josh looked around. The cabin was nowhere to be seen and he sat beside a patch of brambles. Josh pulled his shirt up and removed the electrodes from his sternum. They left a large red mark about his breast bone. The area was tender and he felt like he had been punched. Other than that and a mild headache, he seemed none the worse for wear.

The leaves had begun turning bright colors. Looking around he saw a virgin patch of woods all about. Some of the features of the land looked similar, but no cabin or driveway. The cabin had been built in 2008, so he supposed that he must have been deposited sometime prior to that. If it was not 1997, Josh knew he was in deep trouble. There would be no way of knowing until he was out of these woods. He tucked the time belt into the backpack, pulled it over his shoulders and stood up. It was a three mile walk to the stores, so he'd better start now.

By the time he reached the main highway the sun was sinking lower in the sky. A dirty old convenience store stood about a hundred feet down the road. Josh kicked a rock and headed toward it.

The store was dusty and old. He found a little pocket notebook and an ink pen. Then he walked over to the drink cooler and pulled a bottle of water out. Josh had made sure he got some twenties out of the packet while he was back in the woods and placed them in his front pocket. He laid one down on the counter and looked at his watch. He tapped it twice and frowned.

"What date is it?" Josh asked innocently.

"The fifth," the clerk replied counting out the change.

"Of November, right," Josh smiled. The clerk turned his head to face him. He then counted the change out onto the counter.

"Yep," the clerk replied shaking his head. "I suppose you need to know the year too?" He said with a mocking laugh.

"1997 right?" Josh said. The clerk nodded and gave a disgusted grunt. Josh forced a laugh and breathed a deep sigh of relief. Well, Art's stupid little invention worked after all. It was the only invention of Art's he had ever doubted. Now his life depended on it.

He strolled out to the street and drank his water as he wandered up to the next store. Setting the backpack down beside him he sat on a curb at the side of the store. He pulled a small paperback book from the packet out and thumbed through it until he found the page he was looking for. Josh's finger ran down the page and stopped midway. He quickly transcribed a series of numbers into the notebook then replaced the paperback book into the packet and carefully put it all back into the backpack. Taking another quick look around, Josh saw that no one else was near him. He held his breath, stood and walked into the store. If this wasn't right, little else would matter.

Josh emerged from the store and headed down the street with a small bag of snacks and drinks. After a couple of miles it had grown so dark that he was afraid of stepping in a hole. It would be a shame to break his leg at this point. Howard's research was correct; there was the fleabag motel right where he said it would be. It would be torn down in a few years and replaced with something better, but it was here now. Josh walked to the counter and rented a room for the night. He picked this one because he knew they would take cash. The room was small and musty. He turned on the fan of the heating and cooling unit to air the room out then climbed onto the bed and fell asleep on top of the covers.

Several hours later he was awake and watching the local news broadcast on the small television that sat on the old dresser. The set was ancient even by 1997 standards, but it worked just fine. Near the end of the news, the lottery results flashed onto the screen. Josh's eyes roved between the TV and the ticket in his hand several times, and then finally a faint smile decorated the corners of his mouth. There were five sets of numbers on the ticket. Four were selected randomly, but the last had been carefully filled in to match the winning numbers. Josh showered then retired for the night.

$$ f\ f\ f $$

"Of course, send him in." Buck Fawcett put down the phone. He had been working on a brief, but fortunately he was not with a client. He sure wouldn't want to miss this. In his thirty years in practice since moving down from Richmond, this was a first. A smile spread across his face and he rose to greet the man coming through the door.

"Mr. Mack, come in." Buck waved the man in. James Mack he had told the secretary his name was.

"Thank you for seeing me," the man took his hand then sat down.

"Sounds like you're having a good day," Buck smiled. He had recently brought his son into the firm, making it Fawcett & Fawcett.

"I suppose so," the man answered tiredly. His face was drawn and he seemed a little disheveled, otherwise he was mostly clean and well spoken.

"A hundred and ninety million dollars would make most folks a little more certain that they were having a good day, I would think." The man grunted and smiled at Buck's jibe. "So how may I serve you?"

"I want to claim my winnings through your office," Mack said. "I want as little fuss as possible; I absolutely want my identity protected."

"Family problems?"

The man shrugged, "I just value my privacy."

"Are you sure?" Fawcett asked. "A hundred and ninety million dollar win makes quite a story. I'll have my work cut out for me. Besides, could be your moment in the sun."

"I'm sure it would be…" his eyes bore straight into Buck, "but, no… I don't want the attention."

Buck studied the man for a moment then rocked forward and picked up his pen and began scribbling. "Okay, I see here that you list your address as a motel down the road. Where is your home?"

"I don't really have one," Mack kept his face impassive.

Buck set the pen down and stared at him. "You're awfully clean and educated for a homeless man, if you don't mind my saying."

"I had a run of bad luck," he shrugged, "now I do odd jobs."

Buck waved a hand in the air. "Okay, where do you want the money to go Mr. Mack?"

"I need you to set up a bank account for me," Josh said. "If the taxes aren't withheld already, please escrow the proper amount with some extra to be certain." Josh leaned forward and winked, "I don't want problems later."

Buck laughed and sat back. "I can see you're quite an interesting man, Mr. Mack, why all the mystery?"

"I'm shy," Mack grinned.

"Okay, you're the boss." Buck picked up the pen again and made some more notations. He shook his head as he scribbled with a broad grin on his face. Fawcett & Fawcett would be getting a pretty decent cut for this work. "Anything else?"

"Yes," he said. "I want a car and a credit card."

$$fff$$

Josh walked out of the offices of Fawcett & Fawcett smiling. James Mack was one of three names he could choose from the identities that Howard had made for him. This one felt right, it was the name Howard had bought the cabin in.

His smile faded. This was probably the easy part. He wondered if he could accomplish what he had to do next.

CHAPTER
55

JOSH walked out of the elevator and headed to the parking lot. This place was much nicer than where he had stayed in Danville. Amazing what a few tens of millions of dollars could do for you. Of course he had more than that from Lance & Pike before embarking on this adventure. That was most certainly gone now, even if he succeeded and made it back in one piece. That made him feel less piggish for grabbing such a large lottery win. Besides, that was the payout that week. He wondered how this might affect the future. The next guy to win would get far less than he would have otherwise, but he may have done the guy a favor. The poor sap, his name escaped Josh, would go on to make every mistake a suddenly wealthy person can make. His wife would leave him after catching him with a stripper who would end up in prison for a plot against his life she hatched with a secret lover and his own brother would sue him. Eighteen months later, with nothing left but a two million dollar tax bill, he would be found dead with a whiskey bottle and an empty pill container beside his bed. Perhaps with a smaller windfall he would plan more wisely... perhaps.

He had no idea what he would return to, so Josh had already set up an account in Vanuatu for the money. The Pacific Rim remained out of the grasp of the International Union in his time, so he could retrieve it once he returned. No sense having the advantage of foresight and becoming a pauper.

The Toyota Camry Buck Fawcett had acquired suited Josh

just fine. Good solid car, but not too flashy; just what he needed. Transportation, credit and decent lodging; everything he would use as a foundation to operate from. He sucked in a deep breath and fired the engine up.

His task now was to figure out how to swap the maps on Young Art. It was Tuesday. He had arrived in Virginia the previous Wednesday and it had taken several days to square the situation with the lottery and get down to North Carolina. He had until Friday. He had joked all of his working life about deadlines calling them 'drop dead dates.' He'd had no idea what a drop dead date was until now.

Art had told him before he left that he had eaten alone at a local barbeque joint, Homer's Hog House. Josh had been there and remembered the layout, it was pretty open. Art's favorite food was barbeque and he would eat no other style than Lexington. Many parts of the country prided themselves on their barbeque and believed that theirs' was the only valid kind. North Carolina was no different. In fact it was probably worse. Here they conducted their own civil war over barbeque. The style that hailed from the sleepy central North Carolina town of Lexington versus the kind originating from the coastal region, known as Eastern Style. Violent arguments were known to ensue over such matters. In the years after his injury, Josh and Artemis had bonded over Lexington Style barbeque at least weekly. Art said he had done what he always did when he had something heavy on his mind. He spread it out and studied it over barbeque. This would be Josh's best opportunity; Homer's, that's where he would make it happen.

The dented up Nissan Sentra sat next to the restaurant, Josh smiled. That old car had been a welcome site sitting along side the road as Art pulled him from the water. It had borne silent witness to many great times and grand adventures they had shared. Josh parked across the lot from it and headed inside.

A steaming plate of barbeque was just arriving at Art's table in the middle of the room. He lifted up the blue map to make room for it, unfolded and slid it to one side and continued to read between forkfuls of pork. Josh took the table beside him. Art cast a quick glance sideways. Josh smiled; that was vintage Art, so focused and lacking social grace at that point. Over the years the focus would remain sharp, but the social graces would slowly grow, especially once Julie came along.

"I'll have the Whole Hog special and a sweet tea," Josh told the waitress. He had one eye trained on Young Art as he poured over the blue paper. Josh was relieved that what Art had told him proved true, that he didn't take the blue map seriously until after he saved Josh from the wreck. After that point he would never again be that casual with this document.

The boy's eyes darted about intently. He occasionally smiled or even laughed a bit. Josh reached inside his coat pocket and felt for the counterfeit map. He watched for an opportunity. Darn it! Don't you need a bathroom break? Art would be leaving soon, Josh couldn't miss this chance. He reached out and deliberately knocked his tea glass over on the table and rose up cursing. He fussed and batted at his clothes pretending to wipe the tea away. Art was looking up at him as Josh worked his way behind the young man's chair.

"Dadgumit! Look at what I did," Josh bellowed pointing at the table. Artemis had stood by now and looked over to the table where Josh pointed. Josh knew he would have to move fast, he reached into his pocket with one hand and grabbed the map spread on the table with the other. As he pulled the paper off the table, Art spun around and snatched it from his hand.

"What are you doing?" Art glared, his mouth twisted into a snarl. "That's mine!" Josh said nothing, his face flushed. Idiot, Josh admonished himself. His great plan no longer seemed so simple.

"Is there a problem Pike?" A giant of a man with a substantial paunch covered by an apron waddled out from behind the cash register.

"I don't know Homer." The teenage Art shouted pointing at Josh. "This guy…"

"No problem," Josh reached into his pocket and pulled a twenty and threw it on the table. "I was just leaving."

"I think you better," Homer snorted. "Fo' I call the cops!" Josh watched over his shoulder the whole way to the door and hurried to his car. Damn, he thought, now what? He smacked the steering wheel. He guessed he would have to break into the Pike home to replace the map. Nothing else came to mind.

$$fff$$

Josh sat on the hood of the Camry. It was nearing midnight the next night, Wednesday. A few cars were coming and going from the gas pumps at the travel plaza east of Burlington. He had pulled over to the edge of the parking lot after gassing up to sit and wait. Interstate 85 had moderate traffic for this time of night down the hill below him.

Josh pulled the blue map out and spread it on the hood. He began going over the points, making sure everything was in order. He knew they were, truth was he needed to calm his nerves. Burglary was a new experience for him, so was time travel, he reminded himself. Josh chuckled ruefully; Joshua Lance: time traveler and burglar, what a thought.

He would give it another hour to make sure everyone was asleep. Art slept like a rock, the old man would probably be drunk and snoring loudly, but the old lady Josh didn't know about. Well, either way he would have to risk it. After he blew it at Homer's, Josh knew that Art wouldn't let him near the map again. The plan had seemed so simple before, just grab the map and slip the new one in. He shook his head, what a fool he had been. Too good to be true… Too good to be true…

Everything seemed in order with the blue paper, like there was any doubt. That was the one thing about this trip that had been done right. He'd better be wrapping it up and move on; couldn't afford to arouse suspicions. Josh fished in his pocket for the car keys. He fumbled them and they bounced off his leg then went clattering to the pavement under the car. Damn! He knelt down and reached under the car for them. They were just out of reach so he stretched and just got a fingertip on them. He flicked them toward him. They ended up a fraction closer. He was able to get just enough of two fingertips onto them to slowly drag them toward him.

That ground was a lot further down than Josh had remembered it being. He rested on his knees, getting his bearings. A gust of wind lifted the blue map off the hood of the car and sailed it into the air like a kite. Oh no! He leapt to his feet and jumped up to grab it. He just grazed it with his fingertips as another wind turned it over and sent it over the hill toward the interstate. Josh's heart bounced into his throat as he vaulted over the guard rail after it. He came down at an angle and his heels slipped from under him on the wet grass of the hill depositing him onto his butt. He slid down the hill for several feet and began tumbling sideways hitting rocks, briars and small bushes on the way down. The freefall ended at the bottom in a small ditch beside the shoulder of the road.

Josh scrambled to get upright and regain his breath. His lungs refused to inflate for a few seconds. The paper floated in the air above him, well out of his reach and drifting toward the road. Desperately Josh hobbled after it. It came to rest in the edge of the interstate, he bent and grabbed for it. A car blasted by, running over the paper with the right two tires, narrowly missing his fingers and launching the paper into the air again. It drifted along toward the center of the north bound lanes. Everything seemed to freeze as Josh lunged for it. He only heard the pounding of his heart in his ears; until the air horn of an eighteen wheeler blasted him out of his fog. The wind from the truck blew Josh onto his back. The blue paper was sucked under the truck and never emerged.

Josh scuttled out of the road and flopped down on the shoulder. He smacked the ground, scuffing his palm. No! He screamed. Now what? He rolled over onto his back and looked toward Heaven through his tears. Now what? Stupid! He sat up and stomped the ground. How could he be so stupid? It was all sunk now, all for nothing. Alice, the kids, the future… It was all screwed!

The sound of sirens wailing in the distance drew him back to reality. He realized that they were probably coming for him, but what did it matter now. No, that couldn't happen. Josh wiped his face and scrambled up the hill to where his car waited.

CHAPTER

56

COMFORT food, that's what Josh needed and next to barbeque a big juicy burger was what he loved most and this place had the best. It was one of Josh's favorites from his high school years and here he sat. He had avoided it all week because he didn't want to risk running into his younger self, but this was Thursday and he had never gone out the night before a game. He sipped from a long necked bottle; his eyes sunk into his head from lack of sleep. His whole body was sore from his little down hill tumble and interstate rodeo stunt. When his burger arrived he put his head down briefly; Lord I've already screwed this up, please send me an idea... the right idea. He looked back up and bit a hunk out of the burger. Yum, just like he remembered.

Josh had tossed and turned the remainder of the night, wishing that he had ended up under the truck with the map. But no, that would not have solved anything. Things would still be screwed up. Alice, the kids, Finch, the future... As much as he wanted to, he couldn't give up now. It seemed hopeless, but there had to be another way.

He had kicked around the thought of trying to talk to Art and his younger self after the accident. Maybe show up in the hospital. Tell them something that might dazzle them. It probably had little hope of success. How would it go? *Hi I'm you in forty years! Guess what?* Oh yeah, that would work. Still... he could not totally rule it out. He shifted in his chair and felt a pain shoot from one of the bruises on his butt.

A teen aged girl walked through the front door with two others in tow. Her bright red hair spilled over her shoulders and reached to the middle of her torso, nearly to her waist. The smile framed by the pretty face was as sunny as her hair. Josh wondered if Julie had any clue that she would be just as beautiful at fifty as she was at seventeen; at least to him. Still, here she had youth on top of beauty along with the indomitable spirit that had always shined in her eyes. No wonder Art had grabbed on and never looked back.

Josh took a bite of hamburger as the girls sat down at a table near the entrance. Julie's back was to the door. A group of teenaged guys in football jackets burst through the door, their boisterous voices permeated the room. Connor Finch strutted at the head of the pack, looking about the room. Last time I saw you, your eyes were bugged half way out of your head, you son of a bitch. Josh grimaced and set his burger down. He took a long swallow of beer and stared.

Finch slipped up behind Julie and goosed her under the arm. As she jumped, his hand slid around to the front and cupped one of her breasts. Julie jumped and slapped Finch's hand away and hissed something at him. Finch laughed and walked over with his friends and took a table near Josh's.

Josh finished his beer and sat rolling the bottle between his palms. Finch threw his head back and laughed at something. Josh was sure that whatever it was couldn't have been that funny. Showy little twit. One of the guys, Grady, one of Finch's little butt-hole buddies, he recalled, leaned in and said something. Grady was looking toward Josh as they spoke. Finch turned his head and glared. He knew he should look away, but Josh sat staring back. Finch rose and strolled over. Josh put one foot on the floor as Finch stood across the table, trying on his most menacing look. Josh smirked.

"Can I help you with something grandpa?" Finch's voice was cold and flat.

"No," he shook his head and watched Finch.

"Do I know you?"

Josh laughed and shook his head.

"You got a problem?"

"No problems, sonny boy," Josh kept smiling.

"Well then," Finch leaned in and lowered his voice to a deep growl. "Maybe you'd best keep your eyes to yourself."

Josh finally half looked down, still watching Finch but breaking eye contact and nodded slowly. "Sure, no problem, bubb."

Finch laughed and turned to walk back to his table. Josh's vision focused in on the soft area at the base of Finch's skull and he realized that he was unconsciously gripping the neck of the bottle. One quick whack and all this could be over. Josh slowly relaxed his grip. He knew it couldn't end that way. Finch had to live. Josh walked to the front, paid and left.

Later in his motel, Josh pulled the scrapbook out of the backpack and opened it to a story near the back. It was an interview with General Alexander Birch following his election as president. In the story, it was noted that the people had taken to calling Alex a modern day George Washington. Alex scoffed at the comparison, but noted that much of the credit for his success in the war must go to another man who recruited and led his own band of partisan fighters. If he were George Washington, then this man was certainly Nathaniel Greene. The young general he claimed that he could not have won the war without was a man named Hampton Finch. Connor Finch must live… at least for now.

ƒ ƒ ƒ

Friday night the lights glared over Burlington Central High School. The loud speaker blared and the band boomed. Josh sat watching the team warm up. It was surreal and he knew how the game would end, yet he could still feel his blood begin to pump. Oh yes, football. Josh could never fully get the feeling of the autumn night air out of his system; completing the pass, hearing the roar of the crowd. Number 16, Josh knew, was in for quite a game. He remembered how it felt, the exhilaration of the win, the sweet ache of the tired muscles, much different from the pain his body felt tonight. Then it all would change later on into the wee hours of the morning. The mournful ache in Josh's left foot reminded him of that. By halftime, Josh decided that watching his younger self play football was stranger than he cared to witness, so he left.

Driving away, he threw a glance back at the field. Bitter sweet memories rode with him. This had been the second happiest time of his life, next to his years with Alice. He would go and eat a light supper and decide what to do next. The knot in his stomach reminded him of the only option he had thought of so far. If he didn't come up with something else, Josh didn't like what was ahead of him.

CHAPTER
57

JOSH turned up the old dirt road, one day it would be the paved main road through a subdivision, but tonight the only thing on it was an old abandoned farm house at the end, that was where Josh was headed. He pulled the Camry around to the back, out of sight in case someone else came snooping. There was no other way, he sat gathering his nerve. It had to be. He climbed out of the car with his flashlight in hand and walked toward the back and stepped onto the trail leading into the woods.

An owl protested his presence from above as the tree frogs and crickets serenaded him. Josh plodded along through the darkness being careful of his footing on the trail. He could hear the water flowing in the creek ahead. The trail led downhill toward a shallow spot he could step across. He worked his way down the low creek bank and stepped over the water. The water pooled in a deeper gulley just down stream a few feet. He knew it was there, but it was hidden by the night. A sudden splash in the pool made him jump. Stupid frog! At least he hoped so, either way Josh wasn't waiting around to see. He worked his way up the other bank and climbed the hill upwards.

There, at a sharp crook in the trail, he could see the small clearing leading out to the highway. Josh crept along and found a clear spot behind a tree where he could watch the road. The nights were growing cooler, but it was relatively mild still for early November. He looked at his watch, only a half hour, he was cutting it close.

In Due Time

Sitting down in the still of the darkness, the fatigue crept into Josh's aging bones. His eyelids grew heavy; he dreamed that falling dream. He jerked awake as the ground rushed up and looked around. How long, he gasped. He illuminated the face of his watch. Ten minutes... must stay awake, can't fall asleep. Knuckling his eyes and shaking his head, he felt the butterflies swarm through his belly. Soon, very soon.

The hum of the mustang cut through the night air in the distance. Josh would know its sound anywhere, throughout all time. He was coming.

Josh stood up and hugged the medium sized pine he had been resting against. The mustang purred over the hill and came into site, the headlights cutting through the gloom. As it grew closer the lights began to drift to the left side of the road until it nearly dropped off the pavement then it quickly jerked back to the right and began to fishtail. It finally left the highway on the right side and began to spin until it splashed into the shallow inlet opposite where Josh sat.

The pine bark dug into the flesh of Josh's arms through his coat. He eased his grip and closed his eyes. The pain in his left foot throbbed sympathetically and he could feel the fear of being trapped under the water. His breaths were coming shorter. He had to get control, he had to. The cries for help and the thuds of fists against the car window then began and Josh covered his ears. No, keep your control.

When the Nissan Sentra drove into sight and slowed to a stop, Josh drew in a deep breath. This was what it was all about, he reminded himself. The short figure of a young Artemis Pike emerged from the car with an elbow shaped tire tool in his hand, yelling words of encouragement into the night. Josh felt the blood pumping through his eardrums.

The muscles tightened in Josh's legs. He sprang to his feet and dashed into the road behind Art. The boy looked back in horror as Josh caught up with him. He tackled the young man from behind; the two tumbled onto the asphalt. Artemis thrashed around yelling for him to let go. After a few seconds Josh's grip began to slip and a sharp elbow sank deep into his ribs knocking the wind from his lungs. Gasping for breath, Josh saw the moonlight glint off the tire iron as it flashed toward his forehead. He rolled backwards with the blow and the iron grazed across his scalp.

Josh's head pounded as he crawled about the pavement. He could hear splashing and Art yelling again for the other to hold on. Josh pushed himself up from the road and stood for a few seconds, letting his head clear.

"Hang on," Art yelled as he drew back the tire iron. He let it fly splashing into the water and thumping against the driver's window. He had drawn the tool back to try again. Josh swallowed hard and began his sprint toward the bank. He knew he had to ignore the water… focus on Art. Josh closed his eyes as he pounded the last step springing toward the roof of the submerged car. He opened them again in mid-air and tried to not look down. The gentle lapping of the water against the banks made his heart palpitate. He landed on Art's back as his arm descended again with the tire iron. It missed its mark and splashed in the water.

Art wailed about with his elbows again and Josh rolled with each blow. Instead of trying to hold the young man's arms, Josh instead grabbed his right wrist with one hand and his right thumb with the other, prying the tool loose from his grip. The iron dropped onto the roof of the car with a clunk. Beneath them, Josh could feel pounding coming from inside the car. He ignored it and grabbed for the tool. As he got hold of it, Art struck him in the face with his fist. Josh brought his knees up into Art's sides flipping the young man into the water. Josh stood and flung the tool as far out into the lake as he could manage then dove in after Artemis.

The young man struggled against Josh as they wrestled to the edge of the water. The elbows and kicks were less effective in the water and Josh ignored the blows. Once he reached the shore, Josh pinned the boy to the bank which rose out of the waist deep water. He stood watching the car as Art fought to get loose, but Josh had him pinned with all of his weight. For the first time, he could see the hands against the glass and the face alternating between trying to look out and rising up to get air. Finally the hands went limp and the face sank from the ceiling and settled against the window. The eyes closed peacefully and the face slid down to the bottom.

"No, no," Art sobbed as Josh pulled him from the water and laid him on the bank.

Josh began walking back toward the woods. His stomach ached and his head throbbed; his body one mass of aches and spasms. He had wondered what would happen at this moment. There was the full expectation on his part that he would suddenly go poof and just disappear once his other self drew its last breath, but he was still here.

"Why?" Artemis screamed out, "Why did you do this?"

Josh stopped in the middle of the road and looked up at the moon for a second then turned around. "I had to Art." The boy's eyes went wide upon hearing his name spoken. Josh could only imagine what went on inside his head. In a short span, a man he's never seen appears to predict the future and advise him then another one shows up to stop him and even knows his name.

"Why?" Art's voice barely squeaked.

"Some things shouldn't be tampered with…"

"Who are you?" Artemis choked out.

"I'm nobody," Josh said and gazed at the water filled car in the lake. "Not anymore." Then he turned and disappeared into the woods.

CHAPTER
58

"**A**ND that's how it all happened, Howard," the old man leaned back in his chair and gazed out across the mountain. The shadows were growing long as the daylight faded.

"That's the most incredible thing I've ever heard," I said. He nodded and looked back to me.

"All true," he said.

"I still don't understand why you didn't find another way," I leaned forward. "Why couldn't you have spared yourself?"

"It was probably for the best," he grimaced, "There was no guarantee that the map would have worked anyway. Can't you see Howard, everything bad that happened, happened because of people that I brought into the lives of others? Connor Finch only knew Alice and the kids because he knew me. If he hadn't wanted to get even..." The old man's voice had risen before he chopped off the statement. "Then there's Earl Harper. I brought him into the Council of the Ox."

"Who's the Ox?" I asked expectantly. He smiled and cut his eyes toward me again.

"You'll find out Howard."

"You're the Ox aren't you?" I pointed at the old man. He laughed and sat back.

"In due time Howard," he said with a twinkle in his eye. "You'll know in due time..."

"What will happen to Artemis?" I asked, "It sounds like he doesn't do too well without you."

He smiled sadly, "That's where you come in Howard."

"Me?"

"Yes," the old man sat back, "He's currently in college."

"I thought they couldn't afford college for him."

"They can't," the old man smirked, "He got a full scholarship from a foundation called 'The Fruit of the Joshua Tree.' I understand that this foundation which is handled by the law firm of Fawcett and Fawcett out of Virginia needs a new administrator." He grinned, "I think I can pull some strings and get you the job."

"Why me?" I demanded. At that point I had no intention of leaving journalism. Things were going well in Asheville and with my parents gone now it seemed the best place for me. I didn't realize that within a year things would unfold as the old man had predicted and I would leave the news industry without a second thought.

"Why not you Howard?" He raised a hand with his palm turned upwards. "I can't go straight to Art; he would run the other way. No, he has great potential, but he has to be guided. Oakland is only thinking of football at this point and besides, it took a long time for him to see the truth about all this. Howard, you were the oldest and in many ways the wisest of us all. There is no one I would trust more. Your intentions are pure."

"I don't know about all this," I said shaking my head. "How do I know you're not just nuts?"

"If you're not sure yet," he looked me in the eye, "you will be."

I rose and walked toward my car. "I still think you're the Ox." I called over my shoulder. He laughed and headed back into the house. It struck me as odd that he didn't seem concerned that I was leaving. I expected him to chase me to my car and try to convince me further. I knew I could not write this story, it was too bizarre. I would soon discover why he was not bothered by my exit. He knew I would return. I had to.

$$f f f$$

The General leaned forward on his fists. His arms formed a

triangle from his knees to his chin. "Lance wasn't the Ox, was he?"

I shook my head. "That Christmas one of the surrounding communities invited us to send someone to represent the newspaper in their local parade and serve as grand marshal. The associate editor assigned me to do this. When I arrived in the staging area, I asked the coordinator where I should go. She pointed over to a small wooden cart parked nearby. So I walked over to the man tending it. Hooked to the cart were two of the funniest looking cows I had ever seen. I asked him what the deal was with the cows. He told me that those weren't cows that this was a pair of oxen and that the cart was my ride. I wondered out loud if they extended this hospitality to every grand marshal and he said that this was the first time. In fact, he pointed out that my editor had arranged for this. For a couple of weeks I was the butt of jokes about this around the office and for a while the other reporters would refer to me as the Ox."

"So you're the Ox?" General Birch's eyes lit up. I nodded and he extended his hand to me. I'm sure my eyes registered my surprise, but I graciously took his hand. "Thank you," he said. "You'll never know how much your efforts aided our cause."

"Well, it wasn't just me, but that's another story," I smiled. "I returned and accepted the old man's offer. I no longer doubted him."

* * *

"Howard," the old man said. "Once Art is finished with all of his schooling, the foundation will then guide him into business. You'll have to take an active role in helping Art develop and administer this business. I won't be there for him this time, but you will. I'm counting on you."

I nodded, the gravity of this soaked in. At that point I was just beginning to get a grip on what I had gotten into and how deeply it would change my life. I spent days learning all I needed to know from the old man. Finally it came time for me to go.

"Oh," he said as I prepared to leave. "One last thing. See what you can do to introduce Art to Julie May."

"Now how am I supposed to do that?" I asked.

"You're a resourceful guy," he smiled. "I'm sure you'll think of something."

"I'll try," I held up my hands.

"Now there is more we can do later. I'll try to help you all I can, but…" he looked down. "I have to take a trip and I'm not sure I'll make it back."

"Where are you going," I asked cautiously.

"Montana," he answered.

$$fff$$

"Montana? The bank…," General Birch pursed his lips.

"Yes sir," I answered. "The bank."

"Did he return?"

"He did," I smiled. "I saw him some more. Then one day about eight years after I first met him, I got a call from the sheriff's office up there. The old man had been taken to the hospital and had passed on. Before he died, he had given them a note to contact me. I had him buried in a small cemetery on a mountainside that he had taken me to once. He had told me that was where he wished to be. He wondered at the time about what would happen to his soul… worried that he had become an abomination and that God wouldn't have him. I didn't know what to say." I frowned then waved the thought off, "Well, I respected his wishes and that is where he rests. He gave control of his assets to me. I was to use what I thought prudent for Artemis Pike's business until it became self supporting and to support the revolution. His assets had grown considerably. I suppose being from the future helps you as an investor. These were all held in offshore accounts in the South Pacific like he had originally planned."

I drew in a deep breath and blew it out. "I have one final duty General. The old man told me that when the time was right and he left that up to me, that I was to disburse the remaining assets three ways. To you, your mother and your sister. That time has come. You don't have to worry about income or inheritance taxes, the war took care of that."

General Birch nodded with a raised eyebrow. "It won't be back any time soon if I have anything to do about it. If anyone proposes an income tax on my watch, I'll walk onto the floor of congress and shoot him dead right then and there."

I laughed; I really didn't doubt that he would do exactly as he said. "There is one more thing."

"I had a feeling there was," he answered. "The scandal he mentioned?"

"Yes," I nodded sadly, "the scandal." I reached under my chair and pulled the scrapbook from my briefcase. I flipped it to a page near the end and handed it over. "You'd best read this for yourself."

He looked down and read. General Birch shook his head slowly as he scanned the first story and finally looked up. His face had lightened by a shade. "Nobody knew this." I nodded, "I haven't even told Hampton that I was planning to appoint his father Secretary of Commerce."

"The future knows," I said, "Joshua Lance knew." I flipped the page and pointed to the next story. The General read some more.

"Young girls and drugs again," he said with disgust.

"And he will bring you down along with him," I said. "And if you keep reading you'll see that not only will your opponent beat you for reelection, but that Finch had been a mole in your administration the whole time. It's easy to see, they set him up with the girls and drugs then blackmailed him into spying for them. Then all they had to do was spring the story at the right time. You lose the election and the new president brings the International Union back in. At that point all your work will have been for nothing. Make no mistake, everything that Connor Finch touches, he destroys."

"Dear Lord," the General said quietly. Just then the intercom on his desk buzzed. The General picked the receiver up and listened for a second.

"Send her in," he said then looked at me. "Would you like to meet my mother, Mr. Spence?"

"It would be an honor," I said. There was a certain radiance about Alice Birch as she strode into the office. The General rose and kissed her on the cheek. He smiled and turned to me.

"Mother this is Howard Spence," he said.

"Yes," she smiled. I could instantly see why Joshua Lance was so smitten. "I've read all of your books, Mr. Spence."

"Thank you," I answered.

"I was just telling Mr. Spence about the man that gave you that envelope with the package at the law office in Virginia." The look he shot me left no doubt that he didn't think she needed to hear the whole story, so I just smiled and nodded.

"Very strange," she said, "nice man. I had never seen him, but there was something about him. He looked at me like he knew me and I had the wildest feeling…" Her face seemed to drift into a dream for a moment, "Well, it was almost like I knew him too. He said the strangest thing. He said, hmm…" She placed a finger to her temple, "Let me see… He said that this was something that would be important to Alex…" Her eyes narrowed as she searched for the words then they opened wide and she smiled, "In due time."

Epilogue

IT has been twenty years since my meeting with General Birch. He withdrew his plans to appoint Connor Finch to Secretary of Commerce and helmed the nation for two terms successfully stabilizing and bringing honor back to America. General Hampton Finch retired from his post as Chairman of the Joint Chiefs following the arrest of his father, Connor, for molestation and later embezzlement and bribery. Fortunately General Finch had been allowed the time to lay the foundation for the restoration of our military system. His hand picked successor brought our armed forces might back to the point of solid deterrence from the earlier threats from abroad.

I have continued writing, publishing twelve books since that time. I have kept quiet on the subject of Joshua Lance and the unbelievable story we shared, until now. I had resolved to take it to my grave, having only told General Birch, but now I am very old and time is running out for me. I have reconsidered.

Last night I dreamed that my time had come. I found myself wandering across a meadow filled with flowers. The clean earthy smell was so real that I am not sure it was a dream. Sitting upon a large rock beside a wide river was Joshua Lance. He wore a flowing white robe and was younger than I remembered, but I recognized him instantly. He was gazing off across the river toward a huge gleaming mansion resting atop a gentle rise in the distance.

Smiling he turned and gestured for me to sit beside him. We sat silently for what seemed to be a long time. I was drawing strength and joy from his presence and the peace that pervaded this place. He turned to face me and grinned warmly.

"It's been a long time Howard," he smirked and looked directly at me, "or at least it has for you." I returned his smile. "You've done well my friend," he continued, "but you have more to do."

That's when I knew I had to tell this story. I nodded solemnly gazing at him. He laid his hand on my shoulder and arose. After walking several steps toward the river, he stood at the edge, I opened my mouth and he turned.

"What's it like over there?" I asked. He smiled and looked at me for several minutes. There was a glow to him, youth and vitality like I had never experienced.

"All I can tell you is that you'll really like it."

"Can I come back here?" I wanted to go across the river with him, but knew it was not time.

He nodded, "We'll be waiting for you." He then turned and walked across the river and up the hill. It seems strange now, but then it didn't occur to me that there was no bridge, yet the river seemed no impediment at all to him. At the top of the hill he turned and waved then disappeared through the front door of the great house. That's when I awoke. I could still smell the flowers as I can now.

So, I embarked to tell this story. If you have one-tenth the trouble believing it as I did when Joshua Lance first told me, you will probably dismiss it as fancy. I have, however; told it as I was asked and when I see Josh again, I will do so with a clear conscience.

J. Keith Jones is a native of Georgia who now lives in North Carolina with his wife. As well as fiction he also studies and writes about history. A graduate of the University of South Carolina, he has spent a number of years in the computer industry. His desire to write was sparked by the encouragement of his first English professor in college. *In Due Time* is his first published novel.

To learn more about J. Keith Jones and his upcoming projects please visit his website at www.jkjones-author.com

7476323R0

Made in the USA
Lexington, KY
24 November 2010